CW00872203

SAFE HAVEN:
RISE OF THE RAMS

CHRISTOPHER ARTINIAN

Copyright © 2017 Christopher Artinian

All rights reserved.

ISBN-10:154412063X
ISBN-13:978-1544120638

DEDICATION

To all those people who do the right thing, whatever
the sacrifice, whatever the cost to themselves.

ACKNOWLEDGMENTS

First and foremost I need to thank Tina, my beautiful wife, not just for being a critical eye, not just for keeping me on the right path with this book as she does in life, but for being the reason I get up on a morning.

I would like to thank Annella whose tireless efforts and insightful thoughts helped steer me in the right direction time and time again.

Thank you to Anne for her support and encouragement throughout this entire process. To Gary for showing me where to start. To the numerous people who have conveyed nothing but positivity and shown genuine interest.

And finally to Caroline, my fantastic editor, for making the whole process straightforward and painless. And Jake, a great artist and a great guy. Your generosity will not be forgotten. Thanks man.

1

The light of morning crept into the grey room. The candles had burned through the night, and their wicks were flickering wildly. Each movement could be the last.

Mike and Emma looked from the small flames to the frail shadow of a man lying in the bed. Loud breaths greedily sucked in air, followed by deep hollow rattles as the man exhaled. He had a face as grey as the room. His brow furrowed as if a thousand thoughts were exploding like fireworks in his head, and his eyelids fluttered in laughter, then in sorrow.

Each time the breathing paused, Mike and Emma shot urgent glances at each other. Although Mike looked older than his sister he was just twenty, while Emma was twenty-four.

They had endured this same pain three years earlier. Their mum had died after a four-year battle with cancer: test after test, treatment, remission, and then it had come back, worse than before. It had spread to the lungs. As brave as she had been during the battle, in the end, she just wanted to go to sleep. The day before she lost consciousness, she had said to the two siblings sat around that same bed, "People have only got so much fight in them, and I think all mine is used up."

They knew that their stepdad, Alex, would say the same now if he could. When he had originally come into their lives, he had tried too hard to be a father figure, which had alienated the pair of them. When Sammy, their half-sister, was born, and later Jake, their half-brother, they became even more detached from the family unit.

After their mum was diagnosed, everything changed. Blood became irrelevant and family took on an entirely new meaning. In some ways, the four years that their mother battled cancer were the best four years the family had together. When she died, the family carried on. The fact that Mike and Emma were not related by blood to Alex was not an issue. They were a family. And now, that family was about to shrink again.

"Do you think he can hear us talking?" Emma said. "I mean hear us and understand us?"

"When Mum was in her coma, during the last couple of days, she'd mumble stuff that me and Alex had been talking about the day before. I don't know if she understood, but I'd like to think she did."

Emma moved closer to the bed and took hold of Alex's hand. "Alex, I don't know if you can hear me, but I hope you can." Tears came to her eyes and she took a deep breath to try and compose herself before continuing. "Alex, I just want you to know that Mike and I are very grateful for everything you've done. You were a thousand times more of a father to us than our own ever was." Her voice broke as emotion overwhelmed her.

Mike took over. "I'll miss you Alex. You were a great dad and a good friend." Tears welled up in Mike's eyes as he spoke, but he carried on. "And don't worry about Jake and Sammy. I'd die before I let anything happen to them."

Emma composed herself, took a deep breath and added, "We both would."

For a split second there was a pause in Alex's breathing and it looked like the corners of his mouth turned upward in a tiny smile of recognition, but later both Mike and Emma would deny it happened and just put it down to wishful thinking. His laboured breaths continued and both siblings sat back in their chairs, contemplating the hours ahead.

"What should we do about Sammy and Jake?" Emma whispered.

"What do you mean?"

"Well, they're going to want to see Alex."

Mike leaned forward and spoke softly. "Em, you and I are all they have now. We are going to have to do and say whatever is needed to get Jake and Sammy through this." He paused, realising how strange it felt to be talking to his older sister like she was a child. "The fact is, they're not going to be able to see him again, so we've got to get a reason straight in our heads now and stick with it." There was another pause. "Do you understand me?"

"There's no way they can see him now? He just looks like he's in a deep sleep."

"Remember, you weren't here when Mum died. You weren't here to watch the final breath followed by the death rattle. It's a memory that will stick with me until the day I die. It's one of the most horrible and disturbing things I've ever seen, and it could happen with Alex at any second. There is no way I'm risking Jake and Sammy being stuck with that image of their dad. No way!"

"You love bringing that up, don't you?" Emma hissed, her eyes narrowing, her face hardening.

"What?"

"That I wasn't here for Mum. That it was you and Alex who were with her on that last day. No-one knew how long she'd be like that. The doctors didn't have a clue, nobody did. Do you think I would have gone back down to London if I'd known? That memory might have stuck with you, but it haunts me just as much that I wasn't here." She was almost spitting the last words out.

"That wasn't the point I was making. What I was saying was—"

Emma cut in again before he could finish. "Don't be a dick, I know exactly what you were saying and so do you. I swear, sometimes I can't stand to be in the same room as you."

Mike looked hurt and irritated. "Look, Em," he began, trying not to raise his voice, "my point is that a six-year-old boy and an eight-year-old girl should not see their father die!"

Emma gestured as if she was about to continue the argument but she thought better of it as she calmed down. "Well, can't they see him after? Just for a minute?"

A tear appeared at the corner of Mike's eye, he took a breath, and tried to regain his composure. When it didn't come, he just looked at Emma and slowly shook his head.

She looked down at the floor. Looking at Alex made her too sad and looking at her brother made her too angry. Her eyes followed the pattern of the carpet and she let her mind drift away to less painful thoughts.

In a soft, shaky voice, Mike said, "Em, this isn't the way I want it. I'm not saying this stuff to hurt you, but this is how it has to be. We've got to make the right decisions for Jake and Sammy, as hard as they are."

The minutes passed and the greyness within the room softened as the sun tried to break through. Mike stood up and looked through the thick lace curtains out into the back garden. A small blue tit skilfully edged its way around the bird feeder hanging from the branch of a willow tree. Each manoeuvre the tiny creature made caused a microscopic movement of the willow branch. And each shift coincided perfectly with the bird's next grab at the feeder. It was simple yet ingenious; its methodology was flawless. Mike smiled to himself as he watched. He realised it was the first time he'd smiled in quite a while. For a moment he felt guilty.

*

Noticing that Mike was at the window, Emma finally felt she could raise her eyes without being judged. She glanced at her brother, wondering what was going through his mind, and then back at her stepfather. A sad smile made her lips purse as she contemplated the past. All her work and all her plans were now meaningless. Three years at university and three more working for the largest weekly magazine in the UK. Everything was falling into place, there didn't seem to be any limit to how far she could go, and then, with a thundering clatter, all her plans had fallen around her ears. She shook her head in self-pity and quickly checked that Mike was still looking out into the garden. She didn't want him to see her; he already thought she was selfish and he was good at reading her body language.

Finally her curiosity got the better of her. "What are you looking at?"

There was no response.

"Mike, what are you looking at?" she asked, a little more urgently this time.

Mike blinked several times as if to wake himself from a daze. "There's a blue tit on the bird feeder. It's figured out a way to use its own momentum to work its way right round the feeder and score a nut each time. Clever little guy."

"Sounds fascinating. You really know how to have a good time, don't you?" Emma responded. "It's a mystery why you don't have a girlfriend."

"Well, I'd rather have no girlfriend than one who turned out to be a sarky little gobshite," he fired back at her.

He turned round. They looked at each other, and for the first time in a week they both let out a little giggle, which was quickly diffused by another loud and rattling intake of breath from Alex.

"What time is it?" Emma asked.

"Just after seven," Mike said. "The kids will probably be getting up soon. When they do, will you be okay to deal with them while I stay in here? I mean, get them dressed and fed and just stay with them and try and explain things?"

"Yes, of course, but I think we should take it in shifts. We've both been here all night. You need a break too. It's only fair, Mike. This is pretty exhausting, to say the least."

"I know what you're saying, Em, and don't think I don't appreciate it, but I've got to be here at the end."

"I could call you if it happened while I was watching him."

Mike shook his head, slowly but resolutely. "Em, I've got to be here. I don't think he'll last out the day."

"Are you sure?" she asked.

Almost on cue, a thud came from a neighbouring room as Sammy jumped down off her bed. Mike and Emma shared a knowing look and she stood up to leave. She kissed Alex gently on the forehead and walked over to Mike at the window.

She took hold of his hand. "If you need me, you just shout and I'll be here. You know that, don't you?"

Mike said nothing, but he nodded as Emma left the room.

Mike turned back to look at the bird feeder, but the blue tit had gone. He had little doubt that watching the bird would be the high point of his day, and he reluctantly left the window and sat down next to the bed to carry on the vigil. Alex continued to breathe erratically. With each pause, Mike's breathing also halted, in fear and anticipation.

Mike reached under the bed and removed a small black zipped pouch. On top, in thick white lettering, were the initials RPA. He put the pack on the small chest of drawers next to the bed and then extended his arm to check that it was in easy reach if he should need it quickly. He picked up the paperback that he had put down several hours before when he had found his eyes straining too hard in the candlelight. He looked at the candles; they had all now burned away to abstract lumps on their respective saucers. He glanced again at Alex, to make sure he was still breathing, and then opened his book.

Mike had never been a big reader when he was younger, but after being sent away to a young offenders' institute for eight months he started getting through two or three books a week. They were a fantastic release: first from the fear, then from the drudgery of the place. Now they were just part of his life. He usually read fiction, but his gran, who he thought was the coolest sixty-eight-year-old in the world, had recently sent him one about an American couple who became self-sufficient. They were strict vegetarians, like Mike, and everything about the book lit a fire in his gut. And the way things were going, learning how to live off the land was pretty valuable knowledge, to boot.

He heard noises from the kitchen and assumed Emma had started breakfast. He hoped she'd bring him some coffee.

Mike flipped his bookmark to where he'd left off and began reading, but the stress of the night had caught up with him, and rather than invigorating him, the words on the page had a soporific effect. After a paragraph he started dozing and his eyelids began to feel like lead.

He put the book down and stood up. He slapped himself across the face a couple of times and then got down onto the floor and started doing press-ups. Down, up, clap, down, up, clap, down, up, clap. He had always kept himself in good shape. Before he went away he had played rugby and been the captain of the local under-eighteens cricket team. In the last couple of years, Alex had taken up jogging and Mike had accompanied him. It had been a great bonding experience for the pair of them and they'd taken part in a couple of half marathons. They had been talking about entering the next London Marathon when all this had happened.

He kept going. Down, up, clap, down, up. Then he heard a breath that didn't sound like any that had gone before. He jumped to his feet and looked towards the bed. Alex's last inhalation had seemed louder, more forced, and now there was a pause. A long pause. A very long pause. Then the death rattle. A gurgling exhalation, a disturbing memory rekindled. The sound stopped. Ten, eleven, twelve, thirteen. No movement. Mike gently took hold of Alex's wrist and felt for a pulse. Nothing.

"Alex... Alex... Shit!"

A look of pure anguish swept across Mike's face. He wanted nothing more than to run out of the room, but he knew it wasn't an option. He reached for the black bag labelled RPA. He unzipped it and pulled out a printed document that he had read a dozen times before. The piece of paper gently floated to the ground as he fumbled with the contents of the bag and took out what looked like a clear thick plastic balloon with a hose attached. He carefully placed it on the bed. Although he'd memorised the document, his fastidious nature demanded he had it there while he worked, so he picked it up from the floor and flattened it out in front of him. His finger traced every line at lightning speed. One last, frantic read through before he had to put all his learning into practice.

REANIMATION PREVENTION APPARATUS

IMPORTANT NOTE: WHEN THE VICTIM HAS BEEN SCRATCHED, REANIMATION USUALLY OCCURS BETWEEN ONE AND TEN MINUTES AFTER THE SUBJECT HAS DECEASED. IT IS ESSENTIAL TO ACT QUICKLY AND FOLLOW INSTRUCTIONS ACCURATELY.

- Place protective balloon over the head of the deceased, making sure that the nose bracket clamps to the subject's nose bridge.
- Pull cord around neck until it comes away in your hand. The protective balloon is now sealed.
- Take hold of pump and compress fully eight times or until the puncture delivery plunger is fully extended. Twist the base of the plunger counter-clockwise until you hear it click.
- Place palms over end of plunger and push down until no further movement is possible.
- The procedure is now complete. Please follow disposal instructions on reverse of this document.

Mike performed the task as if he had carried this out a thousand times before. He secured the bag in position, sealed it with ease and began pumping. A thick plastic plunger juddered upwards, almost as if it were growing out of Alex's eye socket. With each squeeze, more of the device emerged from the thick, clear balloon. By the eighth pump, the tube was fully extended and positioned perfectly to punch through Alex's eye and into his brain. Mike twisted its base counter-clockwise until it clicked, just as the instructions demanded. The whole process took only seconds, but it seemed longer. He put his palms over the plunger and then removed them again. He paused.

"I'm so sorry, Alex. I'm so sorry." He was frozen. The horror of what he was doing turned his blood to ice. He heard Sammy's laughter from downstairs and Mike wondered if he'd ever be able to laugh again. He remained motionless, transfixed by the pale, greying face of his stepfather inside the wrinkled plastic balloon. Maybe Alex wouldn't reanimate. Maybe he didn't have to do this to the man who had become his best friend, his dad. Maybe... Suddenly Alex's uncovered eye sprang open, revealing a misty greyness where once there had been brown and white. It was like a cataract had covered the whole surface of the eye, punctuated only by a misshapen pupil that flared like a drop of black paint falling on a hard surface. It was no longer Alex, it was no longer human. Within a second, his face had transformed from one of peace to one of pure hatred for the young man who now stood over him.

With puma-like speed, the thing that had once been his stepfather lurched for Mike. Its arms were outstretched, its fingers clenching like a mechanical grab in an amusement arcade trying to snatch its prize. A low-pitched growl emanated from the back of its throat as it bared its teeth behind the plastic of the balloon.

Mike was caught off guard by the speed and savagery of the creature. He stumbled back, unable to break his gaze away from the ghoulish eye of his attacker and the venomous spit showering the inside of the plastic. As the creature's hands clawed for his neck, Mike's survival instinct kicked in and he grabbed its wrists, pulling them in opposite directions away from his body. Undaunted, the creature began to snap like an alligator, despite the plastic bubble around its head. With each thrust, its mouth got closer and closer to Mike's terrified face. There was another noise from downstairs and Mike realised he had to end this quickly. This thing wouldn't just kill him, it would kill his family too. This abomination, this abhorrent freak of nature, was no longer Alex, and if it wasn't stopped, it would tear Alex's family to bloody pieces.

Mike's muscles flexed as he held the creature at bay, jerking his head out of reach of each attempted bite. The creature was beginning to gnaw at the plastic. Blood dripped from its eye as the struggle slowly forced the syringe further into the socket, but if the vacuum was breached, that would stop. Mike had to maintain his grip on the creature's flailing arms and hands otherwise he risked getting scratched. Their faces were just a few centimetres apart. Sweat began to roll down Mike's forehead, but the creature showed no such signs of strain. Mike took a deep breath, then all his curiosity, shock and fear vanished and was replaced by anger. This virus had taken the man he had loved and now it was trying to take him.

He pulled his head and neck back as far as he could while maintaining his grip on his attacker's wrists. Then, powered by pure fury, he head-butted the top of the syringe with hurricane force. The plunger surged through the soft tissue then slowed down when it reached the denser fabric of the brain. The squelching sound caused bile to bubble in the back of Mike's throat. Eventually the device could move no more. The growling and struggling stopped, and Mike felt the weight of the lifeless creature as it began to fall back. He took the strain and, like moving a piece of furniture across a room, walked it to the bed and let it flop onto the mattress.

Mike collapsed into the chair. Sweat was still running down his forehead and he was slowly trying to get his breathing back under control while studying the figure on the bed.

Blood and gore began squirting in small bursts against the inside of the balloon. Mike watched for a second, saw a small piece of something dirty pink in colour which he assumed could only be brain, fell to his knees with a thud and, without having time to find a receptacle, vomited violently. Thankfully there wasn't much there, but the retching was still loud and painful. Each time he thought he'd finished, he looked back at what used to be Alex and started again. As the final strands of thick saliva dropped onto the carpet, tears formed in Mike's eyes and the retching turned to sobbing. The sobs turned to cries of despair then a violent burst of tears as he doubled over. He wrapped his arms around himself, as if suffering from acute stomach ache, and tried to regain control.

2

The bedroom door creaked open and Emma walked in with a plate of toast and a mug of coffee. At first she was too busy trying to open and manoeuvre the door with only her elbows then, as she stepped into the room, the scene hit her like a tsunami. The coffee and toast fell to the floor, while her hands shot up to her mouth to stifle a scream. She stood there for a few seconds, looking between the clear balloon, which was slowly filling with blood and sediment, and her brother on the floor. She wanted to help him, but all she could do was pick up the small plastic waste bin by the door and heave her breakfast into it. She turned her back to Mike, not wanting to make it worse for him and also needing to hide her view from the horror show playing out on the bed.

Mike realised he'd have to regain his composure. His family needed him. He forced himself to start taking deep breaths. After about five, he was able to stifle his emotions. He wanted to get up and comfort his sister and then deal with Alex quickly and quietly, but before he could, the door swung open again and Sammy burst through.

Sammy saw her father and began screeching hysterically. Her body bent forward and stiffened, her arms and hands clenched by her sides. All her energy was being spent on wails of terror which shocked Mike and Emma out of their grieving.

"Em, get her the hell out. Now!" Mike croaked, as he jumped to his feet and pulled a cover over Alex's head.

Emma grabbed Sammy and tried to coax her out of the room, but her body was rigid.

"Mike, help me!" Emma cried as she struggled in vain to move her sister.

Mike lurched across to help, only to become the target of the screeches. Sammy stood firing screams at him as if she were trying to knock him over with her voice.

"What did you do? What did you do to Daddy? What did you do to Daddy?" she howled at her half-brother, partly in fear, partly in anger. "Don't touch me! What did you do? What did you do?"

Neither Mike nor Emma had witnessed anything like this before. Sammy was behaving like an injured animal. She was obviously in a state of shock and completely out of control. Mike heard Jake start to climb the stairs to find out what was going on. He knew that would make the situation even worse, so he did the only thing he could think of. He'd seen in films and read in books that when someone was hysterical, slapping them across the face sometimes snapped them out of it. She was probably going to hate him for the rest of her life anyway, so what did he have to lose? He raised his hand and slapped her, not with too much force, but enough to stop her screaming. The room fell silent and Sammy's eyes widened in disbelief. Lost in the swell of emotions that was surging through her, she abruptly turned and ran out of the room. Emma's mouth was agape. Mike had never laid a hand on any of them, not even in play. She looked at her brother and then headed towards the door.

"Sammy... Sammy, sweetheart... Sammy..." Emma called pleadingly as she followed her sister out of the room.

The footsteps faded across the landing and down the stairs. Mike heard muffled screams and sobs in equal measure as he stood for a moment, cradling and massaging his forehead. This particular nightmare was nowhere near over and there was a lot of work for him to do before he could think about going downstairs and trying to build bridges with his little sister and brother.

He went to the side of the bed where he hadn't thrown up, reached underneath and pulled out a large black bag. He rolled it out flat and unzipped it.

Inside were two pairs of surgical gloves, two masks and another instruction sheet.

BODY DISPOSAL

CONTENTS:

ONE ADULT BODY BAG
TWO PAIRS OF GLOVES
TWO FACE MASKS

INSTRUCTION SHEET
NB: THIS IS A TWO-PERSON
PROCEDURE. PLEASE DO NOT
ATTEMPT THIS UNAIDED AS YOU
MAY SUSTAIN AN INJURY.

"You have got to be fucking kidding me," he whispered to no-one in particular. "People are dying in the billions and they're worried about me getting backache." He shook his head and stood back to survey the best way to proceed.

Mike peeled back the bed sheets, revealing the frail corpse. His eyes were drawn to the left forearm and four welted scratch marks. That's where the family's personal nightmare had begun, three weeks before, when Alex had tried to help a neighbour whose husband had seemingly gone berserk. They had all seen the spread of the virus on the TV; it had decimated huge parts of the planet. Virtually every country you could name had lost the battle against this remorseless killer.

When the news first came in, people believed it was a huge hoax, something to finally top Orson Welles' "War of the Worlds" broadcasts. But as the reports persisted and were followed by credible video footage by the BBC and CNN, it quickly became a startling reality. YouTube, Facebook and Twitter became survival diaries before going down forever. Science fiction had become science fact. Carriers of the virus died and then reanimated, but they were no longer recognisable as the people they had once been. When they came back, it seemed their sole purpose was to attack the living. And not just to attack, but to bite, to spread the infection. If you were bitten, you were as good as dead. The only variable was how long you would last – often just seconds, minutes at the most.

If you were scratched, there was a slim chance that you would survive but the vast majority of people died then reanimated. The time frame varied massively depending on the previous health of the person and what treatment they had been given, but reports mentioned anything from one or two days to several weeks between the initial attack and reanimation. However, there had been a few documented cases in France and the US where people lost consciousness, just like all the other victims, then, when it looked like they had taken their last breath, they woke up. They were frail from fighting off the virus, but they were alive. These people, these survivors – their blood could have been instrumental in developing a vaccine. But the virus had spread so quickly. Far more quickly than anyone could have anticipated. The scientific infrastructure had been destroyed and there had not been enough time.

All this had been on the news for months. Within a few days of the first cases breaking out in the Far East, America and Australia, the UK grounded all flights and closed all ports. All military personnel serving overseas were immediately recalled, each one given a thorough examination and medical on re-entry. Because of these actions, Britain had escaped much of the horror the rest of the world had endured, but there had been two recent outbreaks: one in Portsmouth and one in Leeds. Those cities had been quarantined, and a huge military presence had been placed in each one with civilian movement kept to a minimum. Houses in the infected zones had been given emergency telephone numbers and kits in readiness for most eventualities.

The only people allowed to work were those deemed vital, such as health professionals and utility and sanitation workers. Refuse collectors travelled with an armed guard. They were seen as essential since in some countries the proliferation of vermin, in particular rats, had exacerbated the problems.

Key to halting the spread of the virus was keeping those infected in their homes, in the care of their families, rather than moving them to a hospital where hundreds or even thousands could be infected if something went wrong. A family member would have to call a dedicated NHS hotline number every four hours to give updates. If a call was missed, a computer raised a red flag, and the details were sent by automated email to a military command post on the outskirts of the city. A military doctor would then put in a call to the house. If there was no response, a "clean-up" team was dispatched.

Mike looked at his watch, conscious of the fact he would shortly have to make a call to the hotline to confirm his stepfather's passing and make arrangements for them to collect the body.

He took hold of Alex's ankles and pulled the body down, positioning Alex's feet at the base of the bag. As he came back up, he caught some exposed skin at the bottom of his back on the corner of the old oak chest of drawers that had been in the family for decades.

"Fuck!" he yelled, as he rubbed the area frantically to try and numb the pain.

When the sting had subsided, he grabbed the lifeless figure underneath the armpits and gently

19

lowered it to the floor and into the body bag. This would have been a real effort just a few weeks before, even for someone as strong as Mike, but now Alex's body had wasted to bones and loose skin, making it all the more baffling that it had nearly overpowered him earlier on.

Mike zipped the bag up but paused ahead of covering the body completely. He would have to keep everything to himself about what had gone on that morning. It was important that his family remembered Alex as the man he was, not a blood-crazed monstrosity. Tears stung at the corner of his eyes again as he began to think of happier times.

"I swear to you, Alex, when this is over, when I know Sammy, Jake and Em are all safe, I'm going to mourn you properly."

He looked at the blood-stained face behind the plastic bubble and cast his mind back to just a few days before. Then, it had been a more comforting face, a more familiar one. The cold, grey, claw-like hand had looked flesh-toned and human as it reached out to take Mike's wrist.

"Don't say anything, Mike, just listen... You and I got off to a shaky start. In the beginning there were times when I thought it might be better if we just stayed out of each other's way until you left home. I'm glad we put the effort in. You know... all I can think of now... is how I want Jake to grow up to be just like you. You have to look after him, Mike. You have to look after all three of them. You're the only person left in the world I would trust our family with. You're the only one who can get them through this nightmare. Always trust your instincts, be strong, and never ever give up." Then Alex had let go of Mike's wrist, taken hold of his hand and finally drifted off to sleep.

How long ago had that been? Two weeks, maybe, but it seemed like a lifetime ago. With that final memory, Mike zipped the bag to the top and clipped a mini padlock through the zipper and a small metal loop. Just as he did, there was a whirring sound and the lights came on. He checked his watch – eight o'clock – right on cue. Like everything else, electricity had been rationed. For the general population it was available from 8am to 8pm each day. He walked over to the bedside table, picked up the phone and dialled the number now etched in his brain.

"NHS Leeds and District Emergency Hotline, please give me your sixteen-digit key card number," a female voice responded.

When Alex had been scratched, the family had been issued with a key card meaning they could get immediate access to help, if and when needed.

"Key card 8312 4442 1616 1687."

"And who am I speaking to, please?" asked the female voice.

"My name's Mike, Mike Fletcher."

"I won't be a moment, Mr Fletcher. I'm just calling up your details now. Okay, Mr Fletcher. Firstly, you are aware that you've come through to the cessation hotline?"

The corners of Mike's mouth raised a little. Cessation hotline, he thought to himself, what a wonderfully impersonal way of phrasing something so very personal.

"Yes, I am."

"I'm very sorry for your loss, Mr Fletcher. If you could bear with me for a few moments, I'll make the arrangements for the collection of Mr Alexander Munro now. Did you use the RPA as directed?"

"Yes."

"Was there any leakage, or did the device malfunction in any manner?"

"No."

"Has the body been placed in the bag provided and sealed as requested?"

"Yes, it has."

"Who has been in contact with the body since the cessation?"

There was that word again. "Just me."

"Okay, Mr Fletcher, I'm sending a collection unit to your address now. They should be there within half an hour. There'll be a doctor with the team who'll take some blood samples from you as well as Emma, Jade and Samantha—"

"That's Jake, not Jade," Mike interrupted.

"My apologies, Mr Fletcher, I was reading from the last entered field notes. Yes, Jake Munro, I'll just amend the screen... There. Now, as I was saying, there'll be a doctor who'll take blood samples and carry out a brief physical examination of each member of the household."

"Is there no way that could be done later? I mean, it's already been a pretty horrific day and it's only just turned eight. I'm not sure how much more I can pile on a six and an eight year old."

"I'm very sorry, Mr Fletcher, but it's essential, for obvious reasons. We do have bereavement councillors available, if you would like me to organise one for you?"

Mike let out a deep breath. "No, that's okay, thanks."

"Well, if you do change your mind, Mr Fletcher, just call back on this line. In the meantime, I've made all the arrangements for you. I've notified your case worker and your names have been removed from the scheduled call list. Once again, I'm very sorry for your loss."

"Thank you."

"Goodbye, Mr Fletcher."

"Bye."

Mike hung up the receiver and headed downstairs. He walked into the living room and found Jake and Sammy nestled either side of Emma. Both children were sobbing, and teardrops were fresh on his older sister's face. He opened his mouth to speak and Emma gave a quick shake of her head as if to say *you'd only make things worse*, so he said nothing and walked through the living room into the kitchen. The kettle on the gas stove was still half full, so he reignited the flame and grabbed a mug. While he was waiting for the kettle to boil, he opened the cupboard underneath the sink and got out a bucket, disinfectant and a cloth. That mess he had made upstairs wasn't going to clean itself up and he was pretty sure no-one else was going to volunteer.

As he walked back, he mouthed to Emma *half an hour*. She nodded. They had discussed, many times, what would happen once Alex died, so when Mike mouthed the words she instantly knew what they meant.

3

The doorbell rang and Mike answered to find that it was the medical team, as promised. He told the two men in hazmat suits to wait in the hall while he ushered a doctor and a young nurse into the living room. As the nurse passed him, their eyes met and Mike couldn't shake the feeling he knew her from somewhere. He looked outside to see if there was anyone else waiting and saw two uniformed, and armed, soldiers in the front of what looked like a military ambulance, but nobody else. He took the hazmat men upstairs while Emma dealt with the doctor.

The doctor and nurse had walked into houses and situations like this more times than they wished to remember in the past few months. They had learnt early on that when there were children involved, the best way to deal with them was to be as disarming and friendly as possible, rather than hiding behind titles and white coats. As the pair of them entered the room, Sammy and Jake looked up, and for the first time in over an hour, they stopped crying.

"Hi, I'm Dr Blair, but you can call me Lucy, and this is Samantha," the doctor announced with a soft New England accent.

"My name's Samantha too," said Sammy, with a quiet and shaky voice.

The nurse bent down and smiled at the child. "That automatically makes us friends. I didn't think when I woke up this morning I was going to make a new friend today. How cool is that?"

Sammy managed a little smile. "This is my brother Jake and this is my sister Emma."

"Well hi, Jake, hi, Emma," said Samantha.

Although her style was a tad saccharine for Emma's taste, the kids were lapping it up, and she was grateful for the diversion.

Lucy took over, and her bedside manner was just as friendly as Samantha's. She placed herself onto a sofa arm and put what looked like a silver briefcase on the floor, then took a laptop bag off her shoulder and placed that next to it. She heard thumps and footsteps directly above, so she began to explain the reason for her visit in the hope that the children's attention would be diverted long enough to get the body out to the vehicle unnoticed.

"Samantha and I are here to give you a little check-up to make sure you're all okay. You've probably heard that some people are getting quite ill at the moment and we want to make sure that doesn't happen to you." She looked towards Emma. "Where's the best place for us to do this? Ideally somewhere with a little privacy."

Emma suggested the dining room. Lucy picked up her bags and asked for a moment to prepare before they began the examinations. Lucy closed the door behind her and leant against it, closing her eyes tightly. "Oh God," she whispered and reached into her pocket for a small plastic bottle. She placed one of the small pills on her tongue and cocked her head back to swallow. She winced a little as the bitter oxycodone tablet caught and dissolved on the back of her tongue on the way down. Okay, now she was ready. She set up the laptop and her equipment and headed back to the door. "Okay, Emma, would you like to come in?" she said, smiling. Just another day at the surgery.

"Okay, this will only take a few minutes. I'm going to do a full examination of you and then I'm going to take a little bit of blood for testing back at the lab. So if you could remove your clothes, please, we'll take a look at you and then get your brothers and sister done."

Emma was taken aback at first but then logic told her it made perfect sense that a physical needed to be done. She stripped down to her underwear and raised her eyebrows as if to say *this too?* Lucy nodded and Emma stood there while some data was entered onto the laptop. Subconsciously she clasped her hands together in front of her groin. Lucy finished and stood up, hiding a small smile as she noticed her patient nervously covering her private parts. Virtually everyone she had ever examined did the same thing, but it always made her chuckle inside.

What contact did you have with your father in the last ten days, Emma?" she asked as she began the examination.

"Well, Mike and I had been sitting with him in shifts, until the last couple of days when we both stayed with him through the night."

"Sorry, I meant what physical contact have you had?"

"Well, both Mike and I have given him bed baths and... you know... changed him." Emma looked at Lucy, hoping she wouldn't make her go into the details about having to change her stepfather's adult nappies. "Obviously whenever we did anything like that, we wore the protective gloves and masks provided." Then Emma took a deep intake of breath and remembered that very morning when she held Alex's hand and kissed him on the forehead. The colour drained away from her face.

"What's wrong, Emma?"

"This... this morning, I held his hand and kissed him on the forehead. Could I have caught anything by doing that, doctor?"

The doctor gave her a warm smile and shook her head. "There are only three ways for this virus to be passed from one person to another: bites, scratches and other exchanges of bodily fluids. Don't worry, you're fine."

Emma breathed a big sigh, but chastised herself for being so careless.

*

Mike closed the door behind the two hazmat men and walked back into the lounge. The young nurse had both Jake and Sammy working on their colouring books. His sister looked up at him and then turned away, still not ready to talk. Jake carried on, completely oblivious.

Mike smiled. "Do I know you from somewhere?"

Samantha smiled back, clearly pleased to have been recognised. "I'm amazed you remember. I'm Claire White's sister."

Mike had gone out with Claire White for about three months before he had been arrested. Her parents had barred her from having anything to do with him again, but with the help of her sister, Claire had managed one visit to the institute before her parents found out. Shortly after, the family moved away from the area.

"Good grief. It's Samantha, isn't it?"

"You know Samantha?" Sammy said, surprised.

"Yeah... from quite a long time ago."

"I like her. She's nice," said Sammy, before going back to her colouring.

Samantha and Mike smiled at each other, then Mike continued. "So, you're in the army now?"

"Good grief, no. Well, sort of," she said, not quite sure herself.

"Erm... okay."

"Well, normally I work at St James, but there are very few people in any of the hospitals now. An awful lot of medical staff have been... well... almost conscripted, I suppose you could say. Lucy – Dr Blair – and I work out of an army base just outside of the quarantine zone. We come in to deal with this kind of thing."

The news was state run these days. The information that filtered through was very limited, so Mike wanted to take advantage of having somebody from the outside to talk to. "So what's happened to all the sick people? Y'know, the ones who have broken bones, inflamed appendix, that kind of thing?"

She looked down for a moment, wondering how much she could or should tell, then looked back up at him, remembering how her sister had been completely smitten, and the reason why he had ended up in the young offenders' institute. She would have done exactly the same thing in that situation, if she'd had his courage.

"Wherever possible, people are treated in their homes by an MMU and then their families are given a care kit, similar to the type of thing you would have had, but with items in it appropriate to that specific problem."

"What's an MMU?"

"Oh, sorry. Mobile Medical Unit."

"And what happens if it's something that can't be dealt with by an MMU?"

"Well, there are very few emergencies that can't be dealt with, but in extreme cases they'll be taken to a field hospital that's been set up just outside the quarantine zone. Unless... y'know... they're..." She mouthed the last word, *infected*.

Mike nodded.

"To be honest, though," she continued, "since they closed all the pubs and brought in the curfew, there has been a massive drop in emergency calls."

The door opened and Lucy and Emma came back into the lounge.

"Okay, you two, come in here for a minute and then I'll make you a nice hot chocolate," said Emma, trying to capitalise on the fact that the children had stopped crying for the time being.

The pair dropped their pencils and walked into the dining room with an air of curiosity. The door closed again.

"What about you? How are you holding up?"

"Well, let's see. For the past two weeks I've seen my stepfather and best friend slowly wither away to nothing. This morning I watched him take his final breath as the man I knew, and then he woke up again as some kind of blood-crazed monster, if the news reports are to be believed. So, I stuck a five-inch piece of plastic into his eye socket and extinguished all life from him, forever. Then, if that wasn't enough, Sammy got to see the aftermath of it all. Can't say things are going well at the moment." He hung his head. Putting words to the morning's events gave them a grim finality.

"I'm sorry. It was stupid of me to ask." She got up from her chair, moved across to the sofa and placed her hand over Mike's. "Sammy told me about what she'd seen before you came back down. I tried to explain what had happened and how you had acted to protect everyone. She's a bright girl, you can see her mind whirring away, processing everything."

Mike looked at Samantha, grateful for the comfort. "It doesn't feel like I'm doing a very good job at the moment."

She took a tighter hold of his hand and felt an impulse to help him, to help his family. Things were coming to a head out on the streets and she felt people should be warned, despite the gagging order that was in place. "Your sisters and your brother are all alive thanks to you, so as far as I'm concerned you're doing a great job. Listen to me, Mike, and please don't let a word of this slip to anyone because I could get into real trouble. We don't get many calls that end like this any more. Usually when someone has a member of the family who is infected, it's not a medical unit that goes round to finish things off." She paused, wondering whether to continue, then carried on regardless of the consequences. "We're losing this battle, Mike. According to the news there are only two quarantined zones, but there have been smaller outbreaks all over the country. They're going to announce over the next couple of days that the electricity is going to be rationed further. Rather than 8am to 8pm, it's going to be 10am to 4pm. The food rations will be brought round door to door rather than having collection points, and they're talking about bringing in new measures for scratch victims." She wanted to continue but realised she had already said too much.

"What do you mean? What new measures?"

"Well, the rumour is, they'll be treated the same as bite victims."

Silence hung between them, both knowing bite victims were immediately put down to avoid the risk of the infection spreading.

"And this is just a rumour too, but there's talk that they're going to bring in a national curfew rather than just the quarantine zones."

"So, if there have been other outbreaks, how come more quarantine zones haven't been set up?"

Samantha let out a sigh. "There are a lot of stories going around about the reasons. There aren't official quarantines in place, but there is certainly a bigger military presence in those areas. Here and Portsmouth are the two areas that are being featured on the news, and massive resources have been spent to contain the outbreaks. The fact is though, that the government put all their eggs in... well... two baskets. They were hoping they'd be able to minimise the advance of the infection by cordoning off these two areas. They thought that might give them time to develop a vaccine, but the other outbreaks are just spreading them too thin. I mean, you've seen the emergency kits with the flares, protective masks, goggles and the rest of it. That stuff costs lot of money and takes time to produce. To do what they did was nothing short of a miracle, but things are starting to..." She trailed off, not knowing how or whether to continue.

"So how do you know all this? Where's all this news coming from?"

"Well, like I said, a lot of it is rumour. But most of the rumours I hear at the base end up being true. Plus, I know that a lot of medical staff have been seconded to other areas, to help set up units similar to ours." She looked down and realised she was still holding Mike's hand. She was happy for the comfort it gave her, but realised it would look inappropriate if the doctor came back, so she let go.

"Samantha, are you telling me that it's all over?"

For a moment, their eyes were fixed on each other and then she looked away, unable to answer.

"Samantha?" Mike tried to continue the questioning, but the dining room door opened again.

Jake and Emma came out hand in hand, while Sammy was behind still struggling to slip her sweatshirt on. Lucy stood in the doorway, beckoning Mike into the room.

He entered and sat across from her, unaware of the drill. She typed some information into the laptop, broke off for a second to smile and apologise for the brief delay and then quickly finished off her typing before closing the laptop.

"Emma's been telling me you've had quite a time," she announced, then tilted her head sideways as if weighing up her patient.

"You could say that."

"Well, this is going to be very brief, you'll be glad to hear. I'm going to take a little blood from you and then give you a physical examination. The whole thing will probably take less than five minutes." She noticed dark circles under Mike's eyes. "When was the last time you slept?"

Mike exhaled deeply and screwed up his face in an attempt to jog his memory. "Two days ago. I think."

"Whoa, you're going to have to get some proper sleep! Do you want me to give you a mild sedative before I leave?"

"No thanks, doctor. As soon as I hit the pillow I'll be out like a light. Plus, I'm not a big fan of taking drugs if I can avoid it."

For a second, Lucy shivered with paranoia. "What do you mean?" she asked, with the start of a frown on her face.

"I just don't like taking drugs. I prefer to let my body sort itself out if it can."

"Shall we ask the black circles under your eyes how they feel about that?" she said sarcastically.

A look of surprised confusion came over Mike's face and Lucy realised that her insecurity was unfounded, that he had just made an innocent off-the-cuff remark. She smiled disarmingly and stood up, placing her stethoscope in her ears and onto Mike's chest in one fluid action. She then checked his ears and his pupillary response and took a swab from the inside of his mouth. Mike offered his arm instinctively and she doused a little alcohol onto a small patch of skin.

"Okay, you're going to feel a little nip."

Mike grimaced as the needle went into his arm. He looked away, hearing the hiss of the syringe as it slowly filled with his blood. His eye twitched a little as he thought back to the blood he had seen earlier that morning.

"Okay, all done. I'm out of lollipops, though, I'm afraid." She smiled as she put a small plaster over the needle mark. "All righty then. If you could strip down for me while I get this labelled."

Mike was clearly embarrassed but did as requested. Lucy placed the phial of blood in her case next to three others and wrote out a little label which she carefully attached. She entered some more notes into her laptop and by the time she looked up again, Mike had stripped down and was standing with his hands carefully clasped in front of him.

"Head down, please," she said as she flicked through his hair like she was a school nurse looking for lice. She checked behind his ears, gently upturned his chin, moved one hand to the back of his head and kept one hand at the front to angle him towards the light. She extended his arms and checked both sides, hands too.

Mike was impressed by how thorough she was, and the embarrassment of being naked dissipated with the realisation that she probably did this dozens of times a day. The doctor completed her examination of the front of his body and gently turned him round. He felt her light hands touch his shoulders and he could sense the movement behind him as she carried out the physical. Then she stopped.

Mike heard her take a step back and felt the cold air against him when just seconds before it had been warmed by her breath. He heard footsteps move across to the door and the handle turn.

"Samantha, can you come in here a minute, please?" Lucy asked, sounding so casual that for a split second even Mike didn't think anything was wrong.

The nurse walked through the door, closing it behind her. Silence.

Mike angled his head round, conscious of the fact that he was naked. He looked at the two faces behind him. Their eyes were focussed on his lower back and he noticed that Lucy had unclipped a walkie-talkie from her belt.

"What's wrong?" he asked.

Samantha slowly looked up. Her eyes met his and where there had been compassion and warmth just a few minutes earlier, now there was sorrow. Her mouth opened slightly but nothing came out.

"Before using the RPA this morning, was there any contact between yourself and Mr Munro?" Lucy asked clinically.

"No. Why?"

She raised the walkie-talkie towards her mouth, but Samantha gently grabbed her arm. "Mike, you've got a scratch just above your left buttock."

A look of realisation swept over his face and he let out a premature sigh of relief. "Bloody hell, you got me worried then."

The walkie-talkie was inches away from Lucy's mouth. "If you've got an explanation, I want to hear it quickly. Otherwise, I'm going to have to get the guards in here."

"Look, this morning, after... well... I had to get Alex in the body bag by myself. Em was downstairs with the kids and I just wanted the job done. I did the best I could, but I was rushing, and after I got his legs into the bag, I stood up quickly and caught myself on the corner of the chest of drawers. It was just a scrape, honestly."

Lucy lowered the walkie-talkie. "Show us. Show us exactly what happened."

"Do you mind if I put some clothes on first?"

"Hurry up." The two women gave each other a look that Mike couldn't read.

A minute later they entered the bedroom. Lucy noticed the wet patch next to the bed. "What's that?" No compassion. This was still serious. Mike hadn't convinced her.

"That's where I threw my guts up after killing my stepfather." Mike was getting annoyed with the doctor's accusatory tone. "Look, I can't even imagine the horrors you must have seen in the last few months, but this morning I... I did the most horrible, sickening thing I've ever had to do in my life. I wanted to be strong for my family, because they need someone to be strong for them. But that sight, that realisation was too much for me and I was sick. I vomited and retched until there was nothing left. I know that's not manly or brave or heroic, but that's what I did." Mike's voice shook as he relived the memory.

The stern look on the two women's faces eased a little. "Mike, can you show us how you got scratched?" Samantha asked.

Mike went across to the chest of drawers and demonstrated. Lucy walked over and got him to do it again, pausing him at the point of impact and pulling his jogging pants down a little to see if she could marry the wound with the corner of the piece of furniture.

She reclipped the walkie-talkie to her belt and stood there, studying Mike in silence. The seconds dragged into a minute and she walked across to the chair Mike had been sitting in the previous night. She flopped into it and let out a deep breath.

"Well? Don't leave me hanging, Doc," Mike pleaded. "Do you believe me?"

She leaned forward and brushed her hands over her tired eyes. "We got a directive through this morning. I haven't even had chance to share it with you yet, Samantha." She looked at the young nurse and continued. "There have been mutterings about it for a couple of weeks now, but as of zero six hundred hours it became official. Scratch victims are to be dealt with the same as bite victims. No tolerance, no leeway. If a member of an infected household has injuries that are consistent with scratch marks, they're meant to be treated as if they were infected." Lucy looked down to the ground, defeated. "I do believe you, Mike, but that doesn't matter according to the new rules."

The colour drained from Mike's face. "So what are you saying?"

"I'm saying that if I follow the new directives, I have to get the guards in here now."

"I swear on my life, on my sisters' lives, on my brother's life, I was not scratched by Alex. Please, my family need me. Please don't do this." Mike looked at Samantha, who once again opened her mouth but couldn't speak. The tension in the room was palpable.

"Don't worry, Mike. I'm not going to report this. I think the new orders are madness. The measures that were brought in to deal with scratch victims were the best chance we had of developing a vaccine for this thing, but now it's like they've just given up." She sat back in the chair, drained.

"Lucy, are you okay?" Samantha asked, moving towards her.

"No. No, I'm not. Downstairs I was a few seconds away from having someone executed for scratching themselves on a piece of furniture. I honestly don't know what the hell we're doing any more."

Samantha crouched down beside Lucy and spoke gently. "You're doing everything you can. A lot of doctors back at the base wouldn't have paused for a second. You did. You've done the right thing, and you haven't just saved one life today, you've saved four."

Lucy smiled sadly and stood up. "Well, we'd better get back to the base."

"Doc, I owe you one. Stuff that, I owe you a damn sight more than one."

"Keep your family safe, Mike, and we'll call it even," she said and left the room.

Mike and Samantha let out deep breaths simultaneously.

"It was good to see you again, Mike. It would have been nicer if it was in a bar or a restaurant a few months ago, but you can't have everything," she smiled.

Mike put his arms around her and gave her a hug. Samantha was surprised at first but then reciprocated. "Take care of yourself out there, Samantha, and thank you. Thanks for everything."

He released his grip and was about to pull away when she grabbed him and moved her mouth to the side of his head. Her breath was warm and it tingled in his ear, making the hairs on the back of his neck prick up with involuntary excitement.

"Your stepfather was already dead, Mike. What you killed wasn't human. Listen, I've left something for you down the side of the sofa. It was written by one of the troops back at the base. Make sure you read it and don't trust anything you hear on the news."

She released him and without turning back, left the room.

4

Mike collapsed on the sofa, realising that now it was back to the reality of the situation. No outside help. He put his hand down the side of the cushion and felt the edge of a small document. He made a mental note to go back to it later when he had some privacy. For now, Sammy and Jake were absorbed with their colouring, while he and Emma just stared at each other, lost in a maze of thoughts.

Emma took a sharp breath. "Gran!"

Sammy looked up from her colouring for a moment and then put her head back down, pressing the pink pencil on the paper harder than before.

"I'll give her a call in a few minutes," replied Mike wearily. "I just want to rest for a little while." He sat further back in the sofa and spoke quietly to his older sister. "It's ration day tomorrow. This might be the last time I need to go pick them up."

"What do you mean?"

"I was speaking to Samantha and she said that they're having to bring in more stringent measures to stop the spread. They're going to start delivering door to door in the quarantine zones." Then, lowering his voice, "It sounds like things are really getting out of hand."

"They'll get back on top of it. They've got armed soldiers on every street corner, for God's sake. In six months it'll all be different. Things will start getting back to normal."

"Do you honestly think that things are ever going to get back to normal again?" He looked at the children, who had gone into the dining room and were sitting at the table doing their colouring. "Em, Britain is pretty much all that's left, and from the looks of it, things are getting much worse."

"I don't believe that. We would have seen more sign of it on the news. There are only two quarantine zones. That's the way it's been for weeks now. The infection isn't spreading. I'm sure what they're doing is just for added security. And, to be honest, with everything that's happened today, I think we can do without this paranoid bullshit, don't you?" Her eyes narrowed and she turned her head as if to say *conversation over.*

Mike sat there, his mouth open, not believing what he had heard. He wanted to come back with a venomous response, but instead let out a sigh and just looked at his shoes instead. He sat studying his laces for a few minutes, caught himself drifting off to sleep and then realised his tasks for the day were still not completed.

"I'd better go phone Gran," he said, looking at Emma. "Do you want to speak to her after me?"

"No. I'd only get upset."

"Bloody hell, we wouldn't want that would we?" he said in a whisper as he walked out of the room.

His relationship with his sister had never been the same since she had left home. There were times when they were still like best friends, able to read each other's thoughts, but then there were times when they despised each other with a passion.

*

"Gran, it's Mike."

"Mikey, sweetheart. I was going to call you today. How's Alex?" The warm voice on the other end of the phone was just what he needed to hear.

Sue Fletcher was Mike and Emma's paternal grandmother. She would have disowned her son if he had lived long enough after what he had done to the family. But she doted on her two grandchildren and she had been like a mother to her daughter-in-law before she passed away. At sixty-eight she was still very much a free spirit. She had lived alone in the far north-west of Scotland for the last fifteen years; she grew her own veg and kept hens and a goat. She even had her own kiln, making pottery which she sold locally. She was a heroine to Mike, and he wished beyond all wishes that she was with him now.

"Alex has gone, Gran."

"Oh, Mikey. Oh, Mikey, I'm sorry. I'm so sorry, sweetheart. How are Emma and the munchkins?" Despite having no blood link with Sammy and Jake, Sue treated them with the same adoration as she did Mike and Emma.

"Holding up. I think Sammy and Jake are in a state of shock. I think we all are. Em is... Em. She thinks she's going to wake up in a couple of weeks' time to find out that ASDA's reopened and Miss Selfridge has got a sale on."

"It's just her way of coping, sweetheart."

"It's not as if it was unexpected, but there was a tiny little part of me that thought... hoped... he might be one of the few who woke up. But I suppose deep down I knew."

"There's nothing wrong with having a bit of hope, darling... Mikey, how's everything else down there? I mean, outside. How are things?" she asked tentatively.

Mike picked up on the unusual tone of the question. "What do you mean?"

"I mean, what are things like? I'm pretty certain we're not getting the whole story on the news," she said, clearly still trying to hide something.

"A nurse who came here today was the sister of a girl I used to date. She said that soon the rations are going to be delivered door to door rather than having local pick-up points, to reduce the risk of the public getting attacked, which suggests to me that things aren't going too well. She hinted as much in a couple of other things she said. Why? What have you heard?"

"I haven't heard anything. I just wanted to know how things are going down there."

"Gran, I love you to bits, but you're a terrible liar." He paused for a second, ready to go in for the kill. "What have you heard?"

Defeated, she realised she had to come clean. "Well, I haven't heard anything through the TV or the radio other than what they've been saying for weeks now. They would have us believe that the quarantine zones are working, the curfew is reducing the number of new cases and outbreaks are quickly controlled." This was nothing new to Mike as he had been watching the same news. "But when I went into the village the other day, there was talk of several people being infected in Inverness and literally hundreds of cases in Glasgow, Edinburgh and outlying areas. I've trawled through all the radio stations I can find, which, granted, isn't that many, but I haven't heard a word about it. Now, I know what small villages are like for gossip, but my gut's telling me there's something to this." It pained her to come clean because if it was true, it made the situation for her family even more dire than it already was.

To Mike, this was just another piece of the jigsaw fitting into place. "I think your gut and my gut are feeling the same thing, Gran." Neither of them said anything for a few long seconds.

Sue lived in a house off the beaten track, seven miles out of the small village of Lonbaig on the north-west coast of Scotland. Her cottage was just a hundred feet from the shore, up an incline with amazing views out to sea. If she walked down one path, it took her to a tiny sandy beach surrounded by the blackest rocks on either side. Down the other path, she could make her way down to an expanse of rock pools where no end of sea life could be found. All that could be seen of the house from the road above was the gable end of an outbuilding. The place was almost invisible; coupled with the tiny population in the area, it made her home very safe. Her grandchildren, however, were in one of the biggest cities in the UK.

"Mikey," she began, at first not knowing how to continue. "Mike. If things get worse, I mean, if things collapse completely, I want you to try and get here.

And if you can't make it here then at least get out of the city. You've got good instincts, Mikey, trust them. Keep the family safe."

Mike had been thinking of little else since Alex had been scratched. Gran's place would be perfect to ride out the storm and start again, but the more he thought about it, the more he realised the journey was virtually impossible. Roadblocks were in place; barriers had been erected all over. There were armed patrols skirting quarantine zones as well as drones and helicopters. They had a zero-tolerance policy for anyone trying to escape, assuming you could even make it to the edge of the quarantine zone. The problems began as soon as you stepped out of your own front door. The curfew meant you were not allowed to move about unless it was to collect rations. On ration day, you had to put on a fluorescent vest, which was colour coded according to your time slot. You had a window of four hours to go to the local collection centre, pick up your bags and return home. It was impossible to use a vehicle as all fuel supplies had been reserved for the military and emergency services.

All these problems were the tip of the iceberg, though. If there were any "infected" on the streets, they would attack. Mike could probably fend off one or two of them, but what if there was a pack? He and Emma could outrun them, but his younger brother and sister couldn't.

On the other hand, if things deteriorated further, staying put would mean certain death. If the rations stopped, if the streets filled with infected like had happened all over the world... If that happened, they were done for.

"I've been thinking about the same thing every day, Gran. If things get worse I don't think we'll have any choice."

"Well, let's hope it doesn't come to that, but I know whatever happens, you'll make the right decision, sweetheart," she said, trying to brighten the mood. "Thank you for calling, Mikey. Send my love to Emma and the munchkins and look after them. I know they're safe with you."

"Love you, Gran. Bye." He hung up the phone while the last words echoed in his head: *I know they're safe with you.*

Mike collapsed like a matchstick tower back onto the living room sofa. Sammy and Jake were still colouring and Emma was watching the looped news broadcasts. Within minutes he was asleep.

*

When he woke up it was to the sound of gunfire. The room was pitch black. He smelt apples, apple shampoo to be precise, and realised that his little sister was cuddling him tightly. She was still asleep and someone had put a blanket around the pair of them. His mind was a haze as he tried to remember where he was and why. He heard another crack of gunfire and a green emergency flare lit the sky up in the distance. It gave enough light for Mike to see the outline of his older sister at the window. He got up, carefully and gently lowering Sammy onto a cushion in the hope that she would remain asleep. He went over to join Emma.

"There are more every night." Emma's voice was shaky; she had been crying. Mike didn't know if it was for Alex or for them. He put his arm around her and said nothing.

There was a creak of sofa springs and both of them glanced back. In the fading light of the flare, they could see Sammy shifting positions but she remained in a deep sleep.

"She's very bright, our little sister," began Emma, "she wasn't just colouring in today, she was processing everything. Everything that young nurse had told her, everything I'd told her, everything she'd seen on the TV and heard on the radio. After she'd finished her colouring book, she came and sat down beside me. She said, 'Daddy was going to try and hurt us, wasn't he? And that's why Mike did what he did.' I told her that was almost right, but it wasn't Dad who was trying to hurt us, it was a virus, something in him, but not him." Emma paused for a moment. "By the time I'd finished, I didn't understand what I was saying myself, but that's when she decided to curl up next to you and go to sleep. Like I said, she's bright."

"Thanks, sis. I didn't think she was ever going to want to speak to me again after this morning." Mike leaned across and kissed Emma on the top of the head.

The pair stood there staring into the darkness and wondering how long this would carry on.

5

When dawn broke, Mike, Sammy and Jake were sprawled, unconscious, on the large, comfortable three-seater sofa. Mike had always hated the flowery design, but after several nights without any sleep, it felt like being on a cloud.

Emma, however, had only managed small snatches of sleep here and there. For the first time, the true reality of this waking nightmare had hit her like a laser-guided missile. Were denial and stupidity the same? She had had dreams of writing for one of the broadsheets when she was younger. Hard-hitting, ground-breaking news stories, giving the people the truth. But before she could start climbing the Fleet Street ladder, she had got a staff job at the biggest-selling celebrity magazine in the country. The money and perks were great, and her social life was something she could only have dreamed of before as the awkward, nerdy teen she had once been. However, the job had softened her brain, and now she was paying the price. It was time to get back in the game. It wasn't fair that Mike had to deal with all the crap. She shouldn't have left him. He was her brother, and he had stood by her and protected her, even though he was the younger one. He had taken beatings from their lout of a father in order to defend Emma. Then she had selfishly left him to pursue a career.

What had changed? Her job and exciting life were just a memory now. They weren't real, though. They had never been real. They were something she did, not something she was. They were gone, but her brother was still here. He was still doing what he had always done, and it was time for her to start doing her share, starting this very morning. It was ration day, and rather than Mike risking himself on the streets to bring back the supplies, she would go. This would just be the start.

Suddenly, she realised she was starving. The last time she had eaten had been the previous morning, and most of that had ended up in a plastic bag. She threw back her blanket and rose from the armchair.

Emma rifled through the kitchen cupboards but it didn't take as long as it once had. There were a few packets of dried food, some tins, a couple of jars of coffee and a box of biscuits for cheese left over from Christmas. That's what she wanted. So what if they were five months old? If they filled her belly, that's all that mattered. She tore open the cellophane and stuffed two crackers into her mouth. They were good. No, they were great. She stuffed another whole cracker in and slowly crushed and crunched the biscuits in delight. Emma had never been beautiful, but she possessed a prettiness that matched her intelligence and wit. She had been very popular once she had left her awkward teen years behind. The last few weeks, though, had ebbed away at the vibrancy of her looks. But now, the realisation that she was going to take control of her life again made her smile. It was a funny, lopsided smile, due to the three dry crackers that were still tumbling from side to side in her mouth, but the light behind her eyes had been turned back on; a spark had reignited the flame that had once burned in her. She was no longer in London, working all day then partying until the early hours; that life had been and gone. She was back on home turf now. She was Yorkshire born and bred. She had struggled to achieve her success, but that was nothing compared to the struggle that lay ahead.

It was 6.30am by the clock on the kitchen wall. Emma finished a further two crackers then went to the fridge and opened the door. The fridge was a tiny bit colder than the ambient temperature of the kitchen, but not much, and she wondered if they would ever experience twenty-four hour electricity again. She took out a bottle of water. Even though tap water was meant to be safe to drink, since the quarantine started, Mike had insisted that they boil all their drinking water as a precaution. She had chastised him at the time for being paranoid and he had retorted with his stock quote: "When you think you're being too paranoid, you realise you're not being paranoid enough." As far as she was concerned, Mike's default position was paranoia, but she was coming to realise that, in this new world, it wasn't such a handicap.

She took a sip from the bottle and leant back against the kitchen counter, just as Mike let out a loud snore from the other room. On top of everything else, it was hard to believe that but for sheer luck she could have lost her brother yesterday as well. Emma needed a good night's sleep, just to reboot, to process everything, but the rattle of gunfire had kept her awake. There had been sporadic shots most nights since the quarantine had begun, but last night there seemed to have been more than usual. On top of that, the image of Alex with that balloon thing on his head just wouldn't leave her mind, so sleep came only in short bursts. But now... now she felt more awake than she had in a long time.

Mike would not be happy about her going to collect the rations. Then it hit her. Mike usually picked up the rations at about 10am, but the window was from 8am to midday. Her three siblings were still fast asleep in the other room. She could sneak upstairs, get changed, get the ration card and vest out of Mike's room and be out of the door just before 8am. By the time the power jolted back on, she would already be a minute or so down the road and Mike wouldn't be able to stop her. She would leave a short note and deal with the consequences later.

*

Emma tiptoed downstairs, placed the small swipe card for the family's rations into the pocket of the luminous orange vest and then slowly turned the key in the worn brass lock. Sometimes it had a tendency to stick, but today, luck was on her side. She slid the bolt across and unlatched the chain, carefully placing it in position to avoid it rattling. Then she took a quiet, deep breath and pulled down the door handle with one hand, placing the other on the door to minimise the judder as the solid oak freed itself from the jamb. She took equal care closing it on the other side and hoped that the click of the lock wasn't loud enough to wake anyone. She placed the key in her pocket and turned. Once she was through the tall wooden gate, she would be free.

It wasn't until she was about twenty metres down the street that she realised she had been holding her breath. She let it out with a satisfying blow. Made it. Free at last. The collection point for this area was the local high school gym. It was less than a ten minute walk but she would have to remain vigilant. As the end of her street came into view, she saw two armed soldiers standing guard and a police car positioned at the middle of the intersection. There was another person in an orange vest just a little further on.

It was the first time Emma had seen any of this. She had heard about the military and police presence from Mike but it was hard to envisage armed patrols on the streets where she had grown up.

She reached the end of the road and both soldiers nodded. Both looked young and well trained, but they had fear in their eyes. She turned the corner and continued, but then heard someone calling.

"Miss... Miss?" It was one of the police constables who had got out of the car. She stopped until he had made his way over to her. He was an older man – probably close to retirement – and a little paunchy around the middle, but with a warm face.

"Is everything alright?" asked Emma.

"Sorry, I didn't mean to startle you, miss, but I just wanted to suggest you might be better off walking in the middle of the road rather than on the pavement. You see, there's practically no traffic other than military and police vehicles and they're few and far between. It's just... if something happens, miss... I mean if one of the infected are around, you'll have more time to react than if they just come out of an alleyway or a garden while you're walking along the pavement."

"Yes. Yes, of course. Thank you. Thank you very much, I'll do that." Maybe this wasn't the best idea she had ever had. It had never occurred to her to stay on the road, yet it was so obvious now it had been pointed out.

What would she do if she did come across one of the infected? She hadn't even brought a weapon of any kind. "Stupid bitch," she muttered to herself. Mike never talked about arming himself, but then he probably wouldn't have wanted her taking the piss out of him. Now she thought about it, she had caught him a couple of times with a long-handled screwdriver, once shortly before and once just after collecting the rations. He had made some excuse about tightening the bolt on the door or the latch on the gate and she hadn't thought any more about it, but now, it was obvious. That's what he used to arm himself on these journeys. She suddenly felt naked.

She carried on walking down the centre of the street, slightly reassured by the fact that there was someone about a hundred metres in front of her doing the same thing. It felt like speeding on the motorway behind another car. Seeing the flash of the speed camera getting the car in front would give her enough time to slow down before she became a victim too, only now the stakes were a lot higher than speeding tickets. A further hundred metres or so down the street, she could see another police car parked at a junction. There were two more figures, but she couldn't make them out clearly from that distance. As she got closer she saw they were soldiers too.

It was strange walking past the greengrocers and newsagents her family had used for years. Now they were boarded up, just abandoned shells, unlikely ever to opened again.

Two more people in orange vests joined from a side street. The more people the better as far as Emma was concerned – safety in numbers. She heard a shot, and a chill raced down her spine as she noticed the other pedestrians had frozen. She swung her body 180 degrees and saw that the soldiers who had greeted her were talking to the police. There was another shot. It didn't sound that close, but she no longer had the protection of her home, so any distance was too close for her liking. She looked back up the road and noticed the people in the orange vests had begun to move again, so she decided to do the same. Was this normal? Is this what Mike had experienced each time he had come to pick up the rations? Or did he go later for a reason? They always heard a lot more gunshots at night than during the day. Were the attacks less likely during the day? Were these gunshots just soldiers sweeping the last of the night's infected detritus away before the streets were safe again? Mike had shared little about his journeys to collect the rations. Was he trying to protect them all from the reality of the situation?

When Emma arrived at the gym, the tension and fear that had gripped her eased as she saw dozens of military personnel and vehicles. She walked through the double doors of the hall, passing four armed guards, and was greeted by a surly soldier about a foot taller than her.

"Card." She wasn't sure if it was a question or a demand, but either way she just handed the swipe card over.

He ran it through the small device he held in his hand and gave her the card back. "Table four. Next." She knew full well there was no-one behind her, but didn't really feel like pointing this out, so she made her way to table four.

She headed across to a trestle table with a large "4" on the wall behind it and was greeted by a young soldier, who was in a T-shirt despite the chill of the morning. Sweat patches were darkening under his armpits and it was clear that, although this was just the start of her day, the soldier had been working for some time. She handed him the card and he ran it through a swipe card reader. A few seconds later, her information appeared on the laptop screen.

The young man looked at her and smiled warmly; he had kind eyes. "Miss Fletcher?"

"Yes, that's right."

"I'm sorry for your loss, miss," he said, still looking at the screen. "The rations are made up a couple of days in advance, so there's an extra person's weekly allowance in here. Please try and avoid using it, as you'll only get three lots next week." The young soldier looked up to make sure she understood before he carried on. "Your box won't be long, Miss Fletcher." The soldier looked to the back of the hall where a series of metal shelving units had been set up. There was a forklift bringing in pallets from outside and a number of soldiers on mobile safety steps moving boxes around on the shelves. A huge man in khaki came into view carrying a large sturdy box, just a bit bigger than a supermarket's banana case. He said nothing, but placed it down on the table with a thud and walked back in the direction he had come from.

Emma's eyebrows raised; she hadn't even begun to think how she would get the supplies back home. The soldier smiled. "I've got some very strong strapping, miss. I could wrap it around the box and leave some extra so you could have the strap over your shoulder and carry it that way."

"Oh, thank you. Thank you, that would be great. The box never seems so big when my brother gets it."

*

Mike was awoken from his sleep by small hands pushing at him. "Mike, Mike, we can't find Emma." The panicked voices of the two children urged him to wake up.

Mike's eyes flickered open. Was he still dreaming? It was light outside now, the TV was on and the clock on the wall said 8.30. He rose, still not fully awake and still trying to process what he was hearing. *We can't find Emma. We can't find Emma.* What the hell was going on? What the hell were they talking about? Emma had barely left the house in weeks. Where could she possibly go?

"We can't find Emma!"

"Okay... okay... just give me a minute." He rubbed his eyes and swallowed. His mouth tasted like three-day-old Chinese food. Mike stood up and went into the kitchen. He looked out at the enclosed back garden, nothing there. He walked back through the dining room, through the lounge and out into the hallway. He was just about to climb the stairs when he noticed a piece of paper stuck to the door.

"Gone to get the rations, will be back soon. Love Em xxx"

"I'm going to kill her," he blurted, before realising the two children were within earshot. Sammy and Jake looked alarmed and Mike realised that was the worst thing he could have said, considering the events of the previous day. "I'm sorry, I shouldn't have said that. I should have said that I'm going to have to have a long talk with Emma when she comes back."

"Where's she gone?" Sammy asked.

"Emma has gone to get our rations." Even saying the words made the blood start pumping faster through his veins.

*

Emma trudged back through the car park, which was still a hive of activity. The box was heavy, but the strapping had made it much more manageable and she felt good that she was doing something to contribute.

"Emma," she heard a voice calling, but couldn't quite place it. "Emma." There it was again.

She stopped and turned her whole body around, as just moving her neck would cause the strapping to cut into it. Emma scanned the car park. There were a lot more orange vests making their way into the gym now, and the blur of khaki continued as lorries were loaded and unloaded while other soldiers patrolled and guarded the grounds.

"Emma." The call came again, but this time she zeroed in on the voice. It was Samantha, the nurse who had visited the house the previous day. Emma smiled and made her way over.

"Hi, Samantha, I didn't expect to see you here." In honesty, she hadn't expected to see her again ever.

"We got a very early call this morning, so we've just stopped off here to get some chow before the next one comes in." Samantha had black circles under her eyes matching those of Mike and Emma. "How's everyone at home?"

"Well, it's been a bit of a blur since yesterday morning. I don't think everything has sunk in yet."

"I don't think it does sink in. Some days I'm going through the motions and I honestly wonder if I'm in a coma and this is just some bizarre fiction that my mind has created. None of it makes sense. The best you can do is just get through each day."

"I know, it's all a bit surreal." Emma wasn't in the mood for talking. All she wanted to do was get home with the rations before the weight of them dislocated her shoulder. "I'll tell everyone you were asking about them, but I'm going to have to get back. Mike didn't even know I was coming out for the rations. I left him a note."

Samantha laughed, "Oh, wow, I wish I could have seen his face when he read that note. That would be one for the album. Well, I'll let you get off. Give him my best and say hello to Jake and Sammy for me."

"Will do," Emma said, as she turned and began the walk home.

As she retraced her steps, she noticed there was now a steady stream of people passing her with orange vests on, and she felt much safer. There was a heavy military presence back at the gym, the army and police were at all the intersections and there were a large number of civilians marching in unison. If something did happen, she was sure she would be safe.

Despite the weight of the box, she was moving more quickly than before, the trepidation slowly eroding as she became more impressed by the organisation and the huge security presence. No wonder Britain had been more successful fighting this than any other country. The organisation and planning was awe-inspiring.

The junction at the end of her street came into view and she could see the figures of the soldiers and the two policemen still sat in their car. She saw one of the soldiers raise his rifle. He was aiming towards the other side of the crossroads. There was a crack of fire and the other troop raised his weapon. Another crack. The milling bodies in the high visibility vests became welded to the road.

One of the soldiers shouted. "RAMS. RAMS AT TWELVE O'CLOCK!"

The words made no sense to Emma, and she just stood there with her mouth open. She was about fifty metres away from the junction. What should she do? The soldiers continued to fire.

Then she saw one. A fast-moving figure heading towards the troops. It was one of the infected. She didn't know how she could tell from this distance, but there was just something unnatural in its gait. Then another appeared, then another. They were running towards the soldiers. A bullet knocked one back off its feet, but within a few seconds it was up again charging at them. Then came a head shot, and this time the assailant didn't get up. The death of one did little to deter the others, though, and they continued towards the two armed men. Four more infected appeared from the same street and one dived at the soldier closest to her. He fired his rifle and the bullet went through the creature's shoulder, but its momentum carried it forward. The young troop lost his footing as the lunging figure grasped him and before he hit the ground, the teeth of his assailant tore into his cheek. Emma heard an inhuman cry; she didn't know if it was the young soldier or the beast, but she turned to ice.

The police car started its engine and began manoeuvring in an effort to block the other creatures that had emerged from the street. She could make out one of the policemen holding something up to his mouth, presumably a radio.

The private still standing aimed his rifle indecisively at his partner's attacker, then raised it again to fire at another of the infected who was approaching him. It was a clean head shot and the beast hit the floor before the shot stopped echoing. The other four were preoccupied with the police car for the time being, and the young rifleman pulled out a knife from his belt and ran to the aid of his comrade. The man on the floor had stopped struggling and screaming. When the other soldier dived on top of the attacker, Emma could see blood all over the face and neck of the downed man in uniform. The troop with the knife shouted a furious battle cry as he knelt astride the momentarily dazed creature. He raised the dagger and, with a huge effort, brought the knife down with the power of a jackhammer. The blade went straight through the roof of the creature's head and all struggling ceased. The young private stayed there for a few seconds, probably as astounded as Emma at what he had just done.

Emma realised this madness had unfolded in a matter of seconds, maybe a minute or so at the most. She was still frozen to the spot, physically and emotionally. Should she find cover? Should she just run back to the gym? Then she noticed movement behind the soldier and the slain figure. It was the troop who had been attacked. For a fraction of a second she felt a wave of relief, then reality exploded behind her eyes. If he was moving after being bitten, he was now one of the infected.

"Behind you!" she yelled, but no words came out. Was that her brain's way of telling her to shut up and not attract the attention of the other creatures? "Fuck it," she said to herself. "If I'm going to die I'm not going to die a coward."

She took in a deep lung full of air, unhitched the strap from her shoulder and brought both her hands up to her mouth to amplify the shout. "BEHIND YOU. INFECTED. BEHIND YOU."

The soldier kneeling astride his victim looked towards Emma. Realising she couldn't say any more than she had, she simply kept pointing, in the hope that he would look behind him. He turned his head and jumped round from his knees to his feet like an agile teenager in a break-dancing competition. The other soldier, blood still running down his face and neck, was now standing, looking around like a lost tourist trying to get his bearings. She could see from this distance that the colour had drained from his face, and soon he would have the sickening and frightening greyish hue of the other infected attackers. Finally his eyes looked towards his former partner and he began to move mechanically in his direction. The crouching soldier instinctively felt on his belt for his knife and realised it was still in the head of his last victim. He swirled round and tried to remove it before his old partner reached him, but the knife was stuck.

Emma heard the drone of engines behind her, but she couldn't tear her eyes away from the unfolding horror.

The bitten troop reached his former partner and they began to grapple. Emma noticed that in addition to the sound of engines, she could now hear a car horn being pumped frantically. She looked in the direction of the sound and saw it was the police car; the horn was sounding to warn her. Two of the infected who had been previously preoccupied with the vehicle were now heading in her direction. Her shout had jerked them from their folly to pursue a more tangible target. As loathed as she was to leave the family's supplies in the middle of the road, she decided her only option was to turn tail and run for her life. She swung round, ready to sprint, and saw two covered army trucks almost upon her.

The vehicles manoeuvred in a heart shape and formed a V between Emma and the infected. A dozen soldiers leapt out and began sighting and shooting targets as they advanced towards the junction.

An army Land Rover and ambulance pulled up behind the trucks. All the bone and sinew in Emma's legs had been replaced by blancmange. They buckled underneath her and all that stopped her from hitting the hard tarmac was the box she had almost abandoned.

Nobody got out of the Land Rover, but a nurse and doctor dismounted from the back of the ambulance. To Emma's huge relief, it was a pair of friendly faces.

"Emma?" Samantha asked, incredulous, as she bent down to help her.

Emma looked at Samantha, unable to speak. She reached out and took a tight hold of the nurse's hand. She could only look at her as the sound of gunfire proceeded down the road. Lucy came to join the two young women and crouched down next to Emma.

"Emma? Emma? Tell me what's happening. Emma?" Lucy checked her eyes and was about to measure her pulse when Emma snapped back to reality.

"How do you do it?"

The two medics looked at each other puzzled. "Do what?" Lucy asked.

"How do you deal with being out here? Day after day."

"What else is there?"

Emma had no response. There was nothing else now. This was the new way of life, for as long as it lasted.

6

"When will Emma be back?" asked Jake, already missing his older sister. Getting ready in the morning was a lot nicer when Emma was helping. His older brother was fun to play with in the garden, but not so much fun the rest of the time.

"Soon, Jake. She'll be back soon. Look, why don't you and Sammy watch a DVD?"

"We've seen all our DVDs loads of times. They're boring," Jake replied with a whiney tinge.

"Okay, how about this then – I'll let you watch one of *my* DVDs." Jake's eyes lit up and Sammy, who had been happily reading in the armchair, immediately closed her book. Alex had had two unbreakable rules. One, never swear in front of the children and two, never let them watch films deemed unsuitable for children. Mike was not going to break the first rule, but he didn't see a problem breaking the second, providing it wasn't something too graphic.

He ran upstairs and glanced through his shelf of titles. His selection was swift and soon he was back down with his hands behind his back. "Right guys, decision time. Left hand or right hand?"

The two youngsters looked at each other and conferred seriously for a moment. "Right hand," Sammy replied tentatively.

"Good choice, Sammy Bear." When Sammy was younger she had had a onesie that had a hood with bear ears. The nickname had stuck as a term of endearment. "Starring none other than Mr Christian Bale, and the one and only Thomas Hardy, you have selected *The Dark Knight Rises*."

The two children looked at each other like it was Christmas morning. Sammy snatched the DVD out of her brother's hand and ran across the room to the player.

Mike smiled to himself and put the other DVD he had brought down on top of the bookcase. Now his brother and sister were occupied, he wanted to read the document Samantha had left him.

The opening titles of the DVD began and the two youngsters were captivated. Mike snatched the document up, folded it and put it in his back pocket.

"I'm going to make a drink. Do you want one?" He looked at his brother and sister, saw a quick shake of the head, and walked into the kitchen.

Mike took out the folded piece of paper and flattened it. It consisted of three sheets, stapled in the top left corner. It certainly didn't look like anything the government or military would have produced; the printing was a little blurry and the diagrams were badly drawn. In large bold lettering at the top it read "RAMS – HAND TO HAND COMBAT". What the hell does "RAMS" mean, Mike wondered, then carried on reading.

RAMS – HAND TO HAND COMBAT

Hand to hand combat is always a last resort. If there are no other options, there are some essential points to remember.

We all know that the only way to stop a RAM is with a head shot. In hand to hand combat, the idea is the same. With a bullet you don't need to think about a skull's weak points, as they are all weak. If you're fighting with a knife or even with your bare hands, then it's useful to know what your best options are.

1) The Eyes. Very weak. If you don't have a weapon at all, push your thumbs into their eye sockets and keep pushing until they stop moving. Ideally have gloves on because if you've got any open wounds on your hands when you're covered in their blood, you're well and truly fucked.

2) The Temples. These are weaker areas of the skull and are easier to puncture than some of the more reinforced parts. If you're using a knife, screwdriver or other strong, sharp object and it's easier to hit the side of the head than the front, go for the temple.

3) The Throat. If you're in a head-on situation where you can't get good enough leverage to go for the eyes or temple, you can reach the brain by bringing your knife/weapon up quickly through the soft tissue where the throat

is. (Bear in mind, this will only work if you've got a long enough blade.)

4) Base of the skull and soft area at the back of the ears. Your aim has to be spot on for this manoeuvre, so don't try it unless you're sure you can make it.

5) If you have neither the confidence nor the accuracy to stop the RAM by one of the above methods, get hold of a heavy blunt instrument and cave its skull in. This works, but unless you're built like a brick shithouse it will take more time, and if you've got multiple attackers, those few seconds could cost you dearly.

Remember, the key to everything is keeping your head and acting quickly. Hesitation will get you killed. And never try to take these fuckers on in the dark. They've got perfect night vision.

Mike glanced at the crude diagrams that followed and then folded the sheets and put them back in his pocket. He poured water from the kettle into his waiting mug until the almost-black liquid reached the top. When he went back into the living room, Jake and Sammy were engrossed in the DVD.

Behind the sofa, there was a small workstation. Mike picked up the laptop in one hand while still holding his coffee in the other. He sat back, flipped it open and waited for it to spring to life. The internet was not the place it once had been. As countries had succumbed to the epidemic, so had websites, search engines, email servers; and what had once been the centre of the modern universe had turned nearly full circle and reverted to being primarily a device for the military to communicate. Commerce had been tricky, to say the least, and there was now only the UK and Ireland. International trade had ended, but due to some ingenious management, in the early months the British and Irish governments had traded medicines, technology and hardware to countries struck down by the infection in return for stockpiles of food and oil. It wouldn't keep them going forever, but it provided a lifeline while they tried to manage their own situation.

Naturally, unemployment had skyrocketed. Millions had lost their livelihoods in a matter of months, and this had led to another brave move. The government conscripted anyone unemployed and able-bodied between the ages of sixteen and forty into the armed forces. Anyone able-bodied and aged between forty-one and sixty-five was drafted into the food, medicine, textile and arms manufacturing industries or utilities. Coal mines which had been closed for decades were reopened and people were effectively back doing national service "down the pit". Mike had never been so grateful to have a job. He had never had ambitions to be a warehouse supervisor at a packaging company, but it beat being drafted. And since Leeds had gone into quarantine, the warehouse had been forced to close and no-one was conscripted from quarantine areas.

The idea behind the conscription to the armed forces was simple. Britain and Ireland had stayed in contact with heads of state all around the world until one by one they disappeared. Although relatively little was known about the virus and those infected by it, logic dictated that at some point either the infected would run out of food and slowly starve to death or scientists would develop a cure or a way of killing the infected en masse. At which time the largest army the world had ever known would begin to reclaim the planet for humanity.

The civil liberties lobbyists had been virtually silenced since the British and Irish governments had decided that the news would be state run, and although the measures brought in seemed draconian, to say the least, they seemed to work. Most of the conscripts didn't even get to see rifles but were put through rigorous physical training nonetheless.

Mike didn't understand all the logistical and financial aspects of how everything worked, but even though times were very hard, people weren't starving to death.

He looked back at the laptop. His browser had opened to reveal the now familiar search box of "Britfind", the last remaining search engine. It was run and controlled by the UK government. Bookmarks like "Amazon" and "eBay" had long since stopped working. All that came up if he clicked on them was the standard "page not found" message. He typed "what are RAMS".

A few pages came up, but all of it related to farming and male sheep. He was pretty certain what he had read had nothing to do with either. He slammed the laptop shut. He was frustrated at how easy it used to be to have a world of information at his fingertips and now, virtually nothing. He sipped his coffee and looked vacantly towards the TV as Bruce Wayne and Alfred the butler filled the large plasma screen.

*

Emma was about to stand up when she saw three soldiers approaching. Two were armed and one was not. She noticed that the one without a weapon had blood over his front.

"Need to get him checked over, doctor. He's been in a close-contact situation with a RAM." The soldier who had spoken pushed the blood-caked troop forward. He started towards the ambulance then stopped.

"You're the one who shouted out. You're the one who warned me, aren't you?" he said, staring Emma straight in the eyes. She just nodded. "That was very brave, miss. What you did saved my life." He stepped forward and she instinctively took half a step back – he was covered in blood – but then stopped herself. She kept her arms by her sides and he grabbed hold of her elbows firmly, yet with a degree of warmth. "Thank you. Thank you." And with that, he released her and stepped into the ambulance.

Emma was still dazed by the events. "Are you going to be okay to get home, Emma?" Samantha asked.

For a second she didn't reply, but then, she snapped out of her trance. "Sorry... yes... yes, I'm only a few minutes away. I'll be fine."

"You've had a nasty shock. Look, Lucy won't be long in there. When she's done, we'll drop you off in the ambulance. It's the least we can do, considering what you've just done." She gently took hold of her arm. "Look, just come and stand with me against the ambulance for a few minutes and get your breath back, then we'll get you home." Emma was still a little distant, but picked up her rations and allowed herself to be guided across to the ambulance.

*

Mike had been upstairs for half an hour. Most of the time his face had been pressed against the window to get the widest possible view of the street. The rage he felt had turned his blood to magma. Emma should have been home by now; it wasn't as if she could just drop into a neighbour's house for a chat.

The magma suddenly turned to ice water as he saw a military ambulance pull around the bend. His feelings of anger were displaced by fear. He wanted to move, but couldn't. His eyes followed the vehicle and widened as it pulled up in front of the house. Adrenalin kicked in and he turned from the window and ran across the landing and down the stairs, three at a time. He hit the ground floor with a heavy thud, unlocked the door and sprinted up the path. Just as he was about to reach the gate, Emma opened it. The ambulance pulled away behind her. She was startled to see Mike there and knew an ear bashing was due, but she had hoped to at least get inside the house first.

He grabbed her shoulders, his fingers tight like a vice. "What's happened? Are you alright? Why were you in an ambulance?"

She wriggled her shoulders to get him to loosen his grip and then placed the ration box onto the path. "It's okay, I'm fine. There was an incident up the road, but nothing happened to me, I just got a lift back from Samantha and Lucy." She stood there, waiting for a response and expecting the worst.

Mike threw his arms around her and held her close. He closed his eyes, and the anger and fear he had been feeling previously were washed away by a torrent of relief. "Never do that again, Em, please.

Never do that again." His voice came out in a whisper, and for the first time in a long time, Mike and Emma felt the bond that they'd had in childhood.

"I won't. I just wanted to help. You've had to deal with all this shit since it began, and I want that to change. That's why I went for the rations."

He pulled away from her and placed his hands on her shoulders once again, this time more tenderly. "Okay, you've just got to promise me nothing like this will happen again. And I'll promise you we'll start working more as a partnership. Deal?"

"Deal." They shared a smile, then Mike bent down to pick up the box and together they went inside.

7

At just after 2pm, the TV went off. Mike looked at the DVD player and saw that there were no lights on that either. He stood up and turned the dimmer switch on the wall. Nothing.

"It's just a power cut. I'm surprised we haven't had more, really, given what's happening." He walked back to the sofa, sat down and picked up his book again, but his outwardly calm appearance was hiding an accelerated pulse rate.

"Aww. It was at a really good bit," Sammy moaned.

"It might come back on in a minute. Why don't you two play a game or something until it does?" He looked across at Emma to bail him out; she was always much more patient.

When she had got them settled down with a jigsaw puzzle, Mike placed his book on the coffee table and went up to his room. He opened the drawer of his bedside cabinet and brought out a small wind-up radio. He frantically turned the handle a dozen times and began to search the bands but there was nothing but static. He tried the front bedroom to see if there was better reception in there – maybe he could pick up something, anything – but all he got was the same fuzzy crackle. He put the radio away and went back downstairs. Before going into the living room he picked up the phone. Nothing. It was an old-fashioned phone that they'd dug out of the loft when the power had been rationed. He clicked the switch hook five, six, seven times in quick succession but to no avail.

Mike walked back into the lounge. "Em, will you come and help me find some more towels? I've looked three times now and can't find any." The request was inane enough to leave the two youngsters completely disinterested and believable enough because Mike was a typical man and couldn't find something even if it was tickling his nose.

Emma begrudgingly left the jigsaw, which she seemed to be enjoying more than her two siblings, and got up to help. The pair went upstairs, and while Mike was still wondering how to express his concerns, Emma found the towels, pushed them into his hands and began heading downstairs.

"I don't need towels."

"What are you talking about? You just asked me to find you towels." She was at the head of the landing, just about to descend, when she noticed the troubled look on her brother's face. She stopped and lowered her voice. "What is it?"

"I can't get a radio signal and the phone's dead." There was a pause as they both looked at each other blankly. A couple of times, Emma opened her mouth to say something then thought better of it.

"You couldn't get anything? Local or national?" He just shook his head. "And nothing on the phone?"

74

Another shake of the head. "Have you tried the mobile?"

Mike's eyes lit up. "No."

Emma ran down the stairs, grabbed her mobile phone from her jacket pocket and ran back up. She turned it on. NO SIGNAL. She went in and out of every room with Mike behind her and each time the display kept constant. NO SIGNAL.

"It doesn't make sense. What should we do?"

"I can't quite remember who said it, but 'hope for the best, prepare for the worst' sounds like pretty good advice to me at the moment." He leant against the handrail, his mind whirring into action.

"Okay. Okay. So what do we do? What do we do to prepare for the worst?" Emma was starting to panic and Mike began to have second thoughts about whether he should have confided in her, but then he remembered their earlier conversation after she had returned in the ambulance. He realised secrecy was no longer an option, no matter how much of a pain in the arse the truth was.

"First things first. Fill the bath. Fill the sink. Fill all the bowls, glasses, bottles, everything you can with water. Start boiling as much as you can so we've got a supply of drinking water," he ordered, passing her as he went into the bathroom.

"What are you talking about? The water's fine, it's the power that's down."

Mike kept his voice calm even though every impulse in his body told him otherwise. "Em. How do you think the water is distributed? When the power goes off, the water supply gets pumped by emergency generators. When they run down, what do you think is going to happen? And, to be honest, I don't know much about how gas gets distributed, but my guess is we won't have that for too long, either. So, you make a start with that, I'm going to get a saw and some rubble sacks from the garage." Mike spoke as if it was the most natural thing in the world.

"What the hell are you going to do with those?" She looked at him as if he'd gone mad.

"We don't know what's going on. We don't know if this is a temporary disruption or if it's the beginning of something else. Either way, we need to stock up on what we can, while we can. We could be fending for ourselves now, for all we know. I'm going to cut off the bottom part of our down pipes outside and attach the rubble sacks, probably weigh them down with a few rocks for good measure. That way, when it rains, we can collect the rain water that would normally flow into the drains."

Emma smiled, impressed. "How the hell did you figure all this out?"

"I've not exactly been reading Stephen King and Clive Barker for the past few weeks. Now, let's get started. Water's the first thing. We'll figure the rest out as we go."

Inside, Emma was clattering in the kitchen cupboards. She had three pans and a kettle on the hobs. She was grateful that Sammy and Jake were still occupied with the jigsaw.

Mike worked on securing the rubble sacks to the bottom of the down pipes. He knew it was a futile gesture because if everything had come crashing down, they wouldn't be staying in the house long enough to reap the benefit of the collected rain, but he had to be seen to be in charge and to have a plan. That was the only way he was going to get them through this. He finished off and headed towards the garage. The afternoon was still bright, but not enough light could make its way into the dark interior through the one small window, especially with the branches of the old willow tree gently sweeping against it. As he entered, he picked up the heavy Maglite torch and squeezed past Emma's old Ford Focus to reach the shelves at the back. When Mike's mum had still been alive, Alex had taken Mike camping a few times. Initially it was as a way to get to know each other, and then it became tradition. Alex hadn't really been an outdoorsman, but they had both learnt together; they had bonded through mutual ignorance. That was when their friendship started.

He picked up the small camping stove and shook the attached bottle of gas. There was still quite a bit in it, and there were spares as well – Alex always had to have spares. Mike allowed himself a smile as he remembered good times. There were two adult-sized backpacks with sleeping bags rolled up and secured to the frame. They had bought a new two-man tent for the last trip, as the previous one had sprouted holes when they pitched it in a state of drunkenness next to a hedge of wild roses. There were two storm lanterns with a bottle of kerosene, four mess tins and two wind-up torches, and underneath one of the back packs was what he had sought most of all, a hatchet. They had used it for firewood, but Mike wasn't really thinking about firewood now. He picked it up and placed it gently on the bonnet of the car.

He didn't know if Emma had even thought about the possibility of them leaving the house. It seemed obvious to him that staying there could only be temporary once the power had gone down, but he and Emma were very different in many ways. He moved the torch past his weights and punch bag and round to Alex's workbench. He already had a long screwdriver up in his room, but he wanted to see if there was anything else that could be of use. Alex had meticulously laid out his tools on rests he had created from pairs of three-inch nails that had been knocked into a solid backboard above his bench. Mike reached up for a claw hammer. He felt the weight of it in his hand and rolled his wrist to see how comfortable it felt. He placed it on the bench. He took another couple of straight-edge screwdrivers, grabbed a carrier bag from one of the shelves and bundled his newly collected weapons inside.

Mike felt more organised now. If the power had gone down for good – if this was it – then he knew where the equipment was for the road and he had assembled some basic weaponry in addition to the small collection of knives he already had in his bedside cabinet.

As he made his way out of the garage, his foot caught on something. The family hadn't had a car since Alex had had to sell their Audi to help pay for Mike's legal costs. There was some paraphernalia left over though, and a dark blue rolled-up pouch clumped to the floor as Mike brushed past it. He bent down for a closer look, unclipped it and found it was tyre-changing equipment. Smack bang in the centre of the pouch was a crowbar. He slid it out and swished it through the air like a light sabre before placing it into the carrier. He walked back into the house and heard Emma still busy in the kitchen, so he tiptoed up the stairs to his room and placed the bag under his bed.

Impulsively he reached to his bedside cabinet for the wind-up radio again. The handle was slowly rotating, but as the dial swept through the frequencies there was still nothing to be heard but static. From the window he could see a couple of green flares in the distance. The instructions that came with the flares were very clear: they were to be used at night. In fairness, though, that was on the assumption that the phones were working, so he concluded that all bets were probably off on that front.

Mike headed back downstairs to join Emma, who was carefully pouring boiling water from a pan into an old cola bottle via a funnel she had previously made out of another bottle.

"How's it going?" he asked, looking around the kitchen at a vast array of steaming bottles and pans.

"I think that's pretty much everything we've got filled." She wiped away beads of sweat from her forehead. "What's next?"

"I don't think there's much more we can do until we know what's happening," Mike replied, touching one of the bottles then flinching away from the boiling contents.

"Well, how are we supposed to find out what's going on if there's no TV, no radio and no phone? What do we do?"

"We're going to have to wait a little while," Mike said. "If this is just a temporary blip, then the power should be coming back on tomorrow or the next day at the latest. The phones should be coming back on or something." He looked out of the kitchen door to make sure Sammy and Jake were still working on the jigsaw, and he lowered his voice as he continued.

"But if this isn't temporary then we need to get out of here."

"What the hell are you talking about?"

"Em, if this is it, if there's no help coming, then what happens when the food runs out? What happens when the water runs out? What happens when those things, the RAMs, the infected, are roaming the streets like it's bloody Piccadilly Circus on a Saturday afternoon?" His voice kept low, but to Emma it felt like the words were being shouted through a loudhailer.

"Surely someone will come to help." Mike didn't even bother to respond. Silence blanketed them like a shroud. One minute, then two. When she spoke again it was not in argument, but in resignation. "So where do we go?"

"We head to Gran's." He looked her in the eyes to show how serious he was.

"That's over four hundred miles. Surely there's somewhere else." Her breathing was a little erratic and Mike could tell she was beginning to panic again, so he gently took hold of her hands.

"Em, if the government's gone, if the army's gone, if the police are gone, the cities are going to be war zones. It's going to be everyone for themselves. People are going to kill their neighbours for a can of beans or a bottle of water. There'll be gangs, militias, no order, no rhyme or reason, and that's not the worst part of it. The RAMs will be everywhere. Because there are fewer people outside of the cities, all the risks will be reduced." He paused to let all this sink in. "Gran's place in Scotland is perfect. It's seven miles out of the nearest village, which has only fifty-odd residents anyway, and there isn't another one for another ten miles. Gran has a well for water, she grows her own veg, she has a wood-burning stove and she's right next to the sea, which is another source of food, not to mention salt. So you've got safety, food, warmth and the most important thing of all – family. This is it now. You, me, Sammy, Jake and Gran, that's all of us."

"Okay, but you still haven't told me how we safely travel over four hundred miles to get there," she said, leaning back against the cold marble worktop.

"We take your car out of the city as far as we can, which I'm guessing won't be far. There'll be roadblocks and all sorts of shit. But we should make it into the country before we have to abandon it. I mean, hell, we're only a fifteen minute drive to farmland from here, and hopefully we'll be able to find other vehicles along the way, but if we can't, we go cross country. Literally cross country, over hedgerows and through fields. We avoid towns and villages. We take what we can carry, and when we stop to rest we find somewhere under cover. I don't know how long it will take us, there are too many variables, but once we get past the big cities, the further north we go, the fewer people we'll run into." He stopped and took a deep breath. "So, what do you say?"

"You're fucking insane!"

8

For once, Emma relished the darkness and the absence of street lights. Her lined curtains blocked out the moon and stars, and all she wanted was to sleep. Hopefully after a good night's sleep she could hatch a plan that seemed less suicidal than Mike's. Travelling four hundred plus miles with two small children while being chased by monsters and bandits didn't seem like much of an idea, but she was clueless as to another option.

She heard a few cracks of gunfire, not too far away, but the last few weeks had turned gunfire into something akin to white noise. It certainly wasn't enough to stop her from falling into a deep, deep... Then there was another noise. It sounded like laughter – children's laughter. Was she asleep already? No. She creaked up onto an elbow and flicked her torch on. She looked at her watch. Eleven-thirty. She'd been in bed for over an hour. The kids were put to bed at eight o'clock, so why the hell could she hear them laughing? These days, she had taken to sleeping in a T-shirt and a pair of jogging pants, on the off chance she would have to move quickly. She opened the door, and at precisely the same moment she saw Mike's door swing open too.

His torch shone into her face. "Did you hear something?"

At first, she was a little reluctant to say. The sound of children's laughter at eleven-thirty at night, the day after their father had died, sounded like the stuff of bizarre dreams, but then she admitted, "It sounded like Sammy laughing."

No sooner had the words left her mouth than Sammy and Jake's door swung open. They came out still laughing.

"Is it bonfire night?" Sammy asked.

Both Mike and Emma looked at each other as though their little sister had gone mad. Mike shone his torch into Sammy's face. "What are you talking about, Sammy?"

"All the fireworks, silly. All over the sky. Is it bonfire night?" She looked at her younger brother and they shared another laugh.

Mike and Emma moved swiftly passed the children and into Sammy's room. The curtains were wide open and the sky was lit up by hundreds of green emergency flares. The pair hurried back out and into their own rooms, where they flung back the curtains only to reveal the same hopeless glow of a lost war.

Both remained speechless while Jake and Sammy ran from room to room to find which gave them the best view of the night's entertainment. In the end, they settled on Emma's. The two adults left them alone and sat in Sammy's bedroom with the door closed.

"I thought we'd have more time than this," Mike said, frustrated and deflated.

"It's like a war zone out there. One of those flares looked like it was in the next street, for God's sake. What are we going to do, Mike?" She was pleading more than asking, but she didn't care how it sounded, she was scared. For herself, for all of them.

"We'll have to go. Tomorrow, first light. How much fuel have you got in the car?" Mike couldn't take his eyes off the sky while he spoke.

"Maybe a quarter of a tank, but that's not the main consideration. The car's not moved for weeks. It wouldn't surprise me if the battery was dead. Even if it's okay, a quarter of a tank won't get us very far." Her eyes were darting from flare to flare, trying to establish where the closest one was.

"It'll be enough. It'll get us out of the city. If the battery's flat, we can give it a shove. We've done that enough times in the past with some of the bangers Mum used to buy." He tried to smile and reached out for her hand. She took it and held it tight.

"As I remember it, we were never surrounded by an army of dead cannibals before, though." The pair stood holding hands like lost children at a fairground as each flare died, only to be replaced by a new one. They could hear the odd crack of gunfire, but the sounds were becoming fewer and fewer.

"Look," said Mike, determined to take control of the situation once again. "We'll all sleep in the one room tonight. As soon as it's light tomorrow, we'll get everything packed up and then we'll hit the road. We're out of options, Em. We need to go."

Emma nodded reluctantly and released Mike's hand. Although she would never say it, the thought of dying together as a family gave her a little bit of comfort. Mike closed the curtains and left the room, shutting the door behind him.

His room was the second biggest after the master bedroom and so was the obvious choice for the "camp out". Mike and Emma busied themselves arranging bedding on the floor to make it as comfortable as possible.

"Right. Emma and Sammy get the bed, you and I are on the floor, Jakey," Mike said as he ruffled his younger brother's hair.

Although Mike wasn't enamoured with the idea of sleeping on a cold floor, Jake thought it sounded like a great adventure and was keen to tuck himself into his new bed. When everybody was settled, Mike went across to turn off the rechargeable lantern. He wondered if they'd ever be able to charge it up again. Only time would tell, but he thought probably not. His finger pushed in the rubber-coated button. Just as he released it, extinguishing light from the room, there was a bang on the front door. Everyone in the room jumped. The banging came again, louder and more frantic this time.

Mike switched the lantern back on, flew down onto his knees and reached under his bed for the bag of weapons. He pulled out the hatchet and the crowbar, handed the lantern to Emma and headed out of the room with torch and weapons in hand.

She rushed out of the bedroom after him. "Mike, Mike, what do you think you're doing? You can't answer the door. You don't know who the hell it could be," but her frantic plea went unanswered.

As he reached the bottom step, Emma was at the top of the landing, clutching the banister firmly. The children remained in the bedroom, too scared to move.

The agitated knocking came again. "Who is it?" Mike yelled through the thick wooden door, his left hand on the key ready to turn, his right hand raised with the crowbar ready to swing. No answer came, so he asked again, this time shouting even louder, "WHO THE HELL IS IT?"

A scared yet familiar voice answered in a stifled shout, "Mike... Mike, please let us in, it's Samantha and Lucy." Without a second thought, he turned the key and swung the door open. The two women piled inside and he pushed it firmly into the jamb once more.

Lucy went to sit on the stairs straight away, panting wildly. Samantha stood, doubled over with her hands on her knees, desperately trying to get her breath back before she spoke again. Mike stood watching them as Emma slowly descended the staircase.

Eventually, Samantha's breathing returned to normal. "Thank you so much. I'm sorry, I didn't know where else to go. It's all gone to hell!"

Mike took Samantha's elbow and guided her through to the lounge. Emma did the same for Lucy and then went to check on Jake and Sammy.

The two women sat on the sofa in a state of exhaustion and shock. Mike needed to know what was going on out there, but he didn't want to grill them; they were clearly in an emotional state. He went to the kitchen and opened the larder door. At the back, on the top shelf behind cereal boxes, was a bottle of Courvoisier cognac. He grabbed it and took four glasses out of the cupboard. The thick liquid glimmered in the lantern light as he poured ample servings into each glass before returning to the living room. Mike gave Lucy and Samantha a glass each and handed one to Emma as she returned to the room.

Samantha took a drink straight away and began to cough. "You might want to let it warm up a little in your hand before you do that," Mike said, just before she took another huge gulp.

Lucy remained quiet. She sat back in her seat and slowly swished the rusty-coloured liquid around the glass, watching it dance and tumble in the lantern light.

"So what happened?" Mike looked at Samantha with warmth, but he needed details.

Samantha took another drink and began. "At about three o'clock, we got a call down at Cross End Flats, y'know, near the big industrial estate. As we were approaching, we saw a large crowd gathered outside, so we called it in straight away. There weren't any high-vis vests to be seen, and it was clearly a breach of curfew. When we got closer, we realised the crowd wasn't made up of people. They were RAMs, dozens of them. We got out of there as quickly as we could. The driver radioed it in and got more support sent, but, just after that, a similar incident happened in Headingley and another in Beeston. By five o'clock we lost contact with HQ. Everywhere we went, we just saw more and more RAMs. They were like rats coming out of a sewer." Samantha paused and took a hefty shot of her drink. "We checked our calendar and saw that rations were being distributed across in Moortown, so we headed over there. We knew there'd be a heavy military presence wherever the rations were. We had to take a few diversions, as groups of RAMs seemed to be everywhere, but we got there eventually. When we did we wished we hadn't, it was like a battlefield. All the supplies had been looted and there were dead soldiers, dead civilians with weapons, a few dead RAMs as well. It was hellish, literally hellish. We were just heading back out when three vehicles blocked our exit. We had two soldiers and two hazmat guys with us – the hazmat guys carry sidearms as well. All four of them got out of the ambulance and walked across to the 4x4s. They had their weapons raised and they were shouting orders at the men in the cars. Then, one by one, they fell to the ground. Whoever was running this gang had positioned snipers somewhere. Our guys didn't have a chance. All this time we've been so busy trying to protect the public from the infected... We'd heard about this happening in other countries, but the government was confident that the measures put in place would stop it happening here. The conscripts were the problem. Obviously not all of them, but effectively we armed gangs, thinking they would have the same interests as the soldiers they were fighting alongside. There's no cure for human nature, I suppose."

She took another drink and looked around the room. Lucy seemed to be in a daze, but Emma and Mike were engrossed. "Well, after that, the car doors opened and eight guys got out. All of them were armed and they started heading for the ambulance. We knew that the same thing would happen to us as had happened to our crew, so we didn't really have anything to lose. The grounds were all surrounded with reinforced mesh fencing, but we figured if we could get up enough speed we might be able to break through. When the looters saw what we were doing, they started running back to their cars. We heard the pings of bullets hitting the ground around us as we sped towards the fence, but if they hit us, they didn't hit anything that slowed us down. We broke through and lost our front bumper, but, more importantly, we had a good twenty-second head start on them. By the time we hit the ring road, we were doing more than eighty. They started after us but then realised they weren't equipped for a chase. They'd be leaving their snipers high and dry and they'd already gained four more weapons from their ambush, so they let us go. We drove for about ten minutes and parked up on a quiet lane. We had no idea what to do or where to go. We couldn't raise anybody on the radio, so we headed here in the hope that you would put us up until we could figure out what to do next." She took a final drink out of the glass and drained it.

"I'm glad you came," said Mike, looking towards Samantha and then turning to Lucy. "Both of you." He took Samantha's glass and refilled it. "Do you have any family around here?" He knew Samantha's sister and parents had moved away but wondered if there was anybody else. She took another drink from the freshly topped-up glass and shook her head.

"Mum, Dad and Claire moved to Spain and..."

Mike knew that, although it was likely small bands of survivors were dotted all over, most people had either died or been turned. "I'm sorry, Samantha." He looked across at Lucy, who was still swilling the cognac around in her glass. "Do you have anyone around here, Dr Blair?" There was no response. She was clearly still in shock, but Mike needed an answer. He moved across and knelt down in front of her, gently placing his hand over hers and the glass. "Dr Blair. Do you have anyone who you'd like to reach?"

Lucy slowly moved her eyes up to his. Her pupils were huge in the dim light of the lanterns. "All my family were in the States. I came over here to work because ever since I was a little girl I'd wanted to live in England. I have to admit, it's not what I imagined."

Mike pulled back and sat down. "Well, we're going to try and make a break for it tomorrow. You're both welcome to come with us. To be honest, I'd be a lot happier if you came with us, I think there'd be greater safety in numbers." Samantha and Lucy both looked at Mike as he spoke, surprised that he had a plan.

"Where are you thinking of going?" Samantha asked.

Mike leant forward and began to tell them about his gran and her home. When he'd finished, he sat back and let it all sink in.

"What's the catch?" This time it was Lucy who asked.

Emma took over. "It's over four hundred miles away, in the north-west of Scotland, but Mike doesn't think that's such a big deal."

Lucy erupted into maniacal laughter, while Samantha tried to reason with him. "Mike, that's madness. You'd be lucky if you could make it four miles, never mind four hundred."

"What's the alternative? Seriously, what's the alternative? Do we stay here and wait for help to arrive?" He took a drink from his glass. His voice wasn't raised, but it was firm all the same. "We're alone. We have to forge our own path, we have to make our own luck. I'll fight whoever or whatever I have to, to keep my family safe, but I'll be damned if I'm going to watch them curl up and die here. We've got something a tiny handful of people have. We've got hope. We've got knowledge of somewhere that can give us a future. Now, tomorrow morning, we're packing up and heading out. I'd really like both of you to come with us." His voice mellowed a little and he sat down. "I really would. But if you don't want to, I understand. You're welcome to stay here, use this place as your own, because when we leave we're never coming back. I'm not an idiot. I'm not saying it won't be dangerous... But we're out of options"

The four of them sat in silence for a few minutes, occasionally taking sips from their glasses. Lucy gulped her cognac as if it was nothing more than tap water and leant forward to refill her glass. "Fuck it. I'm in. Samantha? How about you?"

"Well, I'm not going to stop here by myself, if that's what you're asking me." Samantha was unnerved by Lucy's willingness to accept what sounded like a doomed plan, but the fear of having to face anything alone won over logic.

"You should have gone into politics, Mike. You've got a psychotic streak a mile long and you're full of bullshit, but people still hang on your every word. You could have made it to the top, kid," Lucy said, taking another drink.

"Well, thanks, Doc, that's one of the nicest things anyone's ever said to me." He smiled, but the smile slowly straightened and it was back to business. "How much fuel have you got in the ambulance?"

"About half a tank." Samantha remembered checking the fuel gauge religiously after the looters fired on them, to make sure that the tank hadn't been hit.

"I'm guessing it runs on diesel?" Mike said, already dismissing the thought of siphoning the remaining fuel from Emma's car. Lucy nodded.

"Okay. We've got a big day tomorrow. I think we should try and get a few hours' kip before we set off. If you ladies would like to come with me, I'll show you to your room."

Lucy picked up her glass and the bottle and followed Samantha, Mike and Emma upstairs.

Emma took them into Jake and Sammy's room where two single beds lay at right angles to each other. Mike put down the lantern for them and retrieved a small penlight from his back pocket. "Sleep tight." With that, Emma and Mike left, closing the door.

When they heard a second bedroom door close, the two women hunched up on their elbows. "What do you think really?"

"Just what I said, I think it's probably suicide, but this way, at least we get to choose. If we stay here, we're just waiting to die," Lucy said, before taking another gulp from her glass. As if scripted, a crack of gunfire sounded from outside.

The two of them fell into silence, listening to the sounds of the house and the sounds from the world outside. Samantha drifted into unconsciousness despite the stress of the day. Lucy contemplated the journey ahead. She clutched the locket around her neck, brought it up to her lips and kissed it gently before placing it carefully back against her skin. She swallowed another mouthful of the thick amber liquid from her glass and turned to check Samantha was asleep. When she was sure, she reached into her pocket, brought out a small plastic tablet bottle and popped one of the white pills onto her tongue, quickly swilling it down with another mouthful of cognac. Minutes passed by and a contented smile crept onto her face. So what if she was taking the coward's way out, letting a twenty-year-old kid make all the decisions for her? She had been through enough, she'd paid her penance and more besides. She would just be a passenger on this ride, and when it all went south, at least the blame would fall at the feet of someone else and not her.

Her breathing gradually became deeper, her eyelids heavier, and she fell into a dreamless sleep.

9

When Lucy and Samantha went downstairs the next morning, preparations were nearly complete for the journey. Mike and Emma had packed rucksacks to the brim with supplies, clothing and camping equipment. Everything was neatly piled by the door.

"Hi," Lucy said, almost as if she was intruding.

"Hi," said Emma. "We've got a couple of empty holdalls for you," she said, picking them up and squeezing past the two women on the stairs. "Do you want to come with me and get a few changes of clothes? We might be on the road for a while."

The pair followed Emma back up the stairs and proceeded to raid all the wardrobes and drawers on the upper floor in order to find some suitable clothing. About ten minutes later, they were all back downstairs and Emma was pouring cereal into a bowl.

"I'm sorry. We've only got powdered milk. It's not great, but it does the job."

Samantha and Lucy hadn't eaten since lunchtime the previous day and they shovelled the food into their mouths. Jake and Sammy watched, delighted that they had house guests.

Emma wrapped the box of cereal and the powdered milk in a plastic bag and squashed it into a holdall.

When the two women had finished their breakfast, Mike cleared the dishes and placed a road atlas on the table. Under normal circumstances his actions may have seemed a little rude, but Samantha and Lucy were both grateful that he had a plan and was taking charge of the situation.

"I think our best option is to divide the journey up into segments. The first one being getting out of the city." He zeroed in on a highlighted part of the map. "Now, I think this will be our best bet to get outside of the city boundaries, and I'll bet that when they set up the roadblocks, they never thought about this place."

"I wouldn't worry too much about the roadblocks," Lucy said, leaning forward to get a better look at the map. "I'm guessing they're long gone after yesterday."

"Okay, but this will also give us the best way to avoid heavily populated areas."

"Well, that *is* worth doing," she replied.

"This road here, Bridge Lane, runs right by Mead Hall Farm. Me and Em used to ride our bikes up there. There's a hidden turn-off that takes you onto a dirt track which is big enough for a farm vehicle. It runs right through the farm. It goes on for miles. When you come out of the other end you're in an open field, but there's a gate at the end of the field that joins a road which takes you north and into the Dales. If we take that lane, we'll cut out miles of road through housing estates and built-up areas." He sat back as the two women studied the map.

"So, how long do you think it'll take to get there?" Samantha asked.

"Normally, it would be a ten or fifteen minute journey. Now..."

"Yeah. Can't help noticing you trailed off a bit there, Mike," said Lucy. He shrugged and Lucy went back to looking at the map. "Okay, so who's driving?"

"Well, I think you or Samantha should drive. I'll ride shotgun and everybody else will be in the back." Mike took charge as if he'd been planning for days.

"Wouldn't it be better if you drove? I mean, you know the way."

"In an ideal world, yes, but there may be situations where the road needs... clearing." He said the last word in a manner that would not alarm the children but would demonstrate to the adults in the room what was meant.

"Okay, let's do this," Lucy said.

"Right. Everything we're taking is piled by the door. There's no way that's getting into the ambulance in one trip. So, Doc, you and I take the first load. You get into the driver's seat and get ready. I'll come back and get the second load with Emma, Samantha and the kids. As soon as you see the front door close, start the engine. Okay?" Lucy nodded, fished out her keys and headed to the door.

She picked up a large backpack and a holdall. Mike took a huge rucksack, put one of the children's rucksacks on his other shoulder and carried a holdall in his left hand, leaving his right hand free to carry the hatchet. He turned back to Emma. "As soon as we're out, shut this door behind us."

Mike and Lucy stood face to face, their eyes locked. Each could feel the other's breath in the narrow hallway. Mike mouthed *one, two, three* and swung the door open.

The hedged garden meant they couldn't see what was outside on the road, but at least the immediate vicinity was clear. They stepped out and heard the door gently close behind them. They were both taken aback at what a beautiful morning it was. The sun made the dew on the lawn glisten, and small birds could be heard chattering in the trees. It was an almost comical juxtaposition with the world that awaited them. The pair reached the wooden gate and quietly lifted the latch. Mike pulled the gate back. The ambulance was there, less than two metres away. He put his hand up to signal Lucy not to go any further and carefully edged his head out to look up the road. Everything seemed clear. Because of the weight he was carrying, he had to physically turn his body to look the other way; it was all clear there too. He turned back, nodded his head, and the pair stepped out onto the street. Lucy rushed to the back of the ambulance and opened the doors. They were much higher than those of a civilian ambulance, which made dumping the bags easy but mounting and dismounting for people a lot harder.

She placed her bags inside and ran to the driver's door, while Mike unloaded his luggage, all the time keeping a watch up and down the street. When he saw that Lucy had safely got in, he headed back down the garden path. He tapped lightly on the glass panel and saw the net curtains in the living room twitch. He put a finger up to his mouth to signal everyone to be silent, picked up two more bags and led Emma and the children down the path. As he took hold of Jake's hand, he noticed movement out of the corner of his eye. It was a RAM. It had spotted them and was running towards them. Then another appeared, and another.

"Shit! Get in now," Mike yelled. He lifted Jake by one arm, almost dislocating his shoulder. Jake began to cry, but Mike just tossed him and the bags into the back of the ambulance. Sammy ran towards him and he did the same to her, but she was smart enough to take some of the strain. The RAMs were less than fifty metres away now and they showed no sign of slowing. Two more had joined them to make five. Emma threw her bags into the back and tried to jump into the ambulance, but the ledge was too high. She tried again, and this time, Mike grabbed hold of her hips and threw her into the vehicle. She narrowly avoided landing on Jake, who was now squealing with pain and fear. Samantha was halfway down the path with the final rucksack on her back when Mike signalled for her to get back into the house.

Her face filled with panic. Mike leapt into the back of the ambulance and pulled the doors shut as the first of the RAMs battered against it.

The children were crying and Emma was gathering herself after landing awkwardly. The sound of the slavering creatures clawing at the door of the ambulance stopped, and Mike knew what had happened. He rushed to the passenger seat and saw over the top of the hedge. The RAMs were now pounding the front door of the house.

Mike's brain started working overtime. He didn't even hear Lucy screaming at him in the next seat. Eventually, he came to.

"What the fuck do we do now?" she shouted. Her hysteria matched that of the children.

Mike took a deep breath. "Em, get up here. Show Doc the way to Bedford Place. Park up outside Mrs Green's house."

"What are you going to do?" Emma demanded.

"Just do it, Em," he said, opening the passenger door and jumping down.

He went quietly to the garden gate, but the RAMs couldn't hear much over the sound of their own snarls and laboured breaths. Mike watched them for a few seconds, noticing their clumsy repetitive actions. Their capacity for thought or even basic problem solving seemed to be negligible. They had seen Samantha run through the door, so that's where they focussed their efforts, mindlessly banging on the thick wood while a large window pane was just a few feet away. He took cover behind the hedge, hatchet raised. As the ambulance moved off, he was concerned that the RAMs might follow, but none did. They had a mouse caught in a trap and it was just a matter of time before they got to it.

Mike was wearing a thick black vinyl jacket. It was the closest he would ever get to owning leather, and the material was just as strong. He zipped it up halfway and quietly entered the garden, never taking his eyes off the growling beasts. The RAMs did not notice him; they were still clawing desperately over each other to get through the door.

He moved along the hedge until he was opposite the living room window and pulled his cuffs down over his hands. Then he counted down: three, two, one. Mike ran full pelt across the lawn towards the window. He caught the eyes of the RAMs but they didn't have time to react. Just as he reached the edge of the lawn, he pulled the jacket up over the side of his head to protect himself as much as he could from the impact, and launched himself at the window. There was a thunderous explosion as the glass shattered all around him and he landed heavily on his side. He was badly winded but he had no time to catch his breath.

He stood up, small shards of glass falling around him. He saw Samantha standing there, mouth open – she had obviously been expecting one of the RAMs, which were now attempting to crawl through the space once occupied by glass. Their clumsy and badly co-ordinated movements wasted valuable seconds in their pursuit of the two warm bodies. Their growls gained volume.

Mike quickly took the rucksack, flung it over his shoulder, grabbed Samantha's hand and began to run through the house, knocking over chairs in the dining room as they heard the first of the beasts gain access through the window. Mike cursed as he had to pause to unlock the back door, losing valuable time. He burst through with Samantha in tow. They were halfway down the garden before he looked back to see three of the RAMs in pursuit.

The enclosed space was surrounded by sturdy six-foot panel fencing, and, although breathless, Mike managed to ask, "Can you make it over that?"

"Too bloody right I can."

Two metres back from the fence, Mike unhitched the rucksack and, despite its weight, flung it over. He slowed and turned as Samantha mounted the hurdle in front of her. Realising she was too slow, and that the RAMs would be on top of them before they got over, Mike turned round fully to face the three assailants while Samantha tried to climb over the fence. Then, rather than aiming for her, they changed target and headed towards Mike.

Samantha paused on top of the fence. Technically, she was safe. She could easily drop down the other side and into the safety of the neighbour's garden, but she couldn't do it knowing the man who'd just risked his life to save her was in mortal danger.

Mike brought up the hatchet in one hand and pulled a screwdriver from his belt with the other. As the three RAMs converged on him, it was difficult to establish who looked more menacing, him or them. He raised his right foot hard and fast, pushing the sole of his boot against the first creature's chest with all his might. Its face did not change expression. There was no frustration or surprise, just the ferocious grimace of a rabid animal. It shot backwards, losing its footing and collapsing to the ground. The other two reached Mike at the same time. With equal power, he brought down the hatchet onto the head of one and pushed the screwdriver up under the chin of the other. Both dropped like bowling balls, and the sludgy mixture of blood and tissue enveloped the shining metal blades.

By this time, the first RAM had regained its footing and was heading back towards Mike. He withdrew his weapons from the fallen creatures and, with perfect synchronicity, dropped the hatchet square in the middle of his attacker's forehead while plunging the screwdriver into its left temple. He held on to them as the beast fell. Its grey eyes flickered and Mike noticed how small its shattered pupils were in the strong morning light. He looked at his hands, expecting them to be covered in gore, but to his surprise, the gaping wounds merely pulsed rather than gushed.

When he was sure there was no life left to extinguish, he withdrew his weapons and wiped them off on the clothing of the fallen. He looked up and saw that the remaining two RAMs had made it into the kitchen. Although adrenalin was pumping through his veins and he was confident he could deal with them as convincingly as he had the previous three, escape was the more sensible option.

He turned back to the fence and saw Samantha, still perched half in, half out of both gardens, her face a confused picture of horror and awe. He signalled for her to go. Mike followed, picked up the rucksack and together they ran through Mrs Green's garden to the front of the house where the ambulance was waiting, its engine running. As he ran by the kitchen window, the house looked like it was long abandoned and he fleetingly wondered what had become of the Greens.

The back doors of the vehicle swung open and the pair dived in, pulling the doors firmly shut behind them.

Inside the ambulance, both children were still crying, but the noise lessened to a degree with Mike and Samantha safely in the back. Mike held on to a support strap on the ceiling as the vehicle moved off. Samantha tumbled backwards, but he caught her around the waist. When he let go, she flopped down onto the gurney and felt her entire body shake. She wanted to cry, she wanted to scream, she wanted to get out of the ambulance and run, run as fast as she could, run back home to her childhood, where monsters were only found in fairy tales, and where her mother would hold her in her arms and protect her from any harm. She looked around at the frightened and confused faces, mirror images of how she felt inside. She looked up at Mike, but he was already heading into the cab of the ambulance. "Thanks, Mike," she called after him, her voice wobbling, but nowhere near as much as the rest of her.

"You're welcome," he said to her, before climbing into the cab. "How's it going, Doc?" he asked as he dropped into the passenger seat, releasing a few more shards of glass from the folds in his clothing. Lucy looked across at him, eager to hear the story of how they had won their freedom, but she knew that it would have to wait until later. Her eyes ran up and down his frame with expert speed.

"Your leg's bleeding," she said, gesturing down to a dark purple patch at the back of Mike's calf.

Mike looked down. He hadn't even felt it, but it must have happened when he went through the window. He took out his handkerchief and pulled up his trouser leg while he tied a makeshift tourniquet.

"You should get into the back and let Samantha look at it."

"When we find somewhere safe I'll get it seen to. I want us to get out of the city first." Mike pulled his trouser leg back down over the temporary patch and realised his hands were shaking. He balled them into fists and placed them in his pockets, hoping Lucy wouldn't notice.

"So where am I going?" Lucy asked, with her eyes nervously flicking from side to side as the ambulance trundled up the middle of the road.

"We need to keep straight on for about a mile to a mile and a half. Then we come to a big roundabout. We take the third exit there and keep going for about another—"

"Whoa! There, boy. Just give it to me a little at a time."

The crying in the back had abated for the time being, but there was the sense it could begin again at the slightest provocation.

"How's everybody back there?" asked Mike, turning round in his seat.

He saw that both Jake and Sammy had red eyes. Emma was rubbing Jake's shoulder frantically. He was obviously still in pain from being manhandled into the back of the ambulance. Samantha was holding Sammy close to her, the fear and uncertainty reflected on all of their faces. Mike decided not to push for an answer and turned back round.

The carriageway was deserted. Once, the same streets would have been packed with rush hour traffic, but now they were clear. Mike guessed that it being a main road explained the absence of movement; the side streets and housing estates would be the real battlegrounds.

"Okay, so we're coming up to the roundabout. We turn right here and then where?" asked Lucy, her eyes less fidgety now and her frame a little more relaxed behind the wheel.

"Stay straight on. There's another roundabout, go straight over that and stay on that road."

The ambulance slowed down and the gears crunched as they navigated the roundabout. Then they crunched again as Lucy changed back up and they gathered speed.

"This is a lot quieter than I expected it to be," Mike said, trying to glean a little information from Lucy, who had been on the road virtually every day since the quarantine began.

"This is pretty much what it's been like, but I thought I'd see a war zone after what happened yesterday. I didn't expect this."

Mike looked back into the ambulance. The two adults were soothing the children with gentle words, but the specifics were not audible over the sound of the engine.

"Tell me, Doc, there are a couple of things I don't understand."

"Jeez, just two? I could fill the Grand Canyon with all my questions," replied Lucy, only half joking. She took her eyes off the road for a moment. "Well?"

"How come these things only go down with a shot or stab to the head? I mean, there are a lot of vulnerable points on the human body. How come it's just the head?"

Lucy sat back a little in her seat. She was happy to answer Mike's questions, because it showed he was thinking of ways to kill these creatures, and that beat hiding under the dashboard hoping they'd all go away. "Significant trauma to the brain stops the RAMs instantly. If enough damage was done to other parts of the body, that would probably stop them too, but it would need to be considerable, and when these things are on top of you, you don't have that kind of time, so going for the brain is the safest option." She looked across at Mike and saw he was taking it all in, but needed a little more information. "The most in-depth testing on the RAMs took place in France. They had a lab based in the Alps. We lost contact with it about a month ago, but they passed on all their results to us. The RAMs do actually have some attributes significantly different to humans." She said the words before realising how stupid they sounded out loud.

"No kidding, Doc. I've been pretty hacked off with people in my time, but I've never wanted to bite their face off."

"Yeah, there is that, but other stuff too. The RAMs have almost perfect night vision." Mike remembered the pupils of the beast he had killed in the garden, and how he had thought they resembled those of a cat caught in sunlight. "So we need to make sure we're not on the road at night. We have to be somewhere secure. There's no way we can outsmart these things in the dark."

"But we used to hear lots of gunfire at night. How did the soldiers fight them?"

"The reason you heard more gunfire at night was because there were more of them hunting at night. That seems to be their preferred time, but there are plenty of them around during the day, too. As far as fighting them at night went, our soldiers had some of the most advanced night-vision equipment available. I don't see any of that around here, so I'm telling you: we do not stay on the road after dark." She looked at him to make sure he'd understood.

"Fair enough, Doc."

Once satisfied he had understood, she continued. "Another big difference is their healing capability. When you or I are cut, our body senses it and produces something called thrombin. It's a chemical manufactured by the liver and it slows down the bleeding and heals the wound, but it takes time. When a RAM gets wounded, its liver goes into overdrive. Massive amounts of thrombin are produced and the wound heals at unbelievable speed; this is why their wounds don't gush like you'd expect. That's another reason you're always best going for the brain when trying to take these things out." Lucy switched from fourth to third gear. Confident there was no risk of running into traffic, she went straight through the second roundabout and was back in fourth gear before fully exiting.

"So how come, when... when Alex died, I had to put that thing on his head to make sure no blood got on me?"

"The blood in a RAM who is newly turned is thinner than those who have been turned for a while. When you... when he died, his blood flow would have been only marginally different from when he was alive. If he'd been turned for a few hours, you wouldn't have needed to worry about it." She tried to be as sensitive as possible, but it was only understandable that the memory was still raw for her passenger.

Mike moved back a little in his seat trying to absorb all this information. They sat for a few moments with just the sound of the engine to keep them company. They drove past a large school that Mike remembered as good opponents on the rugby field. He wondered to himself how everything could turn to hell so quickly. "One more question, Doc."

"Shoot."

"RAMs... Where did that name come from?"

"It rolls off the tongue a hell of a lot easier than 'reanimated corpses'. The soldiers started using it at first and then it just became part of the language."

"Makes sense, I suppose." Mike sat there trying to think of other pertinent questions, anything that could help him learn more about these creatures, but none came. He knew the best way to kill them and that's all he needed for the time being.

They had speeded up to sixty miles per hour. Ahead there was a gentle fork in the road. They needed to veer right, but Lucy slowed down a little, as about quarter of a mile in the distance, on the left fork, they saw an old camper van chugging along.

"Looks like we're not the only ones heading out." Mike squinted at the old camper. His gran had one, with a psychedelic design that she had sprayed herself. From what he could make out, the one in the distance was far more conservative.

"Most people wouldn't know where to go. I'll be honest with you, Mike. I think there has been such a huge presence of trained military in the quarantine zones that we've been protected from an awful lot. I'd heard rumours of some horrific shit going on all over the country, but since the government controlled the news cycle, there was never anything official."

"What kind of stuff?"

"Things along the lines of what we experienced yesterday. Conscripts forming armed gangs, taking over whole cities. Lawlessness, turf wars, ration shipments being stolen, looting. That's before you even get to the problem with the RAMs. Put it this way, if we make it to your gran's place, I honestly think it'll be something approaching a miracle." Lucy took her eyes off the road momentarily to look at him while uttering the last few words.

"So why bother? Why try, if you think it's so hopeless?" Mike demanded.

"I'd rather die trying than not try at all," she answered, with an already defeated look on her face.

"We'll get there, Doc. My whole world is in the back of this ambulance. I don't care what it takes. Whatever I need to do to get them to safety, I'll do it." Mike's face was solemn and serious; he meant every word.

Lucy looked across at him and started laughing. She took his hand and Mike looked confused. "Oh, Mikey, Mikey, Mikey. Oh man, you're beautiful. You've got this whole Norman Bates meets Captain America kind of thing going on in there, haven't you, kid?" She gave his hand a firm squeeze and then let go. "Oh, man. It feels good to laugh," Lucy said, wiping a tear from the corner of her eye.

The ambulance hurtled through the quiet city until Mike snapped to attention.

"Okay, in about a quarter of a mile we're going to turn left. This is where it might get tricky," he said, reaching down to the bag in front of him and pulling out the hatchet and crowbar.

"What do you mean, tricky?"

"I mean, the only way to get to the entrance to the farm is through a bit of a built-up area, but it beats the other routes," Mike replied, with his eyes fixed firmly on the road. "Okay, Doc, start slowing down now. It's our next left."

Lucy crunched down into second and the ambulance lurched a little as it went around the corner. It was only a few seconds before they saw the first signs of trouble.

"Okay, Doc, you might want to put your foot down a little," said Mike, holding onto the support handle above the passenger door.

Lucy didn't need telling twice, and the engine roared as she pressed hard on the accelerator. THUD! THUD! THUD!

"What was that?" Emma asked, unable to see anything and echoing the thoughts of everyone in the back.

Mike turned around and made eye contact with the two women to explain that there was a situation. "There's just a lot of *debris* on the road. It sounds worse than it is because we haven't got a bumper."

The two women understood what was happening, but the children seemed placated. He turned back to the road and spoke in a lower register. "Why the hell do they just run at us like lemmings off a cliff? It's like they're completely devoid of any intelligence."

"I know," replied Lucy. "We've seen this before. I don't know if it's the movement that confuses or angers them or the fact that they don't seem to respond to pain so there's nothing that's off limits. The thing is, when a lot of them do this with a smaller car, they can slow it down or even stop it, and that's when the problems begin. I think we'll be okay in this baby, though, she's armoured and very heavy." She tried to sound confident but couldn't hide a nagging doubt.

THUD! THUD! THUD!

"Okay, Doc. Up ahead, you need to take a hard right and really put your foot down, because we've got about a mile of straight road before we take the final corner that will get us to the concealed entrance to the farm, and I don't want any of these things still chasing us down when we get there." He looked across to make sure she had heard over the thudding and the engine.

She jammed on the brake and the tyres screeched as she turned the wheel. For a moment it felt like the ambulance was going to tip, then it corrected itself and they were heading out of the estate and picking up speed again. There were fewer RAMs visible now, but the odd one still jumped at the ambulance like a fly hitting a windscreen. There were some speed bumps, but they were barely noticeable as the heavy vehicle sailed over them at high speed.

"Okay, Doc, you're going to need to slow down because we've got a tight left at the end of this road." The ambulance began to decelerate and Lucy checked her mirrors to see a few small figures in the distance still heading for them.

She turned the corner and put her foot down hard on the accelerator once again. The road was a narrow, windy country lane with thick, green hedging on both sides.

"Okay, about half a mile along this road there's a concealed entrance on the right. It's going to be a really tight turn. There's a gate which I'm going to have to open and close and we'll have to get away really quickly to make sure we're out of sight before anything that's following us knows where we've gone. So keep the engine revved. Okay?" He looked across at Lucy, who was biting her bottom lip in concentration.

She nodded without taking her eyes off the road.

"Okay, Doc, this is it."

She slowed right down and forced the wheel to the right as hard as she could. There was a scraping sound as hedgerow got crushed and uprooted and a thud as some more sprang back into place. By the time she had finished manoeuvring the vehicle, beads of sweat

CHRISTOPHER ARTINIAN

had formed on Lucy's forehead, her blonde hair almost brown with moisture. Mike was just about to get out and open the gate when there were two muted thumps from underneath the ambulance.

"What the hell was that?"

"Oh no. Shit! This happened to a team a few days ago. They drove through a crowd of RAMs, and it turned out that a couple of them had held on underneath. When the truck stopped and they got out, they were attacked."

"Brilliant."

"We've got a problem, Mike. It won't be long before the ones that were chasing us come round that corner. Some of them are going to head in this direction."

Emma had edged her way beside them and caught the drift of the conversation.

"You can't go out there. We don't know how many there are. We'll just have to turn around and find another route."

"Em, I don't think we could reverse out of here if we wanted to." Mike reached down into his bag. He took out a folding knife with a serrated edge and handed it to Emma. Next out was a kitchen knife with a long blade which he gave to Lucy. He then pulled out his trusty hatchet and checked that his screwdriver was still tucked into his belt. "There are more in there just in case. As soon as I open this door, get ready."

"Mike, don't you dare..." Emma's words broke off as Mike released the door handle and jumped out. He slammed the door shut and looked down just as two arms dragged out a battered body from underneath the ambulance. The creature headed towards Mike but was obviously walking on a broken leg. A second RAM appeared from the back of the vehicle. Mike backed up as the figure with the broken leg closed in on him with a snarl of pure hatred on its face. His back hit the gate and he knew there was nowhere else to go. He was hoping he could take them both out at the same time like he had in the garden, but this time, he might lose sight of the second one while he dealt with the first. It was a far from ideal situation. The creature lurched for Mike, baring its teeth. He swiftly raised and brought down his small axe with a fluid motion, making an almighty crack like the sound of a coconut being crushed by a sledgehammer. The beast dropped to the ground, and Mike tried to bring the hatchet back out but it was buried too deep and he didn't have enough leverage against the dead RAM to remove it.

The second attacker was in better shape. Three of its fingers were twisted, but that appeared to be the full extent of its maladies, other than the fact it was dead. It ran at him, arms flailing. Mike ducked down low and the creature stumbled against the gate. He wasted no time and forced the screwdriver firmly up through the base of the skull. Once motion ceased, he withdrew it, wiped it off and placed it back in his belt. He then returned to the first beast, placed his boot on its chest and pulled at the hatchet with all his might. It succumbed with a sickening squelch.

He pulled both bodies to the side and opened the gate. The ambulance carefully moved through and Mike firmly bolted the steel barrier into place once more. He climbed back into the cab of the ambulance. "Okay, we need to carry straight on this track for a while," he said without missing a beat.

He looked back at Emma. She glared at him but said nothing and turned around to rejoin Jake and Sammy.

10

They drove along the dirt track in silence. Lucy looked into the mirror just as the gate disappeared from view. There were no more pursuers to be seen and she let out a small breath of relief.

The track was dry and bumpy, but it was nothing the ambulance or Lucy couldn't handle. The sun was high in the blue sky, and the furrowed field looked like it was a million miles away from the battleground they had just driven through. Mike turned his head and looked back into the ambulance to see Emma and Samantha still clutching the children, a little more relaxed now.

Mike thought back to how he and Emma used to bring their bikes up here in the summer holidays. They'd pack a picnic and escape the reality of feeling like outsiders in their own family. These fields had once been a refuge for the young siblings, and now they were again. Mike was snapped out of his reminiscing by the ambulance coming to an abrupt halt. The track had come to an end.

"Where now?" demanded Lucy. What used to be a gate was now a hedge. Mike jumped down from the ambulance and went to look. Drainage channels had been dug on the other side of the field. "Well?" said Lucy as he climbed back in.

"It looks like they've changed the layout since we were last here."

"When was that?"

He winced a little as he answered. "Six or seven years ago."

Lucy scowled at him. "So what now?"

"Well, it's not ideal. But if we backtrack to the last field, there's another trail that reaches the farm buildings. If we put our foot down, hopefully we can get through to the main road before anyone has time to react." He looked across at Lucy, waiting for her to say something, but she just crunched the gear stick into reverse, turned the wheel and moved off.

Rather than heading north, they were going west, which they both found frustrating. The passengers in the back were blissfully unaware of what was going on up front, which Mike thought was probably just as well. One woman being pissed off with him was more than enough for now.

"Okay, Doc, slow down a bit. When we get through this next gate, we go up a hill and then over the ridge. We'll see the farm buildings about quarter of a mile in front. The road comes out behind a large barn, then we have to go through a courtyard that leads us to a long driveway and down to a gate where we join the road. We need to get through the courtyard pretty quickly, because I'm guessing they're not going to be too happy about us being here, and with it being a farm, they'll have a shotgun or two kicking around, I would imagine." He waited for a response, but she just looked at him again, her blue eyes angry and a little scared.

Mike opened the gate and this time didn't bother to shut it. He jumped into the cab and they were away. Lucy slowly built up speed, trying to move through the gears as smoothly as possible, cringing each time they grated. The ambulance rounded the barn and she put her foot to the floor as they crossed the stone chip courtyard in front of the large farmhouse. Then she jammed on the brakes. The ambulance skidded and a spray of small stones flew into the air. There was a man lying face down in front of them with dried blood on the side of his head. Another man was leant up against a wall, a big red mass of blood where his heart used to be, his mouth open, eyes closed. The farmhouse door was ajar and a pair of legs lay in the entrance, preventing the breeze from pushing the door shut.

Lucy pulled on the handbrake. "What do you think?" she asked Mike, just as Samantha joined them to find out why they had stopped.

"I think we should get out of here as quickly as we can," Mike said, without any hesitation.

Before he had a chance to stop her, Lucy opened her door and got out. She went over to the lifeless body blocking their exit and felt for a pulse, but the body was cold; he'd been dead for several hours at least. She headed towards the farmhouse and Samantha got out to join her. Mike remained in the passenger seat and turned round to look at his sister.

"Stay here a minute," he said, grabbing his hatchet and dismounting before his sister had chance to ask what was going on.

117

He caught up with the two women and stopped them before they entered the farmhouse. Mike barged through the door and over the other body. His head shot from side to side to make sure there was no-one else in the room, then he signalled for the two women to enter.

Lucy bent down to examine the body in the doorway. This man was clearly older but, from the back anyway, didn't display any obvious signs of trauma.

Mike went from room to room checking for any other inhabitants. Only when he was sure they were alone did he rejoin the women in the kitchen.

"Mike, this one's in bad shape, but he's alive. Give me a hand with him and we'll get him to one of the bedrooms." It wasn't a request, it was an order, and Mike was visibly annoyed. Annoyed she had got out of the ambulance in the first place, annoyed they were taking unnecessary risks and annoyed they were wasting time, but nonetheless he went to help her.

Just then, there was a barely audible but definite thud at the other end of the large country kitchen. It had come from the pantry. The three of them looked at each other and then across to the pine panelled door. Mike tentatively crossed the kitchen, weapon poised in readiness once again, lifted the small wrought-iron latch securing the door and pulled it open as quickly as he could. The cupboard was virtually empty, just some bags of flour and a couple of sacks of potatoes propped up against the walls. He was about to close the door when he heard another small thud. He looked again, and this time noticed a square of panelling at the back of the pantry that wasn't flush with the rest of the wall. He reached for it and pulled. The heavy pine square fell forward followed by the black metal nostrils of a shotgun.

With lightning speed, Mike grabbed the gun and angled it away while he found leverage against the back wall of the pantry and pulled fiercely. The explosion echoed around the kitchen; the smell of gunpowder was overpowering in the confines of the small cupboard. Mike wrestled the shotgun away and threw it across the kitchen floor towards Lucy, who picked it up and cocked it with expertise. He dived into the small secret hollow, ready to do battle with whoever was there. A small torch lit up in one corner, revealing an older woman, whose cheeks were stained with several layers of dried tears, and two boys: one huddled next to his mother; the other, slightly older, clearly in shock at just having had a shotgun ripped from his grip. Panic flared in his eyes as he saw the small axe in Mike's hand. He began to shake and Mike lowered his weapon.

"Bloody hell, kid, what are you playing at? You could have killed someone," growled Mike.

"We thought... we thought they'd come back for us. We thought they'd come back to kill us. Me and my brother and my mum," the young boy answered in a broad Yorkshire accent.

"Who?"

"Them that was here last night. There were five of them. I saw them through the window before I got in here." He rubbed the palm of his hand against his eyes to wipe away a stream of tears. "There were some gun shots and I saw my brother and Francis get hit. My dad locked us in here. He went to get my sisters, but he never came back. We heard shouting and more shots. We heard fighting and laughing. I wanted to come out to fight, but I couldn't leave my little brother and my mum. When you opened the door I thought they'd come back for us."

"Yeah. Well, don't worry, kid, we're not here to hurt you," Mike said, putting his hand onto the young boy's shoulder. "Let's get the three of you out of here."

All four of them slowly emerged from the small pantry. Samantha was crouched over the man lying in the doorway. She had flipped him onto his back and was dabbing at the dried blood on his sun-browned, craggy face. His eyes fluttered with each gentle caress from the wet kitchen towel. She guessed he was probably in his late fifties, but he looked strong, a formidable opponent in a fight. She wouldn't want to meet whoever had done this to him.

"Dad!" the two boys shouted in unison as they rushed over to the figure on the ground.

"Joseph, oh, Joseph!" the woman cried, sweeping past Mike and the stranger holding the shotgun to reach her injured husband.

"We were just about to get him to a bedroom when we heard you," said Lucy. "I've examined him briefly and he seems okay, other than some nasty looking cuts, bruising and possibly a mild concussion, but I'd like to give him a proper check-up.

"Are you a doctor?" the woman asked, looking up from her husband.

"Yes, ma'am, and Samantha there is a nurse. If we can get him to a bed, I'd be happy to check him over properly and get his wounds cleaned up." No sooner had she spoken than the young boys began lifting their father, who had already become more responsive. They limped with him through the living room and into a hallway where sunlight from several open doors lit the way to a master bedroom at the end of the short corridor.

Joseph's face contorted with pain as he was lowered onto the bed. His wife untied his boots and undressed him down to his underwear so that Lucy could examine him.

Mike and Lucy went back out to the ambulance. Lucy grabbed her doctor's bag and a few bits and pieces from the built-in cabinets, while Mike explained the situation to his brother and sisters.

Back inside, Lucy headed straight to the bedroom to perform Joseph's check-up. In the kitchen, the farmer's wife busied herself boiling large pans of water on the range, while Emma helped sweep up the broken crockery and plaster caused by the shotgun blast. Sammy and Jake were put in the living room with the younger of the two boys, while the older one stayed in the bedroom with his father, there to help if the doctor or nurse needed him.

Mike decided to have a look around the property, noticing there were several large corrugated metal outbuildings. In one, he found animal feed stacked high on pallets, although all the animals had been shipped out of the quarantine districts long ago. Now it was just going to rot there in its sacks. There was a larger barn next to it that housed a number of farm vehicles as well as a plush new Land Rover and a large four-berth caravan. There were bags of cement piled up next to the door and two large drums with "Red Diesel" scrawled on the side in black marker, next to five green jerricans filled to the brim with presumably the same stuff. In the largest of the metal sheds there was a flatbed truck, and behind it there was an assembly of metal racking full of tubs, jars, bottles and cans. The farmer had obviously been canning and pickling what he could to provide a stockpile if and when the rations ran out. There were plastic tubs at the end of the racking containing seeds. Mike liked the man's forward planning, and his optimism.

A light scraping sound caused Mike's hand to tighten around the handle of his hatchet. When he got to the other side of the racking he saw a large rat caught hopelessly in a trap, its back end crushed, its face almost pleading. Mike was never that keen on rats, but he wouldn't see any animal suffer, so he knelt down next to it and turned the handle of the hatchet so that the wider metal wedge would come down first.

"I'm sorry, fella," he said quietly and then brought down the tool in a single, powerful motion. The creature's head flattened and movement ceased. "Damn it." The taking of the animal's life pained him. He wiped his hatchet on a piece of sackcloth and went back outside.

He paused as something dawned on him that he felt foolish for not thinking of before. When the raiders left, surely they wouldn't have bothered to stop to close the gate to the farm. For all he knew, there could be hundreds of RAMs storming up the lane. He ran across to the ambulance, jumped inside, started the engine and crunched it into gear, making the vehicle judder before it slowly moved off. As he drove past the windows of the farmhouse he saw Emma, hands outstretched, shrugging as if to ask the question *what are you doing?* He put two fingers up, almost like a peace sign, and mouthed *two minutes* as he moved off.

Mike sped down the winding driveway, but there was no sign of anything out of the ordinary. He pulled on the handbrake and parked up in a passing place just before the final bend that led to the gate. He left the engine running and got out, quietly edging around the corner. The gate was shut. Not just shut: he could see from here that it was bolted. The only reason the raiders would have risked taking the time to bolt the gate was that they intended to come back. Mike realised that he needed to get everybody out of there straight away. He climbed back into the ambulance, did an eight-point turn and headed back.

*

In the bedroom, Lucy and Samantha had cleaned up the farmer's wounds. He was badly bruised and there were some nasty cuts, but nothing too serious. The shame he felt for not being able to protect his family was far greater than the physical pain he was in.

"They took my daughters." His voice was croaky, and Samantha lifted his head so he could take a sip of water. "They took my daughters and they killed my son and my son-in-law. He held back a sob as he spoke. "And I couldn't do a damn thing to stop them."

"How many were there?" Lucy asked.

"Five of them, all armed. We only have two shotguns on the place. I gave one of them to Peter and put him in the hidey-hole behind the pantry with my wife and youngest son. My eldest had the other, and he was the first one they shot. I saw Francis, my son-in-law, rush at one of them with a pitchfork and the next thing I knew, there was a burst of red, and he was on the ground too. My daughters were in one of the barns laying traps for the vermin. I didn't have time to get to them. They were on top of me, punching and kicking me. I saw my daughters dragged off before I blacked out." He stopped as his eyes welled with tears.

"Did you know them? Did you know who they were?" Lucy sat down on the bed and took hold of the farmer's rough brown hand. He shook his head sadly. The young boy who was waiting by the door stared at the floor. His sisters were gone, his brother was dead and his father had become a mere shadow of what he once was.

"How old are your daughters?" It was Samantha who continued the questioning.

"Beth is twenty-two, she's only just got married. Annie's..." The big man broke down in fits of tears that gushed over his craggy face. "She's only eleven, for God's sake. She's only eleven. Who'd do something like that?" He looked up at the two women. "Tell me, who'd do something like that?"

Both women held back their emotions. What kind of a world was this? They stayed with the farmer until he drifted off to sleep, or maybe he just shut out the world. Either way, they removed themselves from the room and went back to the kitchen. Alice, the farmer's wife, had prepared some sandwiches and made some tea. Lucy believed that as well as being in a state of shock and denial, Alice was probably a little slow-witted. Keeping busy was the best thing for her, but at some stage she was going to have to face what had happened.

Mike opened the outer kitchen door as Samantha and Lucy came through the inner one.

"How is he?" asked Emma. Alice stopped stoking the coals in the range to listen.

"He's resting now," Lucy said. "He got badly beaten, but there's no permanent damage." She looked at Alice. "I'd let him sleep for a little while before you go in. He's been through a lot." Alice smiled nervously and resumed stoking the coals.

Mike noticed Lucy had her doctor's bag in her hand and took it from her. "I'll give you a hand with this, Doc," he said, making eye contact with all three women from his group, motioning for them to follow him outside. He led them to the ambulance and flung the bag in the back. "We need to get out of here right now."

"We can't just leave these people, Mike," Samantha said. "They need our help."

"Fine, they can come with us, but these raiders will be back, so we need to move."

"He's not going anywhere. Jesus, after what's just happened to them..." Lucy was a little agitated by Mike's lack of compassion.

"Okay, look, I'll try to convince him. I'll explain to him that if these guys come back it will be his whole family wiped out next time."

"Mike. They kidnapped his daughters. One of them was eleven. Eleven, Mike, that's not much older than Sammy."

"I'm not saying this is an ideal situation, Doc. It's shit. There isn't a part of this that doesn't stick in my gut. But what it boils down to is this: I need to protect my family. I'm not going to risk these fuckers getting hold of Sammy or Em, or you or Samantha for that matter. When I said I owed you, Doc, I meant it. As far as I'm concerned, you're with us now. Like I say, I'll do my best to make him see sense. But *we* have to leave. I'm not prepared to risk our safety."

"We need to help them, Mike," Samantha said once again.

"For fuck's sake, Samantha!" She was visibly taken aback that Mike had sworn at her. "Don't you understand what's going on here? Don't you see how serious this is? This isn't some post-apocalyptic Scooby Doo; we're not trundling around in our ambulance solving crimes and helping strangers. This is literally life and death... Literally! If you want to help them, help me convince them to leave with us." Without waiting for a response, Mike turned and stormed back into the house.

The women stood looking at each other. Everything he had said made perfect sense, but every ounce of humanity within the three of them was shouting in a deafening voice that they needed to help this family.

Eventually it was Lucy who spoke. "He's right. It really hurts me to say it, but he's right. If these guys come back, we could all end up dead or worse. We need to try and persuade them to come with us. I saw that farmer's eyes though; the guy's already dead inside. He won't come, but maybe we can save his wife and his sons... maybe."

The three women slowly walked back into the house. In the kitchen, Alice was mixing something in a bowl, and she seemed oblivious to what was going on. Mike had already gone to see the farmer, and they could hear voices mumbling behind the old pine door.

"Alice... Alice... We need you to listen to us for a minute," Emma said, trying to get the housewife's attention.

"What is it, dear?" Alice asked, smiling. She lifted the bowl up so she could carry on mixing the contents while she spoke.

"Alice. We'd like you to come with us," Emma said.

"Come with you where, dear?" Alice replied distantly.

"Well, we're going north. We're heading to Scotland, but right now, we just need to get away from this farm. We think the people who were here last night are going to come back." She looked at the older woman pleadingly but saw no understanding or acceptance in her face.

"Oh, no, no, no, dear, we couldn't leave. There's always so much to do on a farm, the work never ends. No, no, no, we couldn't leave, dear." With that she turned around and placed the bowl back on the kitchen table.

The three women looked at each other hopelessly until they were jolted by the deafening tirade that erupted in the other room.

"For fuck's sake, Joseph, will you listen to me? The blood of your entire family will be on your hands if you don't come with us. These men are coming back. How you lived through last night is a miracle, but you won't be so lucky next time, and neither will your sons and your wife. Is that what you want? Is it? Tell me, because I'll go out there now and put them all out of their fucking misery so at least you won't have it hanging over your heads." The door opened abruptly and Mike stomped out. "It's like talking to a fucking lump of wood," he shouted, barging down the hall. "Come on, let's get loaded up," Mike said to the three women. They stood silently in the kitchen, their mouths gaping.

Emma went to collect her brother and sister from the other room. The two farmer's sons sat on the opposite sofa. They looked scared. The youngest looked like he was about to start crying again. No doubt Mike's outburst had something to do with that.

Lucy went through to the master bedroom and gently knocked on the door. Joseph was sitting up in bed, staring straight ahead, his eyes cloudy and distant.

"Joseph. I'm sorry about Mike. He's a little... He can get a little... Look, I don't like how he said it, but please think about your family. If those men come back, you could lose the rest of them." Her soft New England accent slowly spilt the words out. "Joseph, you need to come with us. You've got two young boys who need their father. You've got a wife who needs her husband. Please think about that."

The farmer turned onto his side away from her. He said nothing. Sadness crept over Lucy's face as she resigned herself to defeat. She turned and left the bedroom.

Mike already had the engine running and everybody in the back. He was looking at the front door of the farmhouse waiting for Lucy to appear.

Inside, Lucy tried to speak to Alice once more, but to no avail. She went in to speak to the boys, the youngest was crying again, so she crouched down in front of the other.

"Look. We've got to go now. If you hear vehicles after we're gone, get your brother, your mum and your dad into that room where we found you. Take the shotgun with you and take some shells in too.

Don't come back out until you're sure they've gone. Do you understand me?" she asked, holding the boy firmly by the elbows.

He nodded, and just as she was about to stand up, he spoke in a weak, broken voice. "My sister is only eleven. Why would they take her? She's only eleven." Lucy gulped, trying to stifle her feelings. She turned and walked through the kitchen and out of the house. She climbed into the cab of the ambulance and the wheels began to roll.

They were about a hundred metres away from the house when Mike looked across at Lucy. Her head was bowed and tears were falling onto her chest. He slowed down the ambulance and reached over to her. "Doc?"

"She's only eleven, for God's sake," she stuttered, between baying cries. Her eyes overflowed with grief as she looked towards Mike. "She's a little girl. She's a little girl, Mike." Lucy fished around for something with which to dab away the tears but found nothing. Mike took out a wad of gauze he had stashed in his pocket and handed it to her. He pulled on the handbrake and put the vehicle in neutral, opened the door and climbed down.

For a moment he leant against the ambulance with his eyes tightly closed. His breathing gradually became heavier and heavier and his hands started to shake uncontrollably. He crouched down on the floor, hoping to compose himself before anyone could see him like that.

"What's happening?" asked Jake, puzzled at why they had stopped.

The boy's question went unanswered but Lucy decided to find out. She jumped down, wiping away tears as she did, and walked round the front of the ambulance to find Mike knelt down on the ground, his arms tightly wrapped around his torso in a vain attempt to stop the uncontrollable rage that was making his body convulse. His eyes looked wired shut as she approached him, and her words went unheard and unanswered.

"Mike. Mike, what's going on?" She crouched down and tentatively extended her hand to his shoulder. As she made contact, he flinched, as if being woken from a terrifying nightmare. She repeated her question, this time with real concern as she noticed his violent shaking. She put a hand on his forehead to see if he was running a fever, but he wasn't.

Mike didn't speak for a moment. His breathing was still erratic, his face still twitched. He grabbed hold of Lucy's hand and took several deep breaths in the hope that he would regain his composure. Finally he was able to speak. "We do this my way. I know what these people are. I know how to deal with them. We do this my way!"

"Deal with who? Do what your way?" She asked, staring into his bloodshot eyes.

"We're going to get those girls back."

11

Within five minutes, they were stood back around the kitchen table. Emma had taken Jake and Sammy into the lounge, but was standing in the doorway so she could hear the plan. At the prospect of being able to rescue his daughters, Joseph had snapped out of his trance-like state and was perched at the head of the table, keen to hear the details.

"First things first," began Mike. "Joseph. What's underneath the stone chips out there?"

"We've got some thick barrier sheeting, but underneath that it's just earth. Why?" he asked, a little puzzled.

"The raiders are going to come back. Maybe tonight, maybe tomorrow, but it will be soon because they won't want to run the risk of losing what's in this place to someone else. The fact that they closed the gate when they left tells me that they saw what was in your outbuildings. They'll definitely take the food;

they may take some of the vehicles or other supplies as well. The chances are they'll also come back into the house to see if there was anything they missed," he said, looking around the table to make sure everybody was following. Even Alice was looking a little more responsive now her husband was up and about.

"Okay. I'm guessing all these guys will be armed. We've got one shotgun between the lot of us, so we can't get into a gun battle with them. We're going to have to use what's at our disposal. So we'll dig some pit traps, y'know, like bear hunters used to use in America. I noticed there's a mechanical digger in one of your barns, Joseph. How long would it take to dig three holes, four by six and roughly six feet deep?" Mike looked the older man straight in the eyes, hoping he could take up the challenge.

He mumbled a few figures under his breath as he visualised the task. "The digging won't take too long, probably less than an hour for each hole. But we're going to have to cart the earth away and even up the surrounds," he said, looking back up at Mike.

"You've got a flatbed truck in one of the barns. We can use that to clear the earth, yes?"

"Well, it's not a tipper, but yes... yes we could."

"We don't know how long we've got – and there's the chance these guys could come back before we're even ready, in which case we're going to have to just fight for our lives – but the sooner we get started, the sooner we'll be done. We want holes in front of this door, the side door of the barn where your vehicles are and the side door of the building where you've got your food store. The main doors are bolted from the inside, so they'll have to use the side entrances. Take your lads, Joseph, and get started on those." Mike looked at him once more, hoping he'd spring into action.

"Before we do anything, we need to move my son and son-in-law somewhere until we can give them a proper burial."

"Joseph," said Mike softly as he leant forward, "those two men died trying to protect what was important to them. Leaving them where they fell makes it look like there's nobody left here. That will give us an advantage that could save your family and mine. When this is all over, I'll help you bury them myself. I would be proud to help you honour them. But right now, don't let their deaths be in vain." He leaned back from the table and watched Joseph, who nodded, understanding what was at stake, and signalled for his two boys to follow him.

When they had gone, Mike spoke to the women. "Alice, we need curtains, bed sheets, quilt covers and whatever you can lay your hands on that can cover a six by four hole, okay?" At first the farmer's wife looked a little shocked to be included in part of the plans, but she did as she was asked.

"Okay, you two," said Mike, looking at Samantha and Lucy. "We need wooden curtain poles, mop handles, sweeping brushes. Get a sharp knife and whittle them into spears. Then take the chairs apart," he said, pointing at the solid pine seating around the table. "The legs, the spindles, anything you can sharpen and turn into a spike for our traps, use it." No sooner had he spoken than the two women got to work.

"What do you want me to do?" Emma asked, still standing in the doorway.

"I need you to take the ambulance back the way we came and park about a mile away, well out of sight. Then I need you to come back. There's a Land Rover and a caravan in one of the barns. Take the kids, a good supply of food and go park them with the ambulance and stay there. If this all goes south we're going to need a getaway plan." He looked at her hoping she wouldn't argue.

"I can fight too, y'know. I'm not useless."

Mike moved across to her and spoke softly. "That's exactly why I want you with Sammy and Jake. You're the only one I trust to defend them." He hugged his sister tightly and they looked at each other, knowing how dangerous the next few hours would be. Finally Mike smiled. "Now fuck off, I've got work to do."

Emma let out a small laugh and turned to get the children.

*

Within four hours, the finishing touches were being put to the traps. Old sheets and curtain lining was straining under the weight of a single layer of stone chips. Beneath each sheet lay 144 cubic feet of nothing above a bed of sharp wooden spikes standing to attention in quick-drying cement. Mike had salvaged three chairs, some rope and some duct tape and taken them to an open space in one of the barns. If all went to plan he would need them later. The sun was getting low in the sky and it would not be long before darkness fell.

Alice and her youngest son, John, had joined Emma, Jake and Sammy a mile away in comparative safety. Mike was with Lucy and Samantha in the house. They had unlatched the window to the master bedroom; that was the only way in and out of the property avoiding the trap. All three stood at the front window as the farmer and his eldest son, Peter, cleared away the last evidence of the day's work. Mike handed the shotgun and a dozen shells to Lucy.

"I saw the way you handled this earlier, Doc. I'm guessing you were used to guns back in the US." She broke the shotgun to load it like she had done a thousand times in her youth. "You two are the key to this whole thing." He handed Samantha one of the spears that had been fashioned from a wooden mop handle. "On the off chance one of them gets in here, you need to do whatever you can to buy time for the Doc. Me, Joseph and his son will hide wherever we can. Ideally we won't break cover until the first trap has been sprung. What we need you to do is usher as many as you can towards the other holes. If we're lucky, we'll use all three traps, and that will mean there are just two raiders left for us to deal with. Best-case scenario, we want three of them alive, but at the end of the day, do what you need to do." Mike looked at the two women, picked up the pile of makeshift weapons from the bed and made his exit.

"Y'know, as grateful as I am that we have a plan, I can't shake the feeling that Mike got this straight out of an episode of the A-Team," Lucy said, half smiling in the dimming light of the evening.

"Well, at least the A-Team were always alive at the end of each episode," Samantha replied.

The pair watched as Mike went over to the farmer and his son. He handed them spears and kitchen knives and made movements, presumably fighting tips, before pointing to various spots around the courtyard.

*

Darkness had fallen. The temperature had cooled noticeably and both women had their hands tucked under their armpits to keep them warm.

"If it's this cold in here it must be freezing out there," Samantha said, wiping away the condensation her breath had caused on the window. The low moon illuminated enough of the courtyard to see basic outlines, but the three outside were invisible.

"What time is it?" Lucy asked.

"Just after eight," Samantha said, squinting at the display on her watch. "They might not even come tonight. We could be like this for days."

"Yeah, that thought occurred to me too, but Mike seems to think they wouldn't risk losing what's on this farm to someone else, so let's wait and see." She rubbed her eyes to try and ward off sleep.

"Are you okay?"

"Killer headache."

"I'll see if there's anything in the bathroom cabinet."

"No need, I've got some painkillers," she said, reaching into her pocket for a plastic bottle.

Samantha squinted to see the bottle Lucy removed from her pocket, but it was too dark. She watched the doctor take a pill and place it on her tongue before cocking her head back and swallowing.

"Do you want me to get you a glass of water?"

Lucy just shook her head.

The moon slowly rose higher and higher as the night wore on, and the temperature dropped further.

"I found these in the wardrobe," Samantha said, handing a thick towelling bath robe to Lucy and keeping one for herself. The women draped them over their shoulders to fight the cold night air. They had to keep the window open wide enough so as to be ready when the raiders did return, as the creak of a window opening could waste any advantage they had tried to gain.

Mike was warm despite the cold night. He was out of sight of the courtyard, behind a drywall at the back of one of the barns. His ears were tuned to every sound and he was keeping himself psyched up and awake by intermittently doing push ups. He had done this a thousand times before in rugby training, often in weather colder than this. It helped the blood flow, it helped him focus. He was determined that when they came he wouldn't too stiff to fight them.

The farmer and his son were crouched down at the side of two outbuildings. They were used to being in the cold. They spent their lives working outside. They wore woollen hats and gloves and were just as ready as Mike to do battle. Joseph looked at his watch. 11.20pm. Maybe they wouldn't show up tonight. They had been and gone by this time the previous night, robbing him of the best parts of him in a matter of moments. He looked across at Peter and felt overwhelming pride; this young boy was acting so selflessly, so bravely. If he could get his daughters back then maybe they could build a new life together. This farm held too many bad memories now. They would go to his brother's place in Candleton. His brother was an influential man there; he owned a huge farm and other property. He was respected by the village. He had asked Joseph to move there before all this trouble had started. Well, if they got through tonight, his family would leave this place behind and they would start afresh.

And what of these strangers? Well, they would be welcome too. They were risking their lives in the name of decency when they owed him nothing. The fact that they couldn't stomach what had happened was proof they were good people. The sky was falling all around them, but they were prepared to risk their own safety to do the right thing. His brother would welcome people like that. But first things first...

It was past midnight when the drone of an engine could be heard coming up the lane. Mike got into a crouching position and checked his boot to make sure he had easy access to his knife. His hatchet was on the ground in front of him and his screwdriver was safely in his belt. The farmer and his son, Peter, picked up their spears in one hand and their knives in the other. They stayed low and ready to spring. Samantha stepped to the side of the window, one eye peeking around the corner. Lucy knelt down, shrugging off the bath robe; she was invisible to those outside. The shotgun was steady and poised on the window ledge.

The vehicle was a Land Rover, a little older than the one Emma had driven up the road earlier in the day. Four doors opened in unison and five men got out, a variety of shapes and sizes, but all carrying guns of one description or another. The place looked the same as when they had left it. The door to the house was still slightly ajar and the bodies of their victims were in the same places they had fallen. There was no reason for them to think the farm wasn't theirs for the taking. The tall skinhead who was driving said something and the others laughed; the laugh sounded forced, which told Mike that the skinhead was probably the leader and the rest of the gang were laughing more out of fear than being impressed by his comic genius. The skinhead started giving instructions and then pointing towards the various buildings and the men slowly fanned out. They each had a torch or lantern in one hand and a gun in the other. Two headed towards the barn with the vehicles, the leader and a sidekick headed towards the building with the produce and the final figure started towards the house.

Lucy's finger tightened around the trigger as she watched the four heading towards the outbuildings. Samantha's eyes were fixed on the man heading towards the farmhouse. For Mike, it all seemed to be happening in slow motion. He watched the two sets of torches approaching, but he was more concerned about the one moving away from him.

A loud noise of ripping fabric echoed around the courtyard, closely followed by two screams and the sound of falling stone chips. One trap sprung and two raiders down. The leader and his sidekick raised their torches in the direction of the screams but could see nothing. They changed their course and headed towards their fallen comrades. Lucy took aim and fired. Stone chips sprayed up into the air in front of them. They stopped in mid stride and scurried back to the doorway of the barn. The leader almost pushed his sidekick out of the way to get there first. Before he knew what was happening, the ground disappeared beneath him. As his torch fell, he could see a shaft of wood glistening dark red through his right foot. He couldn't see the one that punctured his left calf, but he could feel it. He screamed in agony. His sidekick, who had managed to avoid the hole, thanks in no small part to being pushed out of the way by his boss, dropped his torch and started running back to the Land Rover.

Mike set off after him. He had taken the knife from his boot and was sprinting at full speed. He needed to get to the henchman before he got to the car, and before he realised there was someone other than the sniper to worry about. Lucy saw what was happening and fired in front of the escaping raider. He stopped and aimed his gun in the general direction of the bedroom. He fired a few shots and Lucy ducked down behind the wall. Her actions had given Mike enough time, though, and he dived on top of the gunman, plunging the knife into his neck, right up to the hilt. A dribble of blood from the gunman's mouth looked black in the moonlight as he collapsed first to his knees, then flat on his face. Mike paused for a second, making sure he was dead. It dawned on him that he killed RAMs out of necessity, but this looting, murdering, child rapist: well, he actually *wanted* to kill him.

The courtyard echoed with howls and screams of pain from the two sprung traps.

Mike withdrew his weapon and bolted towards the house. He had lost sight of the fifth man. He glanced over his shoulder and noticed that Joseph and Peter had emerged to stand guard on the off chance that one of the raiders made it out of the trap. On his approach to the house, he saw that the final trap had not been sprung and the door had not moved. He heard a boom from inside and leapfrogged the trap. He ran through the house, his fist clutched tight around the knife. He flew at the bedroom door, kicked his legs out in front of him and burst through in time to see a figure collapsing to the floor.

Samantha had her spear raised towards Mike, her hands shaking wildly, and Lucy was pointing the gun square at his chest. As soon as she saw his moonlit features, she lowered her weapon and let out a breath. She looked down at the body on the floor in horror. Her entire adult life had been spent trying to save lives and now she had taken one. Her throat tightened.

Mike looked at Samantha, who was still shaking, and then at Lucy. "He would have killed both of you, or worse. Think about the little girl this piece of shit kidnapped, and then tell me he hasn't got off lightly. Because I'm telling you now, if that was my sister and I had the time, I'd make sure it took days for him to die." He grabbed the gun from the dead man, climbed out of the window, collected the gun from the raider he had killed and then went to join Joseph and Peter. The screaming from the pits was constant. Mike kept the handgun even though he had no idea how to shoot. He handed the pump-action shotgun to Joseph, who cocked it and pointed it towards the hole where the group's leader had vanished. Peter had collected two torches and together the three of them slowly approached the trap. Mike and Joseph had their guns raised; Peter controlled the light. When they got to the edge, they saw that the once brave leader had fear and pain in his eyes. His shotgun was at one end of the pit, more than an arm's length away.

Mike thought for a moment about leaving them all in the traps, but then realised there was a risk that they could fall unconscious due to too much blood loss, so he instructed Peter to go and get some rope. Getting the three of them out of the holes took more time than he had anticipated. There was no struggle, as they had no option but to put themselves at the mercy of their captors – it beat bleeding to death. They were in no condition to fight anyway; they could barely walk, never mind do battle. With guns in their faces, they got temporary patches put on their wounds.

One of the men from the other pit had fallen in almost horizontally. A spike had broken his collarbone and another had gone through his thigh. The third man wasn't impaled as the cement had not set as evenly as it should have. When he fell, the wooden spikes folded underneath him, but the drop was enough to break his ankle, and the knowledge that he would not be able to climb out of the hole removed any will to fight.

They allowed themselves to be tied to chairs so they could be treated. If they were getting patched up, there was no way these people would kill them – what would be the point of that? They were soft, the kind of people Ripper and his crew had exploited all their lives. Bleeding hearts who always wanted to find the good in people. He'd turn on the waterworks and apologise; he'd plead for his life and they'd lap it up, especially the women. Yeah, he might have to give back the bitches that he'd taken the night before, and he'd probably even suffer a beating. He'd cry some more and beg forgiveness and then, when his crew was back to strength, they'd return here and fuck every last one of them over. Shit! The pain was unbearable, but the prospect of getting revenge on these fuckers was gradually numbing him to everything else. They had no idea who they were messing with. Every last one of them was going to pay for this. The world hadn't changed that much;

dumb fucks like this still thought people deserved a second chance. He could see the weakness in their faces. The blonde who was dressing his wounds and that cute redheaded bitch looked like they'd piss themselves if you shouted boo, and the old man, fuck, he'd shit his pants if you pulled a face at him. Yeah, he was going to get out of this mess like he had all the others and then he was going to get some payback. He'd get payback for them blindsiding the rest of his crew, but more importantly he'd get payback for himself, because nobody fucking messed with him.

When Lucy and Samantha had done what they could, Mike told them to take Joseph and Peter and go and get the others.

Lucy pulled him to one side "Mike, I don't feel comfortable leaving you alone here. Yes, they're injured, but there are three of them, for God's sake."

He pulled Lucy into the shadows of the work lights Joseph had erected, and spoke softly to her. "Doc. I lived with scum like this when they sent me away, and I know how their minds work. I'm going to find out where those girls are and I don't want anybody I care about watching me do it, 'cos it ain't going to be pretty. Now, please go check on my brother and sisters, and throw some water on your face. You look like shit," he said with a cheeky grin. The best Lucy could manage was a strained smile. She glanced across at the three bound raiders and wondered if Mike really knew what he was doing.

When he was alone with his captives, he walked around them and dragged their chairs into a wide arrow shape. The leader faced straight ahead; his two goons faced sideways, opposite each other, but able to see their boss and their captor.

Mike dropped out of sight and the three prisoners looked at each other, puzzled. Had they been left alone? Their thoughts were not their own for long as their captor soon returned with a variety of objects. There was a fire extinguisher, a green jerrican, which was half full by the sound of the sloshing liquid inside, and a rickety white plastic lawn chair, which he positioned facing his prisoners, about ten metres back from them. He disappeared again.

"What the fuck's this? What the fuck's goin' on here, man?" the youngest of the prisoners asked.

"Just keep it fuckin' buttoned," snarled Ripper. "Neither of you two say nothin'. Let me handle this, y'hear me? This fucking prick just wants to scare us, man. I looked in their eyes. They ain't nothin'. None of 'em. Let me do the talkin', you understand me?" The pair nodded and bowed their heads, not sure whether to be more scared of their captor or their leader.

When Mike returned, it was with a bottle of water. He sat down in the chair, casually unscrewed the top on the bottle and took a drink before placing the bottle carefully on the floor.

His three prisoners just watched him. Mike rolled his shoulders and his neck as if loosening up for a gymnastics event. He stood, picked up the jerrican of diesel, walked over to the leader and unscrewed the lid of the container. Translucent red liquid poured over the bound prisoner, who coughed and spluttered. Ripper was confident that all this was just for show. There was no way this guy was going to do anything. He had to play along, though. He had to feign fear.

"Look man! Don't do nothin' stupid, I'll tell you whatever you want." He spluttered and coughed the words as Mike screwed the cap back on the can.

Mike stood, looking down at his captive for a few seconds. Then he thought of his little sister, Sammy. What if this scum had kidnapped her?

He bent down close to the spluttering man's ear and whispered. "No, you won't. But your friends will."

Mike stood back and saw a momentary look of confusion on the skinhead's face as he reached into his back pocket and retrieved some safety matches he had taken from the farmhouse when he had got the bottle of water. He took out three and struck them.

Ripper began to scream even before the first match touched him. It was the realisation of what was about to happen more than anything else. The small flaming sticks seemed to dance in the air for an eternity. Mike stood a good six feet back, but even he was a little surprised at the initial heat blast that rushed towards him as the diesel ignited.

He watched from where he stood for a second then walked back to his chair. Ripper tried to flail and writhe, stopped only by the thick rope that held him down. At first his screams sounded like high-pitched wolf howls. As fabric slowly welded to his body and turned to black, the howling stopped and low-pitched growling yelps of pain took over. His frame shuddered again and again as the flames turned the skin into a burnt, crackling mess. Ripper's comrades were wailing. Terrified that the same fate awaited them, they watched in abject terror, shaking violently beneath the ropes that bound them to their chairs.

Eventually the grating shouts of torment stopped and Ripper slumped forward in the chair. The ropes finally gave way to the flames and the body collapsed onto the floor, life already long gone. Mike took another drink of water and sat for a while cross-legged on the chair, looking at his two terrified prisoners. A few minutes passed and he picked up the fire extinguisher, walked up to the flaming mess and released the white foam over what was left of the body to extinguish the still violent flames.

Mike pulled the other two chairs closer together so he could talk to them both at the same time. Both men, younger than Mike, but obviously old enough to murder and rape, sobbed like terrified infants in front of him.

"This is very, very simple. I'm going to ask you some questions, and you're going to answer me. If you don't answer me or you tell me lies, what happened to your friend here will look like a fucking spa treatment compared to what will happen to you. Do you understand me?" Mike asked in an eerily emotionless voice.

The two prisoners continued to sob and look down at their dead leader.

Outside, the ambulance, Land Rover and caravan pulled up in the courtyard. The doors opened and everyone filed out. Torches clicked on to light the way. Joseph started heading towards the barn, but Lucy went after him. She took him by the arm and guided him into the house. Peter jumped over the trap and opened the large kitchen window. Jake and Sammy found it amusing, being lowered into the kitchen through the window. The adults climbed through with varying degrees of ease.

Although the night was far from over, the mood was slightly more optimistic than it had been earlier. Alice put some logs in the range and lit a few candles. She took a large bottle of water from under the sink and poured it into a kettle which she placed on the range to boil. Joseph walked over to her and held her tightly.

They were an ill-matched couple as far as height went, Joseph nearly six foot two and Alice barely five foot, but their embrace spoke volumes about their love for each other.

They all stood around the black wrought-iron range that had driven heat through the old farmhouse for generations. Its warm glow comforted their bodies, allowed their minds to drift and relax for just a few moments, so much so that a few of them jumped when they heard Mike clattering through the window. All eyes looked towards him expectantly.

"There are only two of them left behind to guard the house. It's a big detached place a couple of miles up the road, just on the outskirts of the village. They said it looked new. No furniture, no appliances, big enclosed gardens, two garages. There's another girl as well as your daughters. They keep them tied up in one of the garages. They've got a lot of supplies, food, water, some more guns and ammunition." He looked towards Lucy. "I know it's not ideal to travel at night, but we need to go up there now. We'll get the girls out and then head back there tomorrow. Supplies like that are too valuable to leave behind."

"How do you know what they're saying is true?" Joseph said.

"Don't worry, it's true," Mike replied and looked Lucy straight in the eye. "We'll take the Land Rover they came in. It's got tinted windows; we can drive straight up to the house and they won't suspect a thing. Joseph, you drive, I'll ride shotgun. Doc, it would be good to have you there just in case."

"I want to go," Peter said indignantly.

"No, lad," Joseph replied, "you keep a watch over things here." The teenager nodded, pleased at being given the responsibility of looking after the homestead.

"Of course I'll go," Lucy said. "I was the one who got you into this anyway." She swapped her shotgun for a pump-action that one of the raiders had brought and headed towards the window.

Joseph freed himself from his wife's grip and followed her. Mike rubbed his eyes. He couldn't remember when he had last slept, when he had last eaten, or even what day it was, but he could remember why he'd agreed to help these people. He went across to his siblings and bent down to give the smaller ones a kiss and a hug. He embraced Emma and smiled reassuringly at Samantha, who was glued to the side of his family. It was time to end this ordeal once and for all.

12

Before the Land Rover even pulled away, Peter and his younger brother were barrowing earth to fill in the traps that had won them victory earlier in the evening. Joseph looked at his sons and allowed himself another guilty moment of pride.

"You've got two good kids there, Joseph," Mike said, but rather than making Joseph feel better, it made him feel worse. He had a son dead not a few feet from where he sat, a son-in-law the same and his girls were still tied up in some garage. Anger overtook his thoughts and the Land Rover sped away.

Mike was worried that they could run into RAMs, but the worries were unfounded. There were far fewer people in rural areas so it followed that there would be far fewer RAMs. Until the food supplies ran out in the cities, that was. Then they would start going cross country to find prey.

It only took them a short time to reach the prison holding Joseph's daughters. Mike put on a baseball cap that had been on the dashboard. In the dark, and at this distance from the house, there was no way that anyone could tell Mike wasn't one of the gang. He opened the gate, allowed the Land Rover to pass through, then closed it safely behind them. He climbed back in and the vehicle proceeded up the long paved drive. It pulled up in front of the spacious property and Mike reached over and honked the horn twice. There were flickers from inside and then two figures carrying torches came towards them. Mike couldn't see if they were carrying any weapons, but he guessed they would feel no need.

"Get ready," Mike said, as the first figure sidled up to the passenger door and bent down, waiting for the occupants to lower the window. Instead, the door opened with brute force. The figure was knocked back, a fountain of blood spraying from his nose, and Mike was on top of him, plunging his knife into the area below the kidnapper's Adam's apple before he even had time to figure out what was going on. Joseph quickly opened his door and aimed the shotgun at the chest of the young man who had come round to the driver's side.

"Take me to the girls." At first the figure, with his hands high in the air, illuminated only by the dropped torch and the car headlights, didn't move, but when Joseph barked "Now!" he headed towards the garage.

They got him to undo a padlock at the base of the door and Mike stood back to lift it. Lucy climbed into the driver's seat and drove the car up to the garage. The lights shone in to reveal three terrified girls, tied together in the shape of a shamrock. Mike took the shotgun from Joseph, keeping an eye on the remaining gang member. "Go free your daughters,

Joseph," he said, gently placing his hand on the older man's shoulders.

Fear continued to pound in the hearts of the three captives. They had no idea what was going on. They didn't know they were being rescued; they thought this was just more of the horror they had already suffered. The youngest girl began to cry again as a tall black silhouette approached them. He was talking, but his words were barely audible above the sounds outside and their own rushing blood. But as the man drew closer, two of the girls recognised a familiar voice.

"Dad?" said the oldest, in disbelief. "Oh, Dad," she said again, this time releasing floods of tears. She'd been told her family was dead, she'd seen her husband on the ground, and now, to hear her father's voice, it was more than she could ever have hoped for.

"Daddy? Is that Daddy?" Annie screamed. She was angled away from the door. All she could see was a shadow on the wall looming larger and larger as the figure got closer.

"It's Daddy, my sweethearts," Joseph said, as he fell to his knees and stretched his arms around his two girls. He wanted to be strong for them, but he couldn't control his own tears. "It's your Daddy, darling. I've come to take you home." All three began sobbing uncontrollably. The third young woman, a stranger, wept too, her ordeal over.

Lucy sat in the car with the engine still running, sniffing, overcome with the emotion of the moment. Mike allowed himself to snatch a brief moment of levity and then looked back at the remaining gang member. Emotion bled away from his face.

"Move. Now," he said and gestured for the terrified teenager to start walking. He still had his hands raised as they walked around the back of the garage. Small splinters of light from the headlights and from the moon illuminated the narrow passage between the garage and the tall bushes enclosing the lawn.

"Please," the young man begged. Mike pulled the trigger. Nothing happened. He really would have to find out how to use one of these things before long. He dropped the gun to the floor and the prisoner turned to fight, but Mike quickly removed his knife, stabbed it hard into the young man's stomach, withdrew it and stuck it fiercely into his throat. Shock and gasping horror swept over the kidnapper's face as he put both his hands up to his neck. He dropped forward on his knees and made a sound like the last slushy drops of a milkshake being sucked through a straw, before falling face down to the ground.

When Mike came back round to the front of the garage, the captives had been released. Joseph's daughters were still sobbing, clinging to him like limpets. The other young woman was unsteady on her feet and Lucy had climbed out of the Land Rover to help her. Mike suggested that Joseph should sit in the back with Beth and Annie for the return journey. The other young woman joined them. Lucy got into the driver's seat.

"There's one more thing to take care of," Mike said. "I just need to get something out of the back of the car and then you can take it down to the gate. I'll meet you there in a minute."

Lucy looked in the mirror but couldn't see what Mike was removing from the car. There was a muffled heavy thud and a clank. He signalled for her to move off. As she drove, she looked back. The red glow of the car's lights did nothing to solve the mystery of what Mike had taken from the back of the car.

He looked down at the wriggling pile in front of him. He had bound the two prisoners from the barn tightly together, back to back, legs to legs and feet to feet. Rope and duct tape sealed their joint fates. Their mouths were stuffed with portions of their own torn clothing and glued shut with more tape. They tried to shout, but the result was akin to the noise of a TV on low in a distant part of the house. Nobody could hear them. Mike picked up the jerrican he had brought with him, grabbed the knot around his prisoners' feet and slowly dragged them into the garage. He picked up a torch that had been left on the ground. It was perfect; the garage was empty, the roof was high and it was made of cement, breeze block and little else. He tugged the two gang members into the middle of the floor and poured the remaining diesel over them. Both men were sobbing beneath their ropes and gags.

Mike reflected on the day. He had done things that hadn't sat well with him in the past. In the last twenty-four hours, he had taken the lives of three men. Not RAMs, but living, breathing men. Society demanded compassion, but society had ended. There were no more courts. There were no more prisons, so it was up to those who were left to right the wrongs and to exact justice. These two men deserved to die, but they deserved to suffer too. A bullet would be too quick for the evil they had done, so this was justice. They would burn and they would die and justice would be done.

Mike walked to the front of the garage and lowered the garage door just a little, took the box of matches from his back pocket, removed three, struck them and tossed them towards the diesel-soaked mound. He was further back than before, but still the whoosh of the flames took him by surprise. The screams were barely audible beneath the gags, and the tight ropes allowed little in the way of writhing, but Mike watched as flames engulfed the bodies and the plastic of the duct tape fused to their skin.

"Fuckers!" He spat towards the flames as he pulled down the door and clicked the padlock back into place. Mike ran back down to the gate, opened it up, let Lucy drive through, closed it safely behind them and off they went, back to Mead Hall Farm.

*

By the time the former captives were being tucked into the safety of their own beds along with Tracey, the young woman they had been bound with, it was 4am. Lucy and Samantha had tended to them as best they could, and all three had been embraced until their bones ached.

While Joseph was on the rescue mission to save his daughters, Alice had been making up rooms for the new guests, who, considering what they were doing for her and her family, were welcome with them as long as there was food to eat and air to breathe. As the mild euphoria died down and the younger children were put to bed, the adults began to say their goodnights and retire as well. Joseph, an old-fashioned man, whose handshake and word had been enough for all who had known him in his fifty-odd years on this planet, gripped Mike's shoulder tightly with his left hand. He took Mike's right hand in his and squeezed. Mike thought he could feel the circulation to his fingers stop.

"What you did... what all of you did for us, Mike, we'll never forget it. I'll never forget it. You're a good man. I'm going to bury my boy tomorrow, and my son-in-law. We'll go back to that house and take what they took from others and then I'm driving my family to Candleton where my brother lives. It will be a lot safer there. It's about fifteen miles north of Skelton, and I'd like you to think about coming with us, Mike, you and your family and friends. Trust me, they'd welcome the likes of you with open arms." He paused and looked at Mike's tired face. Lucy was sitting at the other side of the large kitchen table, finishing off her tepid cup of coffee and eavesdropping on the conversation.

"That's very kind of you Joseph, it really is, thank you, but—"

"Just have a think about it. Discuss it with your family and your friends." He released his vice-like grip, nodded and took his leave from the room.

Mike looked across the table to Lucy. They were the only two left in the dimly lit kitchen.

"They've given us the master bedroom and the room next door to it. Joseph and Alice are on camp beds in the girls' rooms. I doubt they'll ever let those girls out of their sight again," she mused while taking another sip from her mug.

"Well, you get off to bed, Doc, I'm going to keep watch," he said, stopping her mid gulp.

"Keep watch? I thought they were all dead," she said, her eyebrows arching in concern.

"They are, Doc. But we're on a farm. Everyone knows there'll be food and supplies on a farm. Just because we've got rid of one group of raiders that doesn't mean another one won't come along."

"Mike, you need to get some sleep. You'll burn yourself out."

"Look, when everyone's up and about again, I'll catch a few hours, but I'm not going to take any risks with our safety." He forced a tired smile. "Go get some sleep, Doc, we've got another hard day ahead of us."

Lucy stood up and walked across to Mike. The bumping and footsteps from the other rooms had died down as, one by one, the others had succumbed to well-overdue sleep. "After the first time we met, Samantha told me about why you were sent away." She said the last two words almost guiltily. "She explained the circumstances to me and I made the assumption that you had some pretty serious anger management issues."

Mike lowered his eyes and laughed a little. It was something he'd heard more than a few times before.

"Then when I heard your plan to get up to Scotland and I saw you in action, I thought it went beyond that. I thought to myself, this guy isn't all there – the way you dived through your living room window, the way you kill the RAMs with that kind of explosive violence – well, I thought there was something a bit deeper than just anger management issues. But everything you've done has been bang on the money. You're the only one who has adapted to this situation. My excuse was that I didn't want to adapt. I didn't want to make those kinds of choices because that would be giving up on the person I was and the values I had. But that was cowardly. I was prepared to go along with what you suggested because it relieved me of the responsibility. If things went wrong, I wouldn't be the one who had made the decision. My hands would be clean." Mike stayed silent as she struggled through her thoughts. She had black rings under her eyes, her collar-length golden hair was dishevelled and there was a dark smudge on the side of her face, but for the first time Mike noticed that Lucy was an attractive woman. Granted, she was a few years older than him, but before this entire nightmare began, she probably turned heads whenever she walked into a room. He waited while she tried to find the words she so desperately wanted to say.

"I understand now. Thanks to you, I understand what needs to be done. I can see that if someone starts a fist-fight with us, we need to finish it with a grenade. I understand that this is the way things need to be now for us just to survive. You figured that out straight away. I just wanted to let you know we're on the same page. And I wanted you to know how grateful I am." She smiled at him. The words didn't come out quite the way she wanted them to, but her point was made.

"We did it together, Doc, you don't need to thank me."

"Yes, I do." With that she turned to head for the bedroom. Before she left the room she looked back at him. "Don't get me wrong. I still think you're crazy, you're just the right kind of crazy."

They shared a lingering smile before she turned again. Mike walked over to the kettle. It had been a long night and it still wasn't over for him. He made himself an instant coffee and wondered how much there was left. Not in the jar, not in the kitchen, but in the country. This might be the last cup of coffee he ever had. He closed his eyes as the warm black liquid rolled over his tongue. It wouldn't be long before the caffeine began to buzz through his veins, giving him the burst of energy he needed just to get through the last few hours of the night.

13

It was past nine before anyone stirred. Mike could hear movement from several rooms, but the first person to appear was Samantha.

"Go to bed now!" Mike just stood there. "I mean it, Mike, you need sleep. Lucy told me you were standing guard all night. If you make any excuses, we've got some stuff in the ambulance that can put an elephant to sleep for a week, and don't think we won't use it."

"Morning, Samantha," Mike said dryly. "Sleep well?"

"I'm serious, Mike," she said, reminding him of a ward matron he had encountered when he was having his appendix out.

He put his hands up. "Okay, okay, I'm going." He walked down the hall. Peter appeared from one of the rooms, his eyes barely open and his head down. Mike carried on to the end door. Emma was dressed and in the process of getting the children ready. They exchanged hugs and hellos, but Mike was unconscious long before they left the room for breakfast.

The morning was well organised, like most days at Mead Hall Farm. After breakfast, which was plentiful but solemn, Joseph began preparing two graves with the mechanical digger while his boys respectfully and carefully wrapped the bodies of their brother and brother-in-law.

Alice and the girls, along with Jake and Sammy, made a start loading the truck, which had now been swept clean of all the dirt and rubble from the previous day. The first job was to pack it with the food and supplies from the barn. Annie, Beth and Tracey worked well together. The latter even managed to raise a small smile from the other two now and again.

The range in the kitchen almost superheated the water, which for the time being was still flowing. Emma, Lucy and Samantha each had a scalding shower followed by a change of clothes. All revitalised and each with a mug of steaming black coffee in their hands, they sat around the kitchen table.

"We should be out there helping," Emma said.

"We will in a minute," Lucy replied. She leant forward, elbows on the table, hands clasped around her coffee mug. "Look, just before I turned in last night, Joseph invited us to join him. He's convinced that his brother's place will be a safe haven. We're heading north anyway, so I think it would be an idea to tag along. If it's as secure as he thinks we should stop there a couple of days and get ourselves a bit more prepared."

"What do you mean, more prepared?" Emma said.

"For a start, we've got weapons and ammo now, and unless I'm mistaken, I'm the only one in our group who's ever used a gun. I could show all three of you how to use one. And judging by the last twenty-four hours, we could be on the road a long time before we get to where we're going. We need to make a few repairs and modifications to the ambulance. Having no bumper makes it a lot easier for the RAMs to get underneath. In the back of the ambulance, you're completely blind to anything other than what you can see through the windscreen at the front. If we had some tools and a bit of time, we could put some peepholes in. That's just for starters." She leaned back, drawing her coffee with her, and looked at the two women to gauge their reactions.

Samantha nodded gently; it was obvious that Lucy had already discussed this with her. Emma's left eyebrow arched, her eyes fixed firmly on the black liquid swilling gently in her cup.

"You're right, it makes sense," she said thoughtfully.

Lucy was a little surprised. Up until now, she hadn't had a lot of interaction with Emma, but was of the opinion she did whatever her brother told her. She felt somewhat guilty that she had jumped to such a conclusion. "Okay then."

The three women finished their drinks in silence and emerged into the morning light. The area near the supply barn was a hive of activity, so they headed across there. They joined the human conveyor belt that was loading and securing the truck. This was nothing new for Lucy – she had grown up in a rural community back in New England. Her father had been a chemist, but his brothers had carried on the family farm. She had often helped out in her holidays and at harvest time. The days were long and the work was exhausting, but the sense of community on the farm always kept her going. She felt that now, a single purpose.

At midday, Peter came across to tell them that they were ready to bury the bodies.

The service was short and unceremonious but full of emotion. Before the earth covered the blanketed body of her husband, Beth removed a locket from around her neck and gently dropped it into the grave. "I'll always love you, Francis. You were the best thing that ever happened to me. My heart will belong to you forever," she sobbed. As she walked away, Joseph and Peter picked up shovels and began filling in the grave. Although the holes had been made by a mechanical digger, the dead at least deserved the earth on their bodies to be replaced with the sweat of their own.

After a short pause, the work began again. There would be time to grieve properly when they were in Candleton.

Before long, all that remained in the supply barn was empty racking. The team of women and children went back into the house and Lucy thought to herself that this must be a little like the "spirit of the Blitz". Everyday people in a terrifying situation, all working together doing their own small part to help win the war. Of course, the war now was very different.

Soon afterwards, Joseph and Peter joined them in the farmhouse kitchen. Both of them scrubbed their hands clean in the large sink before accepting warm drinks from Alice and Beth.

"We should be thinking about getting back to that house soon. Get what we can while it's there," Joseph said, to anyone who was listening, but mainly to Lucy.

She nodded. "It's probably an idea to go in two vehicles, just in case."

"Aye, well, we've got a box van that we use for the farmers' markets, holds plenty, pretty nippy too," he said, looking towards Lucy for approval.

"Okay, well, I'll wake Mike and we'll take the Land Rover up front. We'll clear the way for you in case there are any..." She was about to say RAMs but, noticing there were still children in the room, opted for "problems".

At that moment, the bedroom door at the end of the hall opened and Mike stepped out, stumbling a little. He carried on down the hallway, leaning on the wall and limping. All eyes were on him as he entered the kitchen. Emma was the first to stand and go to her brother.

"What's wrong, Mike?"

"It's my leg. I cut it yesterday, but didn't think any more of it. I've just woken up now and I can barely walk on it," he said, wincing as he leant on the worktop.

Lucy pulled up his jeans. "That's pretty nasty, Mike. We need to get that cleaned up to make sure it doesn't get infected. You probably didn't feel anything yesterday because of the amount of adrenalin shooting through your system. You need to stay off it as much as you can and we need to get it bandaged up." Lucy stood and started rolling her sleeves up.

"Don't worry," Samantha said, "I can take care of it."

"I think we'd better put off getting those supplies until Mike's leg's a little better," Joseph said.

"I'll be fine," Mike replied, wincing again as he put weight on his leg.

"You're not going anywhere today, Mike," Lucy ordered.

"Look, I'll go with Lucy, Joseph and Peter to the house, and Samantha can stay here and sort Mike's leg out," Emma said, a little nervous but conscious of the fact she had said just two days before that she wanted to take more responsibility.

"No. No way are you going out there, sis."

"So it's okay for Lucy to go out there but not me. How does that work, Mike?" Emma snapped.

"The Doc's... the Doc can use a gun, for a start." It was all he could think of at that moment.

"Mike, I'll drive. Lucy will have the gun in the passenger seat. Joseph and Peter will be right behind us, they'll have weapons too. We won't be gone for more than an hour, an hour and a half at the most. This isn't something I'm arguing about, this is something I'm doing." Mike opened his mouth to reply, but before he could, Emma was already making her way to the car. He went to follow her but winced as he tried to walk and instead put an arm around Samantha, who was already in position to support him.

Lucy raised her eyebrows in surprise and smiled at Mike. "Don't worry, we'll be fine." She headed towards the door. "Ready when you are, Joseph."

Joseph nodded and signalled for Peter to join him. Before leaving the house he turned back. "Please don't worry, Mike, I won't let anything happen to them."

Mike's frustration finally gave way to acceptance. He was in no position to argue.

*

Emma looked nervous behind the wheel as Lucy got into the car, still smiling.

"Way to go, girl," she said, playfully slapping Emma on the shoulder.

"He can be so maddening."

"That's what little brothers are there for. Hell, I felt like murdering mine sometimes." Her joviality left her as she realised her brother was probably gone now, along with nearly everyone she knew. Even at his most annoying, his most enraging, it would be better to have her brother there than not have him at all. She placed her hand over Emma's, which was resting on the gear stick. "It's only because he loves you that he's like that."

"I know, but he thinks I'm just some useless idiot. He treats me more like a liability than an equal."

"Well, you're certainly paying your way today."

An engine revved behind them. Emma looked in the rear-view mirror and noticed a large white box van had rolled out of the second barn. She took a breath and turned the key in the ignition. The stone chips crackled as the two vehicles slowly moved off.

*

Samantha guided Mike back into the bedroom. She sat him on the bed and then left him to get some supplies from the ambulance. She returned with an array of items and was followed into the room by Alice, who was carrying a washing up bowl of steaming water.

"Thanks, Alice." The older woman smiled and left the room, shutting the door behind her. "Jake and

165

Sammy are with Beth and Annie. I think Sammy has a new best friend there." She smiled to herself. Amidst this nightmare, two little girls could still strike up a friendship. It gave Samantha a little hope. She removed Mike's boots and then started undoing his belt buckle.

"Whoa!" he said playfully. "I'm not sure what you've heard, Samantha, but I'm not that kind of boy."

She smiled. "A joke, Mike? You made a joke. I think that's wonderful."

"Hey, I make lots of jokes, I'm funny, ask anyone."

"And just for the record, I've heard you're exactly that kind of boy and I'm warning you, any funny business and you'll get a cold sponge bath. That's what we used to do on the wards." This was the first time the two of them had been alone since the previous morning. It felt so good just to joke around for a minute after everything that was going on outside.

"I have to say, I'm not impressed with your bedside manner." Mike looked at her face as she struggled to loosen his belt. She was a lot like her sister, the blue eyes, the pale complexion, the red hair. If he squinted, it could be Claire in front of him. She finally loosened the belt and slipped his jeans carefully down his legs.

"Too bad. Now I need you to get on the bed and lie face down for me." He was about to respond and she brought a finger up reproachfully like a stern parent.

He did as he was told and Samantha examined the wound. "Jesus, Mike, I'm amazed you were able to walk around on this at all yesterday. Now this is probably going to sting a bit," she said as she took a sponge from the steaming bowl.

*

"Okay, if my memory serves, it's a little way after the next bend," Lucy said, attempting to recall the location of the kidnappers' lair from the previous evening. Emma took the bend steadily and then she saw them. Two RAMs were wandering in the lane. On noticing the Land Rover, they began to run towards it. Lucy pumped the shotgun ready, but rather than slowing down to give Lucy more time to aim, Emma put her foot on the accelerator. As the car and the beasts got closer, she could see the creatures' teeth as they bared them in anticipation. At the moment they were ready to pounce, she speeded up even more, giving them no time to get the height they would need to land on the bonnet. As metal crunched against bone, the two RAMs scattered like bowling pins, their legs barely recognisable as the jagged bones broke through flesh and cloth, rendering them unusable. The Land Rover had accelerated at such a pace that the box van was now some way behind. Emma jammed on the brakes. Lucy watched as the younger woman got out of the car and removed a crowbar from her belt.

Emma stood over the first RAM. Both its legs were in splinters, yet no pain registered on its face. It still bared its teeth ferociously, and it began to swivel on its hands in a final attempt to reach its prey. It let out a low guttural sound from the back of its throat, similar to the sounds of the RAMs Emma had seen on the street a few days before, but much quieter. She continued to stare down at it as the box van slowly came to a halt behind them. Then, with all the power she possessed, she brought down the crowbar on the RAM's head: one, two, three, four times. The final blow punctured clean through the skull to reveal the brain, the grey matter, but in this case it was crimson. She turned round to the other creature, which was clumsily dragging itself towards her on its hands, its legs as useless as those of its partner. There was no pause this time as she struck the would-be attacker down. Emma wiped the crowbar clean on the verge, placed it back in her belt and returned to the car.

Joseph and Peter sat with their mouths open as they watched her. Emma climbed into the 4x4, released the handbrake and rolled forward the remaining few feet to the house. She pulled on the handbrake again and sat there, her body shaking all over, a mixture of anger, fear and bloodthirsty satisfaction pulsating through her, making every inch of her quiver.

Lucy understood the feeling. She took hold of the younger woman's hand in a motherly manner. "It's okay, you did good, Emma," she said as she climbed out of the car to open the gates. The Land Rover pulled through the opening and Joseph swung the box van as far left as he could in the narrow country lane before locking the wheel right to get the vehicle through the narrow gateway. As he did, there was a noticeable thud. The rear passenger-side wheel left the tarmac and got caught in a narrow trough on the roadside verge. He revved the engine and continued to turn the wheel but it wouldn't come free. The farmer forced the wheel the other way and revved it harder. This time, the van shot forward and Lucy had to leap out of the way as it went crashing into the brick gatepost, demolishing it as if it were made of Lego. The attached gate fell back in slow motion, making a deafening clang as it hit the block-paved driveway. The van was virtually unscathed, but there was no way they would be able to secure the tall black gate. Whatever supplies they were going to take from the house needed to be collected quickly.

*

"That feels a hell of a lot better," Mike said as he slowly walked around the bedroom. "I'm impressed, Nurse White, thank you."

Samantha smiled as she tried to remember the last time anyone had referred to her as Nurse White. "You're welcome. Now, will you be okay to get your jeans back on or will you need some help?"

"Y'know, I think I might need some help," he said, grinning.

Samantha picked up the jeans and threw them gently at his face. "Fine, I'll ask Alice to come in," she said, going to the door.

Mike shuddered at the thought of the rather rotund farmer's wife helping him put his jeans back on. "Y'know what? On second thoughts, I think I'll be fine." Samantha looked back at him, and they both smiled.

Then, almost as if coming out of a trance, she opened the door to leave. "Oh, before I forget..." She took out a small roll of sticky tape and a black plastic bag from her hoodie pocket and flung them towards Mike. "When you have your shower, make sure you cover the bandages. Try and keep them clean and dry for as long as you can." Mike nodded obediently, and Samantha turned and left.

*

"Oh man, these guys have been busy," Lucy said, as the four of them walked into the first bedroom. There were boxes of tinned and dried food stacked up against one wall. Against another were boxes and trays of bottled water and alcohol, spirits mainly, but some beer too. There were a number of pieces of small electronic equipment. The gang obviously struggled to break old habits. Lucy walked over to a large black holdall and unzipped it. Inside was a small selection of firearms with several boxes of ammunition. There were five pump-action shotguns and two handguns, a Glock 17 and a Browning L9A1. Lucy recognised the two handguns as being military sidearms. They were probably taken from dead soldiers, but she guessed the shotguns might have been with the gang for a long time. Underneath was a wide-bladed hunting knife and two 18-inch handcrafted machetes with walnut handles in thick vinyl scabbards. They had clearly never been used and had presumably adorned the wall or cabinet of some collector before being appropriated by the raiders. Lucy pulled one out and looked at it, in awe of the beautiful workmanship. "I think I've just found Mike's Christmas present," she said, smiling, and a small ripple of laughter went around the room.

"Right then, we'd better get this lot loaded up," Joseph said, moving forward and picking up two boxes at once. Peter tried to emulate his father, but in the end settled for just one box.

Lucy and Emma followed suit, but rather than carrying their loads out to the van, they placed them at the foot of the stairs and returned for more. On re-entering the house, the two men realised they were setting up a chain and took the boxes back to the van.

This time though, Peter climbed into the back and began positioning and securing the load while Joseph ferried more boxes from the house. The four of them worked well together. The pile of stolen booty was quickly loaded, and soon all that remained in the bedroom was the bag of weapons and two heavy trays of bottled water.

"Jeez, I'm glad we're nearly there," Lucy said, panting, beads of sweat forming on her forehead.

Emma was about to respond when a large crack sounded from outside. The two women looked at each other, their eyes widening and their weariness gone. Lucy picked up her shotgun, which she'd carefully placed against the wall on entering the room. The pair of them nervously walked downstairs, eyes searching for a clue as to what was going on. A second echoing crack sounded from outside, then a third and a fourth. They rushed out into the afternoon air to find Peter and Joseph with their weapons raised and several RAMs sprinting up the driveway towards them.

There were no bodies on the ground so Lucy could only assume the shots fired had had little effect on the advancing group of snarling beasts. On the contrary, the loud bangs would have had an effect similar to a dinner gong for any other RAMs within hearing distance. The two women stood in front of the house, unsure whether to try and make it to the Land Rover or head back inside, where they would be trapped. When a further six RAMs appeared at the foot of the drive and began tearing towards the property, Lucy grabbed Emma's arm and pulled her back into the house. Before she closed the door, she saw Joseph fling his shotgun into the back of the van and Peter grab his father's hand in an effort to help him climb in. The first of the attackers was only a few feet away. Lucy slammed the heavy door closed and the two women sprinted up the stairs to the bedroom window to see if Joseph and Peter had got to safety. They hadn't reached the top step before they heard what sounded like two bodies thud against the entrance to the house. Startled, they looked at each other then ran along the landing and to the bedroom window.

The box van was high off the ground and the ledge came up to about chest height on an average man. Joseph had managed to get in, but now both he and Peter were trying to lower the roller shutter to stop the RAMs from gaining access. The beasts' arms flailed in their direction as the farmer tiptoed and leant forward to reach the bottom of the shutter. Peter, meanwhile, was stamping on their hands in an effort to make them withdraw, but it had no effect. Just as Joseph caught the ledge of the door and swung it down, one of the RAMs seized Peter's ankle as if grabbing a chicken drumstick. The young boy yelped and raised his weapon to fire, only to find it empty. He turned it around to use it as a club, but before he could swing, a second RAM grabbed his other leg and gathered enough purchase to drag itself over the ledge of the van and take a bite from the sweet young flesh of its prize. Its teeth sunk deep into the soft cotton of Peter's sock and then, piranha-like, ripped away a piece of pink and red flesh. The boy howled in pain. Seeing what was happening, Joseph pulled the shutter down with all his might. The attacker's body fell back as it lost its grip on Peter, the chunk of rubbery flesh still hanging from its mouth. The shutter bounced back up and Joseph forced it down again, this time trapping several forearms and wrists. A few withdrew to begin clattering on the outside of the door instead. Joseph placed all his weight on his front foot to hold down the roller shutter and reached across for his pump-action shotgun. He fired shot after shot, severing hands from wrists, forearms from elbows, to form a gluey, bloody pool. Eventually, the van fell into darkness as the shutter closed fully with a firm click. The banging from the outside was deafening. The black interior of the van made it all the more shocking, all the more frightening. Not knowing was sometimes scarier than knowing. Joseph reached up for the portable inspection light they used mainly in the winter months and turned it on. His son was shaking violently, his eyes rolled into the back of his head. Then all movement stopped. Joseph refused to acknowledge what was happening. He acted as if the boy had been caught on a piece of sharp machinery back at the farm. He tore off his shirt and bandaged the boy's ankle, then, with his belt, tied a tourniquet.

"Don't worry, son, don't worry, I'll get us out," Joseph said, desperately trying to think how. The cab of the van was separated from the back by a solid piece of board that they had put up to avoid loads falling forward if the van ever had to brake suddenly. This added safety feature, that Joseph had been so pleased with at the time, now had him imprisoned. Then he remembered the Leatherman multi-tool that Beth had bought him for his last birthday. At first he hadn't really seen the point – he already had better screwdrivers, pliers and knives in his own tool box – but he gradually became less reliant on his old box of tools and used this pocket miracle his daughter had given him more and more. Now it could very well save his life. He had installed the dividing board using normal wood screws; they had been perfect for penetrating the reinforced plastic surround of the cab. It would take him a while, but he'd be able to unscrew the board and drive the van out, then that young nurse could fix his boy. Joseph was shifting boxes to get to the board when he heard some movement behind him. He turned around to see Peter slowly getting up. He approached his son and then stopped abruptly. The boy's eyes were no longer his own. The pupils flared angrily in the dull light, the irises and whites now an eerie opaque grey. Peter's face, once rosy like a freshly picked apple, was draining of colour as each second passed. A guttural gurgling started in the back of the boy's throat as he limped towards his father. Then he pounced, pivoting from his good leg, but Joseph had time to get out of the way and the creature that had once been Peter fell on a pile of boxes. The farmer wasted no time and climbed on top of him. The beast twisted and writhed, snapping at Joseph's hands and arms with its teeth.

"Don't worry, son. Don't worry. I'll get you some help," he said desperately, madly, hopelessly. Although only in his late fifties, his face had assumed the look of an octogenarian. This was one tragedy too many. He glanced around and saw the sturdy lashing straps they used to secure loads, then looked down again at his son. "I'm sorry I have to do this, son, but it will be for the best, you'll see." Joseph manoeuvred one of Peter's hands down by his hip so he could kneel on it rather than hold it, then did the same with the other. It took him the best part of ten minutes to weave the straps around Peter's body, but in the end, his son was almost immobile. The immediate danger was over. Joseph left him snarling and writhing like some trapped reptile and began to remove the partition.

14

Inside the house, Lucy and Emma had not been able to see the events unfolding in the van. They hoped that the fact they had heard the shutter slam down meant that Joseph and Peter were safely in the back. As Lucy had feared, the shots had attracted more RAMs. The total number was probably around thirty now and even more were appearing at the driveway entrance. From the direction they were coming from, she assumed they were residents of the village down the lane. They heard the sound of breaking glass from downstairs.

"Oh shit, they're inside," Lucy said. Emma rushed across to close the door.

"Have we got anything to wedge it shut with?" she asked. All they had left in the room was some bottled water and the weapons bag. Was this really how it was going to end for her? She then remembered the hunting knife in the bag and slid it across the floor to Emma. "Try this," she said, less than optimistically.

Emma placed the knife in the small gap below the door and then kicked it repeatedly, creating a solid wedge. "It won't last forever, but it'll give us a bit of time."

"Great, we've got a few extra minutes to think about how horrible our death is going to be before it actually happens. Thanks," Lucy said, beginning to show real terror for the first time since Emma had met her. She wanted to reply with something reassuring, but what could she say? There were dozens of RAMs heading their way and nothing between them but a wedged door.

"We've still got the guns and ammo," Emma said, pointing to the holdall.

"Yeah, I suppose we can take a few of them out before they get to us," Lucy replied and reached into the bag.

Emma stood with her back against the door, her chin leaning against her chest, her eyes downcast. She heard the first footsteps on the staircase. Thud, thud, thud. She gripped the crowbar she had taken from her brother's stash of weapons. "I wish Mike was here," she said, not even realising the thought had turned into words.

"I don't think even Mike could get us out of this one, sweetie."

"Maybe not, but he wouldn't give up. He'd never give up."

"We're not giving up, but when they get through that door, and make no mistake, they will get through, I don't rate our chances," Lucy said, carefully checking the magazines in the handguns.

An idea hit Emma like a hard slap across the face. She pulled the crowbar from her belt and knelt down, jamming the straight edge into the tiny gap between two floorboards. She levered one up slightly, then turned the crowbar round to the claw end and completed the job, pulling the floorboard clean off the joist. Now that there was a hole, the second board was even easier to get up. She looked underneath. There was a gap of about eighteen inches and then a typically flimsy piece of plasterboard forming the ceiling of the room below. Lucy looked at her as if she had gone insane. Emma looked back, wide-eyed, and the older woman couldn't determine whether it was madness or excitement.

"Are you okay?" she finally asked.

Emma began pulling up more floorboards as quickly as she could while the first of the RAMs thudded against the bedroom door. "Give me a hand, quick," Emma shouted.

"What the hell, Emma?"

"Don't you see? Underneath the floorboards all you've got are some narrow joists and then plasterboard. That can't take a person's weight and those things don't have the intelligence or co-ordination to balance on the beams. If one of those things steps on the plasterboard, they'd just fall straight through to the room below. If we can take up enough boards before they get that door open they won't be able to reach us," she blurted between grunts as she pulled up board after board.

Lucy didn't waste time talking and knelt down beside Emma. The pair tugged and pulled at the boards, throwing them into a corner of the room. The banging on the door was getting louder as more hands beat the wood, sensing live prey inside. The two women carried on. Looking towards the doorway would do no good. They had one chance and this was it.

*

Joseph's hands developed blisters as he used all his brute strength to remove each screw. They had been put in using an electric screwdriver, then tightened with a large Stanley from his father's tool box. It was fifty years old and could easily last another fifty. It was a sturdy tool, and although what he had in his hand was ingenious and useful, it was hard going when it came to loosening some of the screws. Eventually he levered the last few turns and pulled the final one free with his fingers. The board had been measured and cut well, so it remained wedged in place. The noise outside was growing louder. Although he was sure the creatures became more vocal as their agitation grew, he was equally sure that the increasing volume was also due to more of the beasts joining their ranks. He sat for a moment to get his breath back and looked at what had been his son still jerking around in the confines of the strapping. "Don't worry, son. We'll get you patched up. You'll be as good as new."

*

The door began to give with the force of the RAMs pushing against it. Emma and Lucy paid no attention to the cuts and splinters on their fingers and continued as fast as they could. Sweat was dripping off them onto the dry wooden floorboards and they were panting like thirsty animals, but they were nearly done. Emma triumphantly pulled up the last board of the row and stood up to survey their work. There was boarding just in front of the door, extending into the room by no more than two feet. Other than five

179

narrow joists, set equally apart across the length of the room, and the plasterboard ceiling of the lounge below, there was nothing between them and the door but the five by four corner they had left themselves. The two women slouched down, exhausted, with their backs against the wall. Lucy reached across and grabbed two bottles of water. They took large gulps, eyes glued to the entrance. All they could do now was watch and wait as the door slowly shifted forward.

*

Rather than tearing away the partition and escaping as quickly as the van could move, Joseph stood and looked mournfully towards what had once been his son. He climbed back over the array of supplies Peter had secured and sat down opposite the writhing figure trying to break out of the strapping like a lunatic attempting to escape a straightjacket. The farmer leaned against the side of the van, which was shaking with each punch and slap from the marauding pack outside. He felt no fear of the creatures. He felt no fear for what might happen to him. He just looked towards Peter and grew sadder with each passing moment.

The beast continued its violent struggle, occasionally pausing for a second to lock eyes with the man on the other side of the van. Where there had once been admiration and love, now there was only the same piercing malevolence that was to be found in the eyes of any of the infected creatures. Joseph's sadness slowly turned to anger. Not with Peter, but with himself, for allowing this to happen. With himself, for just a few moments ago promising his son it would all be fine, that he would get him patched up. There was no cure for what Joseph saw in his son's eyes, and the pounding and battering outside was just a further validation of that fact. The noise became more deafening, but Joseph became less and less aware of it as he watched the figure across from him pull two, then three fingers free from underneath the strapping.

*

The first few fingertips crept their way between the door and the frame. A human would be in agony, as the pressure created by the wedge was still great enough for the bottom of the door to be flush with the frame. But these fingers, these creeping, grey tendrils, had forced their way through, and the small gap they had created amplified the guttural, choking growls from the landing.

Emma was twenty-four years old and Lucy was thirty-four, but they each instinctively reached out for the other's hand like frightened children reaching for a parent.

At first, the creeping digits, having made their way through the gap in the door up to the knuckles, froze like the legs of a giant spider trapped beneath an encyclopaedia. Then they slowly began to move, clenching and unclenching, clenching and unclenching, as if gradually waking up from a deep slumber. The pallid colour alone was enough to send spasms of fear through Emma. All the vigour and resolve of a few moments before, when she had been tearing up flooring like the Tasmanian Devil in the old cartoons, had now gone. She clutched Lucy's hand tightly and Lucy reciprocated. They had bought themselves time, but that wasn't going to protect them from the slideshow of horrors they were about to endure. They could close their eyes, but what if one of the beasts happened to run towards them and managed to step on the joists rather than fall between them onto the plasterboard? The odds were against it but then again, twelve months ago, what were the odds of a person dying from a virus, only to come back as some terrifying monster hell-bent on feeding on the living?

*

Joseph's reanimated son lay across from him, tirelessly stretching and wriggling beneath the straps. One hand was free and it balled into an angry fist, seemingly shuddering with pent-up rage. The creature's second hand was working its way free too, one finger at a time. Joseph didn't know whether it was by design, by reason, that the beast had started to liberate its other hand or whether it was simply that the body was moving so violently that it had jerked free. Regardless, Joseph just sat there, watching what had been his son's flesh turn from a healthy pink to a milky grey hue.

*

A high-pitched screech broke through the low growls of the creatures on the landing as a hand and then an arm followed the fingers into the bedroom, forcing the wedge to scrape against the floorboards. The two women watched in horror as more of the ghoulish limb became visible. Another screech as the shoulder pierced the threshold, and then part of a face. The mouth opened slowly and deliberately, teeth bared, jaws flexing in anticipation of feasting on the two women. Emma looked away; if this was going to be her last day, she did not want that to be the final image burned into her memory. Lucy watched, her face crumpled, her eyes resigned. The RAM forced its head, then its chest, through the door. It was side-on and making slow headway, but the wedge wasn't going to stay in place forever and it would not be long before the RAM broke through completely. It got stuck momentarily between the door and the frame, and that enraged it still further, its army green T-shirt and cropped hair the only clue to who it had been in its previous life. Its eyes and head convulsed like someone having a seizure. Globules of thick saliva dripped over its bottom lip as the low growl from the back of its throat intensified. The other RAMs outside joined in, sensing that the prey was closer, and Emma pulled her hand free of Lucy's to cover her ears and block out the sound. Tears streamed from her eyes. Lucy picked up her shotgun and pumped it, ready for action.

*

As the monstrosity worked its second hand free, it pushed itself off its back and began sidewinding towards Joseph like a desert snake. Its eyes locked on his, its grey flesh thirsty for a fountain of dark, red blood. The excited gurgling in the back of its throat became more frantic with each jolting advance. Joseph continued to watch, his demeanour unchanged.

*

Finally the wedge was knocked across the remaining floorboards and fell onto the plasterboard. The creature ran towards the women. Emma sensed Lucy stiffen; she opened her eyes and uncovered her ears. The beast was in mid leap and everything slowed down as if it were being played out frame by frame. Lucy brought the shotgun up ready and Emma reached for the crowbar, wrapping her fist tightly around its cold metal shaft. She could see behind the leaping figure more grey flesh, grey eyes and gnashing teeth making their way into the room. The toe of its boot landed on a joist. Lucy and Emma held their breath in anticipation as that split second seemed to puncture time.

*

Finally, Joseph stood up, with his back still against the pounding metal of the van. What had been his son was now just twelve inches away, still desperately shuffling towards him. "If there's any part of you still inside there, son, I want you to know I've always been proud of you, I've always loved you." The creature carried on struggling, unmoved by the emotional outpouring. Joseph took two steps away, forcing the RAM to change course. "I'd give my own life to bring you back from this, son, but there is no way back, I can see that now. I've got to protect what's left of the family, and to do that I'm going to have to do things that only God can forgive me for, because I know for a fact that I'll never forgive myself."

*

The boot twisted and slipped down the side of the joist. The former soldier's heel punched through the plasterboard ceiling as if it were a sheet of dry pasta. The beast's other foot caught on the next joist, and its teeth punctured its upper lip as it hit the solid wood of the first beam at full speed. It felt no pain as it plummeted through the thin plasterboard ceiling, but Lucy and Emma winced, not out of any sense of pity, but simply imagining how painful it would have been for them. A large hole was left as the flailing hand of the RAM disappeared to the floor of the lounge below. The rest of the horde advanced swiftly from the landing. Some hit joists, like the first; others landed straight onto the plasterboard. All of them fell hopelessly, leaving a flip book of monstrous images shooting glances of pure malevolence towards their potential prey before vanishing through the floor. More advanced until there was nothing between the doorway and the small area where the two women sat other than the exposed joists. Eventually the attacks stopped. Were the creatures learning? Were they reasoning? Or was it just an animal instinct? There was no roaring engine or moving vehicle to confuse their senses, just two frightened women. The RAMs massed outside the room, watching the trapped prey. The door was now fully open, the floor was gone, and Emma and Lucy could see the beasts shoving and jostling on the landing and stairs, trying to get closer to their quarry. Below, the women saw bloodthirsty creatures looking up, some crippled with broken limbs after their falls, some reaching upwards with unbridled hate and energy. The growling and the gurgling, the snarling, the anger, the hopelessness. The hopelessness consuming them.

*

The young RAM finally freed an arm and dragged itself towards Joseph, who was up at the partition looking for his weapon. He picked it up and stepped towards the struggling beast. "I'm so sorry, son," he said again as he raised the shotgun towards the creature's head. One last lunge and the RAM's hand clamped onto Joseph's ankle for leverage. Its fingers dug deep, but Joseph felt nothing. The emotional pain far outweighed any physical discomfort. He stared down the barrel and felt for the trigger, then hesitated. He turned the shotgun around and bludgeoned the monster instead. The creature eased its grip as it lost consciousness, and Joseph freed his foot, unaware of the tiny scratch that the RAM's nail had made through his wool socks. The bereaved father set to work applying more strapping; he put a burlap sack over the beast's head and tied its neck and body firmly to the metal shelving in the back of the box van.

*

Emma stood and looked out of the window. She couldn't see any more RAMs on the driveway, but the house and van were both surrounded. "There aren't any more coming in," she said to Lucy.

"When the firing started, these were probably the ones within earshot. Guns can be as much of a liability as they are a necessity." Lucy looked into the bag of weapons, knowing as she said it that they were the only protection the two women had, but that they could also alert other RAMs to their whereabouts. "I guess this is what they call a catch-22, kid." Without realising, both women were having to speak louder to hear themselves over the houseful of low, choking growls and grunts.

Joseph worked his way to the front of the van, took three deep breaths and then pulled the partition away, but he wanted to put it right back when he saw the monstrous gathering outside. The side mirrors had been battered beyond use, but he imagined they would show even more monsters behind. As he leapt into the driver's seat, the volume of the creatures increased with fevered excitement and the van began to shake more and more. Joseph fumbled the keys into the ignition. A quick turn and the engine fired. He put his foot down on the accelerator again and again just to drown out the inhuman sound of the RAMs. The van jerked away, some creatures rolling underneath, others hanging on for a while before losing their grip and falling away.

*

Lucy and Emma looked at each other in shock as they heard the van's engine. They sprang to their feet and watched as it rolled down the drive followed by a small posse of hunters. "Oh, shit!" Lucy exclaimed.

"What do you mean? That's the first bit of good news we've had. At least they're alive. Once they get back to the farm, they'll figure out a way to help us. Our chances are better than they were five minutes ago," Emma said, baffled at Lucy's reaction.

"If you saw the house full of RAMs, the downstairs windows broken, no sight or sound of human life, would you think we'd survived? Our only hope was being so long overdue back at the farm that they came out looking for us. Babe, we're royally screwed." Lucy slumped back down, banging her head softly but repeatedly on the wall as if to ignite a spark of an idea. Emma watched as the van turned left and out of sight with just a couple of stragglers still chasing. The others began to make their way back to the house.

*

Joseph sped along the lane, putting as much distance between him and the wretched house as possible. His mind was awash with sadness. How could he tell his wife that he had failed his son? How could he tell Mike his sister had died? Or Samantha that her friend had died? What was he going to do with the creature in the back of the van? How would he live with being the only one to escape the house without injury? As he pulled up outside the gate of Mead Hall Farm, all was quiet. He found it hard to believe that just moments ago he had been within touching distance of a horde of bloodthirsty beasts eager to rip the flesh from his bones. Joseph remembered what one of the women had said about the RAMs hanging on to the underside of the vehicle and grabbed his shotgun before opening the door. He jumped out and bent to look under the van: all clear. He opened the gate, drove the van in and closed it again, checking in all directions to make sure there were no unwanted pursuers. He drove slowly up the winding private road to the house.

*

"How many rounds have we got?" Emma asked, wiping another tear from the corner of her eye and trying to compose herself in spite of the fear.

Lucy looked in the bag at the boxes of cartridges and the magazines. "All told, I'd say we're looking at about one hundred and twenty, give or take."

"How many RAMs would you say there are?" asked Emma.

Lucy stood up and leaned over to look down at the malevolent creatures snarling up at her. She looked towards the door and beyond to the landing. She looked outside. "I don't know. I don't know what's in the rest of the house. The whole ground floor could be overrun with them. From what I can see, I'd say seventy or eighty. Why?"

"Don't you think it would be worth trying to shoot our way out?"

"Not for a second. Firstly, I'm the only one who can shoot, and I'm not great, so the chances of me getting a headshot every time are slim. Secondly, every shot fired means that any RAM in hearing range is going to start heading this way. And thirdly... I don't have a thirdly..." She saw the look on Emma's face become more disheartened with each word she uttered. "We're going to have to face facts, Emma. The only thing I've got the power to do is stop us turning into them. I can do that for us."

15

Mike, Samantha, Tracey and Beth were standing in the kitchen, drinking coffee and talking about anything but the previous few days, when the van rolled up. The children were in the living room with Alice.

Mike went to the door and saw that there was no-one in Joseph's passenger seat and no Land Rover following. He ran across to the van, ignoring the pain in his leg, as the others filed out of the doorway. Before Joseph had a chance to pull the parking brake on, Mike had ripped open the door.

"Where is everybody, Joseph?" he demanded.

"Mike... Mike." He swallowed, trying to hold back emotion. "We were overrun."

Mike grabbed hold of the older man's upper arm. "What do you mean, overrun? Where are they, Joseph? Where's my sister?"

"They're gone, Mike. They're gone – my boy, your sister, Lucy. They're all gone." He placed his head in his hands, muffling his words. "There were dozens of those things, dozens of them. They got my boy. They got the girls. There was nothing I could do." He began to sob.

Mike released his grip on Joseph and walked straight between the three women who had come out to listen. Beth wept as she went to hold her father. Tracey looked uncomfortable. Samantha stared in pure bewilderment then followed Mike back into the kitchen, passing Alice, who was rushing out to her husband.

Mike picked up his mug of coffee and sipped slowly as the first howls of Alice's pain sounded outside. The children came in from the other room but Samantha immediately ushered them back. Mike stood there alone in the kitchen, the bitter black coffee making his lip curl with each sip. A familiar sensation slowly crept over him. His breathing became heavier and his hands began to shake. Samantha walked back into the room and leant against a kitchen unit. Her words "Are you okay, Mike?" went unheard as blood surged through his body, gushing like white-water rapids in his ears. He took another sip from his mug only to bang his bottom teeth on the china because his hands were shaking so violently.

Mike looked down at the mug then flung it across the room with venom. Shattered pieces of pottery sprayed all over the kitchen and the remaining dark brown liquid dribbled down the wall. He lunged at the solid kitchen table and flipped it over in blind rage, as if it were a piece of plastic patio furniture. The sturdy wood clattered as it fell on the quarry tiles. Samantha impulsively went to him, to try and calm him down, but she pulled back when she saw the vein throbbing on his temple and the look of unbridled anger in his eyes. Mike glared towards her and marched out of the front door into the courtyard. He passed the grieving family, not even sharing a glance with them as he went by, and stopped when he reached the wall where he had been lying in wait the previous evening. He looked down, saw the hatchet he had left lying there and picked it up. The sun glinted off the blade and shaft. Like a human time-bomb he ticked his way back to the ambulance. Samantha could only stare from the doorway.

The last time he had been consumed like this was after his mother had died. His little sister, Sammy, had asked the priest if her mum would go to heaven. The self-righteous horror of a man had replied that she wouldn't because she had broken her sacred wedding vows made before God, but he would pray for her soul nonetheless. It took three strong men to pull Mike off that priest. If they hadn't he would undoubtedly have killed him. Everyone thought Mike was lucky to get away with eight months in a young offender's institute, but he knew it was the priest who was lucky to get away with his life.

He climbed into the driving seat of the ambulance and reached down into the passenger footwell. His bag of makeshift weapons was still there, including various screwdrivers, two of which he placed in his belt. He hunted for the crowbar and when he couldn't find it, that just infuriated him further. Mike was an intelligent man who prided himself on being resourceful and living on his wits. He was able to think logically and plan well, which is why he'd been put in charge of people nearly twice his age at the warehouse. But when this feeling took hold of him, logic vanished. All that was present was a single-mindedness for revenge. It didn't matter that the RAMs had no more understanding of who they were killing than a snake in the desert or a shark in the sea: Mike wanted to hurt them, needed to hurt them. The engine started and chips flew as the ambulance shot out of the courtyard, the violence of the exit jolting the grieving family from their mourning.

Samantha began running after it as quickly as she could. She hadn't thought for a moment that Mike would head back to the house, but when she heard the engine start, she realised what he was doing.

"Oh my God! He's going back there," Joseph cried as he held his wife's weeping face to his chest.

*

The pair sat, deflated and defeated, their fingers once again entwined for comfort. Lucy held a handgun in her other hand, looking at it with contempt.

"I'm really sorry it's come to this, Emma. I thought for a while yesterday that we might have had a fighting chance. I thought we might have made it to that sweet little home by the sea where we could have lived in safety and tried to start again. Man, was I a fool."

Emma tightened her fingers around Lucy's. "Don't be so hard on yourself. I thought the same." The younger woman looked at the gun in Lucy's other hand, thinking it would all be over soon. "Do you pray, Lucy?"

"I haven't prayed in a long, long time. You?" she asked, her eyes still transfixed by the weapon.

"No, but I think I'd like to now." Emma began to cry, still looking at the handgun.

"I don't see how it could do us any harm," Lucy said, her eyes tearing up as well.

"Mike would be furious if he knew I was doing this," she said, letting out a small sobbing laugh.

"Mike's not here, sweetie. You say whatever you want to say." Lucy put down the gun and put her other hand over Emma's. They both closed their eyes.

"Dear God, please look after Mike, Sammy, Jake and Samantha. Please give them safe passage. Don't let this be the future. Give them something more, something to live for, and if you can't give them that, then at least allow them to live without fear and death hanging over their every waking hour." Both women sobbed uncontrollably, their hands clutched tight, the sights and sounds of the RAMs blocked out. "And please, God, forgive us for what we are about to do. Amen."

"Amen," Lucy whispered in response. The pair remained for a moment in the same position. Their heads bowed, their eyes closed, their hands squeezing each other's for strength. Finally Lucy released her grip and used the back of her hand to wipe away the salty, watery streams from her eyes. She picked up the gun and took a deep breath, then turned towards Emma. "Are you ready, sweetie?" she asked, her voice full of sadness. Emma nodded, and Lucy brought up the gun to the side of the younger woman's head.

*

"I've got to go after him," Joseph said, breaking away from his wife.

"No, Joseph, no!" Alice cried in protest.

"That lad, those women, they saved us last night, they had no reason to. Lucy and Emma would still be alive if they'd just minded their own business and carried on. But no, they stayed and helped us, they risked everything, and look where it got them. I owe it to them." His grief subsided as a sense of duty took over. "Take your mother back in the house, Beth." His voice was stern but compassionate. The two women began to walk away as Joseph climbed back into the van.

The mother and daughter suddenly stopped. Beth ran to Tracey and whispered something in her ear, then climbed into the passenger seat of the van. The tear stains were still evident on her face but her voice was resolute. "I'm going with you, Dad. I know how to shoot, and I owe those people as much as you and more besides," she said, picking up Peter's shotgun from the footwell. Joseph looked across at her with pride and started the engine.

Before the van reached the gate, Samantha flagged them down. "I was too late. I thought I could catch him, but he'd already gone by the time I got to the road," she blurted, out of breath.

"We're going to see if we can talk some sense into him," Joseph said.

"I know Mike, Joseph. You won't be able to talk him out of anything."

"I've at least got to try. I've at least got to try," he repeated as the van moved off once again.

*

Emma felt the frigid metal pressed against the side of her head and shuddered. This was it.

Her eyes closed. A deep breath – decaying flesh. Not what she wanted her last smell to be. She could even hear the gun shuffling in Lucy's hand. All her senses were at their peak. That sound, was it Lucy's finger moving over the trigger?

"No!" Did she shout it or just think it? Her hand moved with lightning speed to push the cold metal from her head.

The gun made a deafening bang as the bullet pierced the wall over the side of Emma's head. Neither woman heard anything but ringing. Both recognised, though, that the instant before there had been a noise, a split-second screech, from outside the house. It was the sound of rubber against tarmac, the sound of a vehicle being driven at speed. It was the sound of hope.

The pair looked towards each other, the pain in their ears dulled by the anticipation of what they would see out of the window. They jumped to their feet. The ambulance. How they both loved the sight of that ambulance now, tearing up the driveway, battering everything in its way.

A group of RAMs began running towards it and the vehicle answered in kind, speeding up towards them. Figures were strewn in all directions as they were hit by the improvised battering ram. The odd ones not too severely damaged got up to pursue the ambulance, but were soon flattened, more conscientiously this time, as the vehicle reversed over them with malice, creating a nightmarish trail of gore.

More creatures stormed out of the house, excited by the prospect of easier prey, and the ambulance charged relentlessly towards them. Blood, flesh and sinew painted over the camouflage front and the underside of the vehicle as it moved.

"He's got no idea we're here," Emma shouted, barely able to hear herself over the ringing in her ears.

Lucy's hearing wasn't as badly affected as the gun had been at arm's length when it went off. She picked up the shotgun and used the butt to smash the window, then raised it and fired at some of the creatures that were running towards the ambulance. One down, two down.

Small explosions of red caught Mike's eye as he looked towards the house. Two figures dropped. Then, like a balloon filled with thick red paint, another head exploded. This time, he heard the shot over the loud thuds of the RAMs hitting the ambulance. He looked up and saw Lucy and Emma at the bedroom window, and every fibre of his being told him to drive straight to the house, drive straight towards his sister and Lucy – but he knew that wasn't the smart play. He could see figures in the room below them and others elsewhere in the house. Mike didn't have a problem battling these monstrosities, he'd wrestle alligators if it meant saving his sister, but the more of these beasts he could lure out and kill with the ambulance, the better chance they would all have.

He drove up and down the long, wide drive, picking them off sometimes one at a time, sometimes more. A few died instantly. Others were knocked to the ground with shattered limbs, their advance slowed to a snail's pace. Still more ran out of the big, luxurious property, the downstairs rooms emptying slowly but surely. There was enough space in front of the building for a tennis court and the drive itself was long enough to reach third gear without unnatural acceleration, but Mike concentrated his efforts in the middle section, as this gave him the best vantage point for seeing what was heading towards him.

Lucy and Emma looked on with glee as each RAM fell, but they allowed themselves to enjoy the sight for just a moment before Lucy turned back towards the door, her face menacing, bitter. She pumped the shotgun and began to fire. Pump, fire, pump, fire, pump, fire. Over and over again, bloody explosions decorated the walls, doorway and floor. The beasts were beginning to thin; some had already gone outside to see if they could get to the driver of the ambulance. Lucy became so bent on destroying them that she failed to notice the holes appearing in the thin walls of the house where the shot had spread. The small gaps gradually revealed the part of the landing to their right. Like the rest of the house, it had been crawling with RAMs. Before, these creatures had known the women were there but could not see them. Now, catching glimpses through the holes created by the shotgun, they began to scratch and dig feverishly, like giant rats clawing their way into a cardboard box full of breakfast cereal. Grey hands broke through, then heads. Lucy did notice those, but her reaction was simply to fire at them, making the problem worse. The shot spread further and the walls became weaker. The digging hands multiplied and moved further along the wall from the doorway. Some of the scratching was now opposite where they were standing; the gap between them and the beasts had become frighteningly narrow. One good leap and any attacker would be upon them.

"Shit, I didn't think this one through," Lucy said, realising that in her zeal to battle the creatures she had significantly compromised their safety. She picked up one of the handguns and gave the shotgun to Emma. "Take this. You've seen me use it. If I say so, start firing." Lucy pulled the slide back on the Glock 17 and extended her arm, cupping her other hand underneath to support the gun. Although she hadn't used handguns in a long time, her father had insisted on teaching her. It was just like riding a bike. Lucy rolled her neck and held her breath as she lined the first RAM up in her sights. The snarling faces were appearing from behind the decimated plasterboard with more haste now, but Lucy kept her cool and remembered the times her father had taken her to the firing range. Relax, aim, squeeze, relax, aim, squeeze. Each shot landed square in the forehead, stopping the feverish digging. But other beasts, seeing the advancement of their fallen brethren, began to take their place.

*

Sweat was dripping down Mike's face as he worked through the stiff gears and locked the wheel left, then right, then back again, reversing and then shooting forwards. He was meticulous in his destruction of the creatures but noticed that the shots from inside the house were attracting more RAMs. He reversed at full speed down the paved drive, skittling beasts this way and that. He jammed on the brakes as he reached the road, desperate to see how many more were heading their way. Mike squinted into the distance and saw only the odd few. If he could wrap this up quickly, they might just escape before a whole army of these things attacked. He looked ahead and saw that more menacing figures had left the house and were running towards him full pelt. What they lacked in intelligence they made up for in resolve. He crunched into first gear again, ready to advance, and then caught sight of movement out of the corner of his eye. It was the box van. He looked more carefully and saw Joseph and Beth. It pulled up and Joseph began to climb out but

Mike vigorously shook his head to say *no*. He motioned with his hands to signal that he was going straight ahead, but Joseph needed to stay there. He then pointed at the few advancing figures working their way up the road. Joseph urgently wanted to speak to Mike, but to climb out of the van with RAMs advancing would have been more than foolhardy. He nodded reluctantly as Mike raced back up the drive.

Joseph pulled the box van forward, blocking the driveway. He was angry that Mike was putting them all at risk just for the chance to get revenge. Then he heard the shots. One, two, three, four.

"That was from inside the house," Beth said, narrowing her eyes to see if she could see anything up the long driveway. She saw nothing other than Mike mowing down beast after beast.

"Oh, my God. Oh, sweet Jesus. They're alive. The girls are alive." The realisation gave Joseph renewed vigour. The RAMs working their way up the country road were at least a hundred metres away, but he decided to follow Mike's lead. He put his foot down and used the van like a battering ram, pummelling the advancing creatures. When there were just a few left in the distance, he reversed back up and blockaded the drive once more.

Shots continued in the house, but Mike couldn't see any more RAMs coming out. The driveway and garden looked like the gateway to hell: blood, bone, eviscerated bodies shuffling on broken limbs, arms outstretched, still grasping hopelessly. The soundtrack of the creatures choking back phlegm-filled growls of anger would shoot terror through most, but Mike didn't have time to be terrified. He parked behind the

Land Rover and picked up his small axe in one hand and a screwdriver in the other. He climbed down from the cab and was greeted by arms reaching out from beneath the ambulance. The movement was painfully slow as the body they were attached to had clearly been run over a number of times. When the head finally emerged, Mike plunged the hatchet into it without hesitation, and thick red and pink tissue squelched up the sides of the blade. He walked towards the house, pushing the screwdriver through an eye socket here and slicing into a forehead there, as damaged, beaten creatures still desperately reached out to seize their prize. Mike's limp was virtually non-existent due to a combination of bandages, painkillers and adrenalin. He paused at the door, banged on it, then took a jump back, ready to fight if anything came towards him, but nothing did. He looked back and noticed that Joseph and Beth were both in the entrance to the drive, holding up shotguns and ready to fire if anything came their way. It was quiet inside the house and Mike carefully made his way up the stairs. Bodies were strewn everywhere. The occasional reaching hand was quickly dismissed with a sharp blow from the hatchet. Finally he made it to the landing, where the broken creatures were piled three high in places. He looked towards the room where he had caught sight of Emma and Lucy. Through the doorway he could see them: Lucy, her hands still clutched around the Glock pointed in Mike's direction, and Emma holding the shotgun, bracing it against her shoulder. On seeing Mike, they lowered their weapons.

"For God's sake, be Careful!" Emma yelled, pointing to the floor.

Mike didn't understand what she meant, but when he got to the doorway he saw the gaping hole down to lounge below. He pulled bodies away and began smashing the door hinges with his axe. As the second brass fitting came loose, he took the thick piece of pine and placed it down over two joists with an echoing clatter, creating a makeshift bridge. He leapfrogged over to where the two women were standing and grabbed them both, pulling them tightly to him. Emma took tight hold of him and Lucy impulsively kissed him hard on the lips before wrapping her arms around them both.

"I thought I'd lost you," he said to Emma, kissing her forehead. She pushed her head further into him. "I thought you were both dead."

"Oh boy, Mikey, you have no idea," Lucy said, looking into Emma's eyes and thinking of a few moments earlier when she had almost put a bullet through her brain.

"There'll be more coming. We need to get out of here now," Mike said, eventually breaking his grip on the two women.

"No arguments from me," Lucy replied, replacing the guns in the holdall and gathering the supplies.

"I'm so glad you girls are alright. I didn't see how you could have survived in there. The place was swarming," Joseph said as the trio emerged from the house.

"It was a close thing. Trust me," Emma replied, looking knowingly towards Lucy. "Where's Peter?" Joseph and Beth simultaneously looked towards the ground. "Oh, no. Oh, I'm so sorry."

"Joseph, Beth... I'm so sorry," Lucy echoed, any other words of condolence escaping her.

"Thank you. Both of you. Thank you," Beth said, seeing her father struggling to fight back emotion.

"Look, I was wondering if you girls wouldn't mind driving the ambulance back? Beth can take the car. I need to have a word with Mike." Joseph looked at each face for approval. His voice was croaky but understandable.

"Fine with me," Lucy said, a little baffled, "but we'd better get moving."

The women boarded their assigned vehicles and Joseph and Mike ran back down to the van before any more RAMs materialised.

Once inside the ambulance, Emma turned to Lucy with a concerned look on her face. "What the hell do you suppose that's about?"

"Well, I'm guessing it's nothing good. But, hey, why would we want good news to spoil a perfectly shitty day?" Lucy replied, crunching the gear into first.

*

"Okay, we're alone now. What's all this about, Joseph? What's going on?" Mike asked, with equal measures of bemusement and worry.

"It's about Peter."

"Of course. I'm sorry, Joseph. I didn't get chance to tell you before. I'm so sorry. Peter was a really nice lad. He was brave as well, more than you could expect any boy of that age to be," he said sincerely.

"Thank you, Mike," Joseph said. The van began to trundle along the lane with the Land Rover and ambulance following close behind. "Mike. Peter got... Peter got bit and turned." He said the words like it was poison on his tongue.

"Oh, no. Oh, Joseph. Did you have to...? Did you have to take care of him yourself?" he asked, knowing only too well the pain of having to finish off a loved one.

"I couldn't do it, Mike. I tried, but I couldn't," said the heartbroken father, remembering the hideous creature his son had become.

"So you left him back there?"

"Mike. I've got no right to ask this, and I hate myself for it." He turned to look at his passenger as they drove along.

"Ask what? What are you talking about?" Their eyes met, one pair empty, the other confused, and then realisation struck. "Oh, shit! Where is he?"

"He's in the back." Joseph saw the immediate look of panic sweep across Mike's face as he turned towards the storage area of the vehicle. "Don't worry. He's tied, bound and covered. There's no danger."

"I'm begging you, Joseph. Please don't ask me to do this." He looked across at the grieving father and thought he seemed to be ageing with each moment that passed.

"Mike, I can't do it, I can't. And the killing seems to come so easily to you." He regretted the words as soon as they left his mouth, but it was too late to take them back.

Mike looked hurt. Joseph's words made him sound no better than the men who had raided his farm. When he responded there was bitterness in his voice.

"These things are already dead, Joseph. I don't know what it is I do to make them stop exactly, but you can't kill what's already dead. And I don't do it because I want to, but because there is no alternative. And if you're referring to what happened last night – well, yes, that did come easy to me. I suppose it's just a personality quirk, but I've never had a lot of time for child rapists and murderers. I don't understand how anyone who's a brother or a father wouldn't want to take their pound of flesh from scum like that. It might sound self-righteous, but we still have to have some moral absolutes. I don't want my brother and sisters living in a world where that isn't the case. We can't let every grain of goodness dissolve in a steaming pot of venomous bile just because we're trapped in this madness where rules no longer exist. They figured that out first. They thought they were untouchable, that they could take what they wanted. That's all they'd ever done all their lives, only now, guess what? No consequences. The weak still think human life is something sacred and to take it is wrong. Let me tell you, there is nothing sacred about human life, Joseph. We're living, breathing animals, and like with any animals, you put the rabid ones down."

The younger man paused for breath and his anger left him, recognising the apologetic expression on the farmer's face. "Fuck it! Fuck it! When we get back, reverse up to the furthest barn. I'll take care of it and then we'll get the body out and wrapped in a blanket before your family has to see. Fuck it! I really liked that kid, Joseph. You don't know me well enough to know how hard this will be for me. It feels like shit when it's someone you know."

"I'm sorry, Mike. I'm sorry for asking you and I'm sorry for what I said. I'm just not strong enough."

"You don't need to be strong. You just need to remember why you're doing it. I'll do whatever it takes to protect my family and if that makes me someone I don't like very much then tough luck, it's the price I have to pay." The van came to a stop outside the gate to the farm. "But we're all going to have to learn to play our part, Joseph, because this fucking nightmare has only just begun." With that, he opened the door and jumped down to push the gate back to allow the three vehicles entrance.

Mike signalled for Lucy to wind down the window as she drove through the gate. "Joseph and I have something to take care of. We'll be in when we're done, but keep Alice busy."

"What's going on?"

"I'll tell you both later. Just please do as I ask." His face was tired, but he was clearly agitated.

"Okay, Mike," Lucy replied, "but I want to know everything when you come in." Mike nodded and closed the gate behind them.

16

Mike could hear Joseph pacing up and down outside, the stone chips crunching beneath his feet each time he turned. Mike switched on the light in the back of the van and saw the bound creature, barely moving beneath the layered strapping and the burlap sack. He pulled the coarse material from the captive's head and tore the duct tape from its mouth to reveal lips curled in hatred. Haunting grey eyes with shattered black pupils flaring in the dim artificial light of the van sent a shudder down Mike's back. He dropped his head and gazed at the hatchet grasped firmly in his right hand.

"I'm sorry, Peter, you were a good kid," he said as he drove the once-shining blade through the top of the RAM's skull. He wiped the metal clean on the creature's clothing then replaced the sack over its head before opening up the back of the van. Joseph stood there despairingly with a thick grey blanket in his hands. He climbed into the van and together the two men carefully wrapped the body and tied the blanket securely to make sure no-one could see the gruesome remains within. They lifted the bundle down and placed it gently and respectfully on the ground.

"There's probably a couple of hours of daylight left," Joseph said. "I think I'd like to get him buried today."

Mike just nodded. "I'm sorry, Joseph. I mean that."

"I know you do. And it means a lot to me, lad."

"I'll leave you to be with your family, Joseph. You know where I am if you need me."

"No, don't go," Joseph said, grabbing Mike's arm. It took him a moment to regain his composure before he could speak. Mike stood there in an uncomfortable limbo as he watched the grieving father struggle to bring his emotions back under control. "I wanted to ask you if you'd thought any more about what I'd said about you coming to Candleton with us?"

"We're heading north, you're heading north. I know it's not far, but it will probably take us the best part of a day to get there, safely I mean. Maybe your brother wouldn't mind putting us up for the night before we set off again the next day," Mike said, with the beginnings of a small smile on his face.

"You'd be welcome to stay there with us, all of you. Permanently, I mean." Joseph grasped Mike's hand in order to shake it.

"Thank you, Joseph, but we're heading north of the border. A bite to eat and a safe place to sleep for the night would be much appreciated, though." He released his grip. "Do you need a hand with the digging?" Mike asked wearily.

"I think I'd prefer to do it myself. By God I never thought I could lose two of my boys... You get back to your family. Thanks again, Mike." The pair of them walked across to the house.

The kitchen was empty, but in the living room Alice was sobbing, her arms around John on one side and Annie on the other. Both of their faces were dry for the moment, but tear stains glistened on their cheeks. Beth and Tracey were squashed onto the ends of the sofa, desperately trying to comfort Alice with soft words and kind touches. The denial she had been living in was unable to shield her from this latest shard of reality.

"I'm so sorry about Peter, he was a good kid," Mike said, looking around each of the faces. He wanted to say something else, but words failed him. He left the lounge and headed down the corridor to the master bedroom.

Although hardly euphoric, the mood was noticeably more upbeat once the door was closed. Emma and Lucy, although saddened by Peter's death, were beginning to appreciate how lucky they were to be alive. Samantha felt a guilty joy that her friends had returned safely, and after spending part of the day devastated that their sister had been killed, Jake and Sammy were now in a state of elation to have her back with them and safe. As Mike leant back against the door, firmly shutting it behind him, his two younger siblings ran up to him. He collapsed to his knees and recharged his strength through their embraces.

"You brought her back," Sammy said, with a look on her face like a thousand Christmas mornings had all come at once.

"The Doc and your sister seemed to do pretty well looking after themselves. I just helped out a little bit," he said, smiling. Sammy kissed him on the cheek then returned to the king-sized bed with Jake where they had laid out an array of crisps and snacks.

Before Mike could say another word, Samantha gave him a towel and some clean clothing. "We've got wine, crisps and chocolate. Go get yourself cleaned up," she said, still trying to hold back her giddiness that the group were all back safely. As if under orders, Mike turned round and headed towards the bathroom. Samantha followed him out, gently closing the door behind her. "Oh, and Mike, before I forget..." Mike turned back, waiting for her to say something else, but instead she took hold of his hand, stood on her tiptoes and kissed him gently on the cheek. Her normally pale face was blushing bright pink. "Thank you. Thank you for keeping us all together." She turned and went back into the bedroom.

Mike stood for a moment, still breathing her comforting aroma, still feeling her delicate hands on his face. The crying from the other room roused him from his momentary reverie and he went to take his shower and get a shave.

When he returned, Jake and Samantha had started a jigsaw on the floor. They were carefully mulling over where each piece belonged while chomping on packets of unhealthy fried snacks. The three women were sitting beneath the window, their backs against the wall, a bottle of red wine and a large packet of crisps being passed back and forth.

"So, is this just a girl thing or can anybody join in?" Mike asked playfully.

"You come and sit next to me, Mikey boy," Lucy said, pushing up against Emma and creating a space between herself and Samantha.

Mike sank down between them and was handed the bottle. He looked carefully at the label, took a couple of swigs, then winced a little as the dry red fluid ran over his tongue and trickled down the back of his throat.

"So, tell us everything," Lucy said, snatching the bottle back from him. She took a drink and then handed it to Emma.

"Not really a good idea," he replied, nodding in the direction of his younger brother and sister, who were far too immersed in their snacks and puzzle to even hear him.

"Well, at least give us an idea, Mike, we shouldn't have secrets. What did Joseph want?"

"Well, let me see. How can I put this? Peter wasn't as still as you would expect a corpse to be."

"You're kidding me?" Lucy replied, "Joseph didn't..."

"He asked me to do it." Mike snatched the bottle and took another hefty gulp.

"Sorry, Mike. That's a really shitty thing to have to do," she replied.

Mike shrugged. "What the hell. Have hatchet, will travel. What's one more skull to crack open?" he asked bitterly under his breath.

There was a pause in the conversation as the wine passed up and down the row.

"Y'know, Doc, there's something that's been bugging me, something I don't understand about the RAMs," Mike said, and Lucy let out a small groan. "Barring the odd one here and there, they nearly all have single bite wounds, or only one that's visible, anyway. I find it strange that the RAMs go to the effort of chasing and killing their prey simply to take a single bite of flesh. I mean, I've watched a lot of wildlife documentaries and I don't remember seeing one where a predator just takes a single bite out of its prey. What the hell is that all about?"

Lucy and Samantha looked at each other. "You noticed that too, huh?" Lucy took a drink from the bottle and continued. "The fact is, Mike, we don't know. If we'd have had more time to study these things, I'm sure our scientists could have come up with some ideas. I can give you my theory if you want to hear it," Lucy said, passing the bottle to him.

"Please," he said, turning sideways to listen.

"I believe there is an element of feeding during the attacks, but to a greater extent I think it's to do with spreading the virus. If you want to give your genes the best chance for survival, what do you do?" she asked, looking at Mike.

"Mate?" he replied, almost apologetically.

"That's right. Only, the more women you mate with, the better your chance that some of those women will fall pregnant with healthy offspring who'll carry your genetic code. Of course, for the purposes of this example I'm assuming that all your little guys swimming around down there are fit and ready for service rather than sleeping at the wheel." She smiled at the opportunity to tease him, and Samantha and Emma both giggled childishly.

"Nice, Doc, thanks. Anyway, moving along," Mike replied.

"Well, for us, sex is how our genes are passed on. For the virus, a simple bite or scratch is enough for the genetic code to survive, to spread, to take over. So yes, I think there is a nutritional aspect to the bite, although these things seem to be able to last a hell of a long time without food. But I think, and like I say, Mikey, this is just my theory, I think the primary reason, or certainly an equally valid reason, is to make us all one big happy family."

"How long can they last without food?" Mike asked, carefully listening to everything she said.

"Jeez, can't we just enjoy the wine and talk about, oh, I don't know, music, films, books, anything but this?" she pleaded.

"Please, Doc, one last question and then I'm done, I promise," he said, taking the bottle for another drink.

"The French had had one for six weeks when we lost contact with them. It hadn't had anything to eat for that period. It had slowed down a little, but all its other characteristics remained constant. We don't know how long they can last without food. The one saving grace is that the virus doesn't seem to be able to jump species, and the RAMs aren't interested in anything other than humans. Can you imagine having to deal with reanimated rats and dogs and birds? Whoa! I don't even want to go there." She pulled the bottle back out of Mike's hand and took a drink.

"Thanks, Doc, I appreciate it. I won't bother you any more with my questions tonight," Mike said, smiling.

Emma unscrewed the top to another bottle of wine and took a drink, then placed her hand in a bag of crisps and shoved them in her mouth. Like Lucy, she just wanted to forget about the day. To forget about the RAMs, just for a little while, to feel normal.

"So, Lucy – music, film, book," she said, as bits of crisps fell from her mouth.

"Huh?" Lucy replied.

"Music, film, book. What's your favourite piece of music? Your favourite film? Your favourite book?" Emma asked, brushing the crisp fragments from her top.

Lucy smiled. "Oh, man. Let me see. Oh, I'm going to have to think about this one. You go first, Samantha," she said, handing the first nearly empty bottle to the younger woman and relishing the prospect of having something approaching a normal conversation.

"Well. It would have to be 'It's You' by Zayn," Samantha said, beaming as she remembered the song.

"Oh, good grief," Mike said quietly, but not quietly enough, as Samantha flicked his knuckle with her middle finger. "Ow!"

"Favourite film would have to be *Titanic*," she continued proudly.

"Oh, good grief," Mike repeated. This time, she dug him in the ribs. "Ouch," he yelped, pushing up harder against Lucy to try and avoid any further injury.

"Favourite book has to be *Wuthering Heights*." As soon as she said it she balled her hand into a fist, ready to jab Mike.

"Actually, that's a pretty good choice, I'll give you that," he said, before she could get her punch in.

"You've read *Wuthering Heights*?" she asked incredulously.

"Yeah, so?"

"You? You, Mike Fletcher, have read *Wuthering Heights*?" she asked again.

"Yes. Yes, I have. I don't know how many other ways I can say it, Samantha. Yes, I've read *Wuthering Heights*. It's a great book."

"Well I never," she said, smiling to herself and taking another drink of wine.

"That's nothing compared to some of the books he's borrowed off my shelf." Emma chuckled, leaning forward to see how red her brother's face turned.

"Aww, poor Mikey, are you getting embarrassed, sweetie?" Lucy chipped in, making him turn even redder.

He took a deep breath, a drink of wine and composed himself. "No, I'm fine, thanks," he replied, handing her the bottle. "Y'know, Doc, it's funny, you remind me a lot of my gran. I think you'll like her."

Lucy paused in mid gulp and turned her eyes but not her head towards Mike. "How so?"

"Just little phrases and expressions, and the fact you call me Mikey. She's the only other person who ever calls me that," he said, remembering fondly.

"How old's your gran, Mike?" Lucy asked, curiously.

"She's sixty-eight. Sixty-nine next month," he replied.

"So, you're telling me that I remind you of your sixty-eight-year-old grandmother?"

Mike was unaware that the other two women had put their heads down and were giggling away as he dug himself into a hole.

"Erm, just... just with some of the things you say." It dawned on him that, despite not meaning it as an insult in any way, comparing Lucy to an old-age pensioner could easily be seen as such. "I mean, not physically. I mean, hell, you've got all your own teeth and your face doesn't sag and erm..." Mike gulped, took the bottle out of Samantha's hand and drained it.

"Girls, get the kids out of the room. Seriously, that is the hottest thing any guy has ever said to me," she said, still straight-faced.

Worried that he'd offended her, Mike soon realised he was the butt of yet another joke as he noticed Samantha and Emma shaking with laughter.

"I've got all my own teeth and my face doesn't sag." She rubbed her hand up and down his thigh and rolled her tongue provocatively over her lips. "I want you now. Get over to that bed, no, in fact, screw the bed, we'll do it right here." She pretended to unbutton her shirt. Emma snorted wine through her nose and began coughing and spluttering.

"What's so funny?" Sammy asked from across the room, noticing the two women wobbling in hysterics.

"Nothing, sweetie," Lucy replied. The young girl thought about pressing for more information, but then went back to her crisps and jigsaw. "I bet you had women lining up at your door. Man, if my prom date had known how to woo a girl like you do, he'd have ended the night a lot happier." She smirked and took a drink from the second bottle before passing it on to Mike.

"Okay. Point made, Doc. So go on." Mike said, taking a drink.

"Go on what?"

"Music, film, book?" Mike replied, wanting to get back to the original conversation.

"Oh, right. I'd forgotten. You got me all hot and bothered for a moment there. Let me see. Music? That would have to be 'Paradise City' by Guns N' Roses," she said contemplatively.

"You're a rock chick?" Mike said, surprised.

"You betcha, babe. Film? Film would have to be *The Shawshank Redemption*. Everybody stayed silent but nodded appreciatively.

"Book..." She trailed off and a look of melancholy swept across her face. "Book would have to be *Charlotte's Web*." Lucy grabbed the bottle back and took a drink.

Emma leaned forward to look at her. "*Charlotte's Web*? The children's book? How come?"

Lucy took another drink. "It was my daughter's favourite book."

This time Samantha turned to look at her friend in surprise. "You have a daughter?"

"Past tense. She died three years ago," Lucy answered sadly.

"I'm so sorry," Samantha said. "I had no idea. What happened?"

"We'd gone up to see my folks for a few days, and one morning they took her into town while I had a lie in. They were in a head-on crash with a guy who was coming home from his friend's all-night bachelor party. Mom and Dad and the other driver died at the scene. Charlie died later on in hospital. She was six." Lucy gulped and then took a drink. "That was her favourite book. I used to read it to her all the time. Out of everything we left behind at the base, that's the thing that I miss the most." She passed the bottle across to Samantha and unclasped a gold locket from around her neck. She opened it up to show her friend.

"She was beautiful. She looks just like you," Samantha said, smiling sympathetically. She passed the locket to Mike and Emma who echoed the sentiment.

"Well, I might not have the book any more, but they'll have to pry that photo out of my dead hands before I give it up," Lucy said, taking the locket back and refastening it around her neck. She took a deep breath and, in an attempt to lighten the mood, turned the questioning around. "So, anyway, Emma. Music? Film? Book?" she asked leaning forward to look at her and handing her the bottle at the same time.

Emma was still shocked and saddened to learn of Lucy's misfortune, but taking her cue to change the subject, she responded. "Okay, music would have to be 'Hymn for the Weekend' by Coldplay and Beyoncé," she stated confidently.

"Ugh!" Mike said.

"Do me a favour, Samantha," said Emma. No sooner had she said it than Mike got poked in the ribs.

"Favourite film would have to be *The Notebook* with Ryan Gosling," Emma said, and quickly fanned herself with her hand.

"Sometimes I am stunned that you're my sister."

"Samantha," Emma said.

Samantha responded by giving Mike another sharp prod in the ribs. "Ow!"

"Book would have to be *Fifty Shades of Grey*," she said finally.

"Ooh, ooh! I want to change my favourite book," Samantha said, like an excited schoolgirl trying to get the teacher's attention.

"Okay guys. Rule number one, is strictly no take backs. Your first choice is your only choice," Lucy replied, acting as moderator.

Mike just shook his head despairingly, for which he got another painful prod in the ribs.

"Okay, buddy boy. Music? Film? Book?" Lucy demanded, turning to look at him and handing him the bottle.

"Music? 'Octavarium', by Dream Theater," he replied.

"Who is Dream Theater?" Samantha asked.

A look of exasperation fell across Mike's face and he was just about to tell her when Emma leaned forward and replied instead. "They're an 'extreme metal' band."

"They are not an extreme metal band," responded her brother indignantly.

"Well, they sound extreme to me," Emma retorted, clearly a little tipsy as she began to struggle with her diction.

"Bloody One Direction are extreme compared to the bland shite you listen to," he replied curtly.

"Children, children. Play nice," Lucy appealed, slowly beginning to enjoy herself again.

Mike took another drink of wine and handed the bottle to Lucy. "Anyway, they're a progressive metal band," he stated, oblivious to the fact that Samantha and Emma had started laughing at him again. "Film? that would have to be *The Seven Samurai*." He stopped this time because Lucy was leaning forward and chuckling. "What? What is it now?" he asked, frustrated.

She took hold of the top of his hand in apology. "Oh, Mikey, I'm sorry, sweetie. It's just I knew you were going to say that film before it even came out of your mouth. That is like the perfect Mike film. Emma and I got you a little gift earlier. You'll understand when you see it." She turned to the younger woman and they both continued to laugh knowingly.

Mike was baffled by the whole exchange and was just about to ask more questions when a loud crack of gunfire sliced through the merriment like a white-hot blade through butter.

The children looked up, the relaxed and contented smiles on their faces gone in an instant. "What was that?" Jake asked fretfully.

Mike jumped up and Lucy extended her hand and gestured that she wanted him to help her stand. She got to her feet with a groan and the pair headed towards the door. "Stay here a minute," Mike said to Samantha and Emma, who were already heading across to the children.

"What the fuck is it now?" he asked quietly as the two of them headed down the hallway and out through the kitchen.

"My question exactly," Lucy replied, pulling the Glock out of the back of her jeans.

Mike ran across to the ambulance to get his weapons and rejoined Lucy. The courtyard was deserted except for the vehicles. The pair looked at each other, wondering which way to go. Then they heard a scream, followed by another echoing blast from a shotgun.

"That came from behind the barns," Lucy said, beginning to run. Mike followed with just the merest hint of a limp. They reached the corner of the building and Lucy put her head round to see if she could catch sight of what was going on. A split second later there was another violent crack of gunfire and she went toppling back, knocking Mike off his feet. She was motionless on top of him.

"Doc? Doc?" he said a second time, with more concern in his voice.

A figure came rushing around the corner. "Oh, my God. I'm sorry, I'm so sorry. I thought it was more of those things," Joseph said, looking down at the pair of them.

"Yeah, well, as you can see, it's not," Lucy replied, pulling herself to her feet. Mike let out a huge sigh of relief. For a moment he was convinced she had been shot. "Jesus, Joseph, you've got to check your targets. You can't just fire at anything that moves."

"You're right. I'm so sorry. Are you alright? Are the pair of you alright?" he said, clearly flustered.

Mike stood up. "What's going on, Joseph? Why are you firing? Every RAM in earshot is going to be trying to find us."

"We'd just finished burying Peter. We were all saying our last goodbyes when one of those things appeared. If I hadn't fired it would have been on top of us, on top of my family. Then just now another one came out of nowhere. I don't understand. There must be a fence or hedge down somewhere," Joseph said. His hands were visibly shaking.

"Is everybody okay? Nobody got attacked?" Lucy asked.

"We're all fine." Beth was breathless as she joined them. "Mum's very shaken, the kids are crying, but nobody's been hurt physically."

Mike looked past Beth and saw the two creatures on the ground. One with half its head blown away, one face down with a large exit wound at the base of its skull.

"What do you think?" Lucy asked, ignoring Joseph and Beth and looking towards Mike.

"Well, if two got in, more can get in. It won't be long until dark and we're getting out of here at first light tomorrow, so I think we should move out of the house immediately. We'll get the vehicles into the largest barn, sleep rough in them tonight, post a guard and head out as soon as we wake," said Mike, rubbing his hand over his face.

"I don't understand. Why sleep in the barn? If we're posting a guard, why not sleep in the house?" Beth asked.

"The barn has two sturdy, lockable entrances. The house has lots of windows. If a few of those things attack at the same time, we'd struggle to defend it," he said, with a little more patience than he would have had with Joseph, whose weaknesses were starting to annoy him. "Right, so I just want to confirm, we're taking the box van, the flatbed truck, the ambulance, one Land Rover and the caravan. Is that right?" he asked, looking at Joseph and Lucy.

"Yes," Joseph said. "Only, I've been thinking. I think we should hitch the caravan to the truck. We're going to be going over some rugged ground and it will be able to handle it even better than the 4x4." Mike and Lucy nodded, impressed that Joseph had actually been thinking.

"Okay, good. We'll figure out who's in what vehicle tomorrow, but bear in mind, when we're on the open road, it's not just the RAMs we need to worry about. A truck and a van full of supplies are going to be a real target for thieves. The four of us are going to be the first and only line of defence. You three can shoot and I can fight, so we need to think smart about who goes where." They all looked at each other. "Now, let's get the vehicles moved, get everything out of the house that's going and get everyone safely in the barn. Joseph, Beth, can you organise that while the Doc and I patrol in case there are more of those things around?"

"Already on it," Beth replied, and headed back towards the funeral party.

"Once again, I'm sorry, Lucy. I'm not really cut out for this," Joseph said.

"It's okay, you were just trying to protect your family. I understand," Lucy replied, considerably calmer than she was a few moments earlier.

"No, it's not okay," Mike interrupted sternly.

"Mike, there's no need—" Lucy began.

"Look, Joseph, I understand where you're coming from. I know how much you've lost, but people are depending on you. Your family and my family." Mike placed a firm hand on Joseph's upper arm and a soft hand on Lucy's shoulder. She took a small intake of breath as the gesture was uncharacteristically tender. "You're a good person and a good father, Joseph, but you're going to have to 'man up' if we're going to get through this. We won't get any second chances out there, any of us." Mike let go of Joseph, turned round and walked away. Lucy smiled weakly, a little embarrassed, and followed.

When she was certain they were out of earshot, Lucy leaned in to Mike and spoke softly, so as not to be overheard. "Y'know, if a twenty-year-old kid spoke to me like that, I'd slug him so hard, he'd think he'd been hit by a train."

"That's exactly the reason I don't need to speak to you like that," he replied. Lucy shrugged as if to concede the point and the pair continued across the courtyard.

"Come here a second," she said, speeding up a little as she went towards the back of the Land Rover.

She opened it up and unzipped the weapons bag. "When we get to where we're going, I'll show you how to use one of these properly, but for now just look and listen," she said, pulling a pump-action shotgun out of the holdall. Lucy turned it upside down, pulled some shells out of a box and pointed to a black metal shaft underneath the barrel. "This is a tubular magazine," she said, placing the shells into the receiver. "Your shells are stored here." She finished loading and turned the gun over. "Give this slide a good pull," she continued, cranking the pump-action mechanism with a satisfying clunk. "Then aim and press the trigger." Lucy depressed the slide release then repeatedly pulled and released the pump to empty the chamber and the magazine. She turned it over to double-check it was empty and then handed the weapon to Mike. "Okay, hotshot, your turn."

The pupil studied the gun for a moment and then put into practice what he had seen. Like a well-programmed robot, he loaded, readied and unloaded the shotgun.

"Okay, that's good," Lucy said. I'm going to show Samantha, Emma and Tracey how to use one as well. We've got enough weapons, so if nothing else, we can look menacing with them if it gets tricky out there," she said, getting three more shotguns out of the bag.

"Good idea, Doc," said Mike, putting a few shells in his pockets. He was about to set out on a short patrol of the grounds when Lucy stopped him.

"Oh, before I forget," she said, reaching back into the bag. "Emma and I saw these and we just thought of you straight away." She smiled and removed the two large machetes from the bag.

Mike's eyes lit up. "Doc. I don't know what to say. They're beautiful."

"I wouldn't quite go that far," she replied, letting out a small laugh.

"No, Doc, you don't understand. These are beautiful. I remember seeing a programme on the makers of these. They're genuine works of art," he said, caressing the metal like it was the face of a loved one.

"Wait a minute. You actually know where these were made?"

"Too right I do. It's a small company in Sheffield. There are these two old guys who are well past retirement age and everything they do is handmade, they're proper craftsmen, old school. These knives aren't cheap knock-off shite from China, these are serious pieces of equipment. They would have cost a small fortune. Seriously, these are awesome, Doc. Thank you," Mike said, genuinely grateful. He leaned across and gave her a kiss on the cheek.

"You're welcome, Mike," she said, quietly laughing and shaking her head to herself as she went back into the house to get her next pupils.

Mike continued to marvel at the blades for a moment then placed them in his belt. He picked up the shotgun and started his reconnaissance of the immediate area.

Joseph got to work moving the vehicles into the largest of the barns, while Beth helped Alice empty the house of all they would be taking on the journey. After Tracey, Samantha and Emma had had their weapons training, they joined in to complete the task before darkness fell.

The sun was low in the sky and night was approaching quickly. Lucy and Mike stood at opposite ends of the courtyard while the others scurried to and fro. They watched carefully, their eyes darting around, looking for any alien movement, anything out of the ordinary.

Alice came to the kitchen door with an apron still hanging around her neck. "Joseph? Joseph? I think there's something wrong with the pipes. The water's stopped running," she said, as if it was just any other day on the farm.

Joseph knew there was nothing wrong with the pipes. He knew the generator working the water pump had finally run out of fuel, but he wanted to see it for himself. He turned the tap. Nothing. That was it, he thought to himself. That's the end of civilisation. No order, no laws, no power, no running water. We're back in the Dark Ages now. He turned to Alice with a sad smile on his face. "It's alright, dear. We've got plenty of bottled water, we've got a full tank in the caravan and we've got the chemical toilet. We'll be fine." He put his arm around his perplexed wife and guided her into the courtyard. "Now, how about cranking up the gas stove in the caravan and making everybody a lovely hot cup of tea before we all turn in for the night?" he said to her gently.

"Oh my word, tea bags," she said, annoyed with herself and marched straight back into the house. She came back out carrying a large tea caddy and walked purposefully towards the barn.

Joseph walked up to Lucy. "Okay, we're all set. All the vehicles are in and all the supplies are loaded and secured."

"Great," she said, signalling across to Mike. "Let's make sure we've got everybody in and then get those doors locked."

17

With the doors locked and bolted, it was dark inside the barn. The skylights allowed the last rays of the sun to penetrate, but it was hard to see anything other than outlines of figures and objects.

"Anyone for tea?" asked Alice from the door of the caravan. Everybody gathered round. The lights from inside provided a warm, comforting glow. Joseph went around passing mugs of tea to the adults and hot chocolate to the youngsters.

Mike took his tea and a lantern back to the ambulance and had the odd sip while searching through his holdall. He breathed a sigh of relief when he found the book his gran had sent him. He hadn't seen it since leaving the house the day before. Had it really just been the previous morning? So much had happened in such a short time. He picked up a sleeping bag and his thick jacket and made his way to the barn door. He could hear quiet conversations as everyone warmed themselves with their drinks.

Holding up the lantern to the locks, he made sure they were secure. It was highly likely that no-one and nothing would actually be able to gain access to the barn, but he wasn't prepared to take any risks. Mike would stand guard. It would be nice if he got relieved at some stage, but he'd rather do it himself than force somebody who may well fall asleep on the job. He took another sip of his tea and began reading in the dim light of the lantern. As drinks were finished, the voices gradually diminished and everyone made their way to whichever vehicle was acting as their bedroom for the night. Mike heard two sets of quiet footsteps and put his book down. He knew without looking that he was about to be pounced on. Sure enough, Sammy and Jake flopped down on top of him like they were in a rugby maul.

"Shouldn't you two be in bed?" Mike asked, grabbing them both playfully.

"We're going now," Sammy said, giggling. "Why aren't you coming?"

"I might later. I'm just going to stay up and read a little while."

Jake said, "Samantha said you're keeping watch to protect us from the bad men."

"Oh she did, did she? Well, that's just not true. I don't need to protect any of us, because I know about a secret weapon that would defeat anyone, no matter how bad they were."

The children looked up, wide-eyed. Finally, Sammy asked the question. "What? What weapon?"

"Jake's farts," he replied. "They'd kill anybody."

Both children started laughing hysterically. The word alone always got them giggling, but when the action was attributed to someone, it made it even more hilarious. Unbeknown to the three of them, Emma had been watching in the shadows, enjoying seeing them interact. Her family.

"Very nice," she said as she stepped into the dim glow of the lantern. "You realise that's all I'm going to get all night now, fart this, fart that." The children burst out laughing again as she said it and the sheer joy of seeing them laugh made her giggle too.

Mike kissed his younger brother and sister on the head. "Right, the pair of you, off to bed now." They kissed him back and ran off towards the ambulance.

"Have you figured out the sleeping arrangements?" Mike asked.

"Kind of. I don't think it's going to be too comfortable, but they're sleeping head to toe on the gurney. Samantha and I are head to toe on the floor and you and Lucy can spread out in the cab."

"Ooh, tempting, but I think I'll just stay here the night," he said, putting his hands under the sleeping bag to warm up.

"Lucy says she's going to take over from you at two," replied Emma. Mike angled his watch towards the lantern and saw that it was nine-thirty.

"That's cool, I was hoping I'd get a bit of shut-eye before tomorrow."

"Samantha and I both offered to take turns, but Lucy said she was more than happy just to split it between the two of you." She paused for a moment, not sure how to carry on. "She showed me how to use a shotgun today."

"Yeah, she said she was going to. That's good, we need as many of us as possible able to shoot."

"Do you think we're going to run into trouble tomorrow?"

"Em, we're looking at travelling nearly fifty miles tomorrow. So far we've done about six since leaving home, and look how well that's turned out." They both let out a small sarcastic laugh. "But what I can promise you is that I won't let anything happen to us," he said, beckoning her to sit beside him.

She went to her brother and he unzipped the side of the sleeping bag so she could put her legs and hands under. She leaned into him and he put his arm around her. "You can't promise that, though, can you? I mean really, you can't," she said sadly.

"Yes I can. You've just got to trust me."

"Mike, tell me you won't get cross," she said, leaning her head on his shoulder.

"What?" he asked, already on edge.

"No Mike, you've got to promise me first," she replied.

"Okay, I promise," he said, leaning his head against hers.

"Lucy and I were going to end it all this afternoon. The house was surrounded, there was no way out. We had a choice of being a meal for the RAMs or going out on our own terms. The difference between me dying and not dying was literally a split second. The barrel was pointed at my head and Lucy was pressing the trigger when I heard the screech of your tyres. It's nothing more than dumb luck that I'm sat here. So when you say you won't let anything happen to me, you can't promise, really, can you?" She looked up at her brother, not reproachfully, but like a child looking to a parent for answers.

"When Joseph told me that you were gone, I blew a gasket. I mean, I was as enraged as I have ever been. You know me better than anybody alive. What do you think I would want more than anything at that moment?" he asked, looking down at her.

She thought for a moment and then she realised the answer was obvious. If anyone ever hurt her or Sammy or Jake, there would only be one thing on his mind, "Revenge."

"Anybody messes with my family, I don't care who or what they are, I'm going to take them down." His eyes glinted in the lantern light. "I understand why you and Lucy thought the way you did, but like I say, Em, you need to trust me, because I won't give up fighting while there is a breath left in me. Don't forget that, ever."

They sat in silence for a while, watching the flickering flame. A minute turned into two and Mike tried to listen to his sister's breathing. He gave her a gentle nudge. Nothing. Another, nothing. "Em?" he said. "Em?" This time louder.

"Huh? What? Oh. Oh, I must have drifted off," she mumbled. "I'd better go to bed before I start drooling on you."

"Too late," he said, pretending to wipe his shoulder dry.

Emma smiled warmly, "I love you, Mike," she said, kissing him on the forehead as she got to her feet.

"Love you too, sis. Get a good night's sleep. We've got a long day tomorrow." He watched her as she disappeared into the dark. He was happy inside. A few months ago, he had been at loggerheads with Emma. Their relationship had been at its lowest ebb. For her to fall asleep on his shoulder felt like when they were younger, when they were best friends, when they were each other's only salvation.

*

Alice was curled up to Joseph, her arm clutching his broad chest tightly. Annie and John were right next to her. The master berth in the caravan was only meant to take two, but all of them felt the need to be close. The stress of the past two days sent mother and children to sleep like they'd been given a horse tranquilliser. Joseph stayed awake, staring into the dark, hearing their breathing and thinking about his two fallen sons. The grief was unbearable, but, now more than ever, he needed to be strong for his family. He would get them to Candleton safely and then they would have time to mourn properly.

A painfully hot and itchy sensation suddenly danced around the skin of his ankle. He desperately wanted to reach down and rub his leg. He grimaced and rubbed his other foot against the affected area to relieve the sensation. Slowly the pain dissipated and the farmer began to relax again. Odd. Very odd. In all his fifty-eight years he had never felt anything like that. Then again, he'd never experienced the stress and heartache he'd felt in the past few days before, either. The pain was probably just some quirk of the body, some physical manifestation of all the emotional trauma. He remembered when his father had died of a heart attack. For weeks afterwards, he had felt palpitations. He went to the doctor on Alice's insistence and was told it was very common for that to happen after a loved one had passed away. The doctor gave Joseph some leaflets about coping with loss and even details for bereavement counselling, but the words of the doctor were enough. It was the body's way of coping. He went back to listening to the comforting sounds of his family breathing in deep slumber, and gradually his eyelids got heavier and he drifted into a dreamless fog.

*

Lucy was as good as her word and took over the watch at two. Almost in a daze, Mike thanked her and headed off to get some sleep. She had brought a small flask that she'd asked Alice to prepare earlier for her and Mike but had completely forgotten to give to him before she bedded down. She poured the dark brown liquid into the plastic cup and clasped her hands around it to gain what small comfort she could in the cold darkness of night. She heard the door of the ambulance click closed, followed by silence. When she felt sure she was alone, she reached into her pocket for the small brown bottle of tablets. She turned the safety cap and flicked it open with her thumb before tapping a small white pill into her palm. She stared at the pill for a second. She knew she couldn't carry on taking these the way she was, but right now she needed them, just to make things a little easier. She swallowed the tablet and then shot a nervous glance into the dark as she heard footsteps.

The sound stopped.

"Who's there?" she whispered.

There was no reply and the steps began again. Surely there was no way one of the creatures could have got inside the barn? The doors were locked and secured. But the uncertainty of what was lurking in the shadows of the night made Lucy reach round for her Glock. She pointed it in the direction she thought the sound had come from. "Who's there?" she demanded, a little louder this time. Slowly a figure emerged into the dim light. Lucy put down the gun.

"I'm sorry," said Tracey, stepping out of the shadow, her hands raised slightly as if to say *please don't shoot*. "I need to pee. I thought I heard Joseph had set up a toilet," she said, embarrassed.

Lucy smiled to herself. "Haven't you got a light, sweetie?" she asked. Tracey shook her head apologetically. Lucy reached into the breast pocket of her thick cotton shirt and retrieved a key-ring torch which she handed to her. "I wouldn't exactly call it a toilet. It's more like a big bucket with some pallets round to give you a bit of privacy. There's a sack of sand and some TP if you need it, too. It's over on the other side," Lucy said, pointing diagonally across the barn.

"Thank you. I'll bring it straight back," Tracey said, holding the torch up in front of her.

"You keep it, I've got another," replied Lucy, smiling as she watched the girl disappear around the back of the box van and out of sight. Within a few moments, Tracey reappeared. "It's alright, I said you can keep it."

"It's not that. I don't think I'll get any more sleep tonight. I was wondering if you wouldn't mind if I stayed out here with you?" she asked nervously.

"Hell, no," Lucy replied, "I could use the company. Here, have a drink of this," she said, passing the younger woman the mug as she sat down beside her.

Tracey took it gratefully and gulped the hot liquid before handing it back. Lucy ruffled the sleeping bag that Mike had left behind and placed it over both their knees.

"Thank you," Tracey said, "everybody's been so kind to me."

"You had a rough deal, kid. Nobody should ever have to go through that." Lucy took hold of her hand. "Whereabouts are you from, Tracey?"

"Originally, I'm from Brighton, that's where I grew up, but I was at Leeds University when the quarantine came in. I was in a hall of residence and then a couple of days ago there was an outbreak. I managed to escape with a few others, but we got separated. I found an empty house where I thought I would be safe until help came or at least until I could figure out what to do next, but then..." Her words trailed off as if the rest didn't need to be spoken. "I thought about trying to make it back down to Brighton, but even if I made it, I doubt if I'd see my family again."

"Well, sweetie, you're with us now. I can't say it's going to be a joyride, but at least you don't have to face anything alone."

"What do you think our chances are? Really, I mean?"

"You talking about mankind or just this group?" Lucy asked, smiling.

"Well. Now you mention it, both."

"I think mankind was done for long before this happened, but it sure as hell speeded everything up. As far as we go, well, I think we've got a better chance than most. We're armed, we've got vehicles and we know where we're going. That's three things more than most survivors will have," Lucy said and took a drink from the mug before passing it on.

The two sat in a comfortable silence for a while and then Tracey turned rigid. Lucy looked at her, puzzled, then she heard it too. She immediately dimmed the lantern. The footsteps outside got louder.

Soon they were followed by more. The younger woman let out a faint yelp as the sound stopped not far away from where they sat. Both women looked towards the door and held their breath. The crunching sounds began again but this time became quieter with each step. When they were no longer audible, the pair let out deep breaths.

"Do you think they were people or those things?" Tracey asked.

"I don't know, but there's no way in hell I'm going to open the door to find out."

18

Alice was first to rise in the caravan, quickly followed by her two youngsters who had been cuddled next to her throughout the night. After five minutes or so, Joseph reluctantly turned over; this morning he felt unusually lethargic. He blinked and saw Alice at the gas stove with two kettles on the hobs and several tins of beans, tomatoes and spam next to her. He allowed himself a weary smile. He could always rely on his wife to get things organised in the morning, to get everybody fed and ready for the day. He edged towards the end of the low berth and placed his feet on the bristling nylon carpet. The sensation made them tingle, and his memory of the night before and the strange pain came back to him. He reached down to look at his bare foot, and saw that just below the ankle there was a small red scratch, no longer than a grain of rice. For the life of him, Joseph couldn't think how he had managed to scratch himself there. It was inflamed and yellow around the edges. Joseph treated it as he would any other cut: he took down the first aid kit, rubbed in a little antiseptic cream and placed a sticking plaster firmly across it. His father had instilled in him that on a farm a wound always needed to be treated and covered, no matter how small it was. He pulled on his socks and clothes and slid the folding bed back into its two compartments before joining his wife.

"I've made some tea. I'm just brewing a few more and starting breakfast for everyone," she said, as if it was just like any other day.

He kissed her on the forehead. "Thanks, love. Where are Beth and the little 'uns?"

"Beth was up before me. They're all in the barn somewhere. I heard Annie giggling earlier on. It was so nice to hear. I didn't think I was ever going to hear that sound again." She looked thoughtful for a moment, remembering the previous two days, then snapped herself out of it and went back to the tasks at hand. Joseph kissed her again on the back of the head and stepped out of the caravan.

Breakfast was a hasty affair. The group stood at the door to the caravan, taking it in turns to get a plate of food like they were at a friend's barbeque party. Nervous chatter bounced around as the beginning of their journey drew closer.

After Lucy and Tracey had freshened themselves up and grabbed something to eat and drink, they quietly pulled Mike to one side.

Lucy whispered to him so her voice didn't carry to the rest of the group. "We heard footsteps outside last night. We think two sets, but we can't be sure."

"What time? Where did it sound like they went?" he asked, looking at both the women for answers.

"It was probably about three hours ago. It sounded like they walked off into the distance... And before you ask, I couldn't tell, neither of us could," Lucy said.

Mike thought for a moment. "Look, I've got ideas on how we should do this. I don't just mean how to deal with what could be outside these doors, I mean the whole journey. But everybody's life is at stake here, and if things turn to crap I don't want it to be because of something I didn't think of. We should get all the adults together. I'll gladly tell you what I think are our best options, but I'm more than happy to take suggestions if someone can think of anything better." He looked at the two women who both gave a barely perceptible nod in agreement. Mike turned around and went looking for Alice.

"That's worrying," Lucy whispered.

"What is?" Tracey asked, looking towards her.

"Granted, I haven't known Mike long, but this is the first time I've ever seen him lack confidence in his own ideas. Hell, his arrogance and pig-headedness are two of his most endearing qualities. You take those away and he's just like any other twenty-year-old kid. I think this is the first time I've seen him scared, and if he's scared, we've got problems."

"I don't understand. Nothing's changed since yesterday or the day before, and he didn't think twice about throwing himself into harm's way," Tracey said.

"I don't know if you've noticed, but Mike's wired a little differently to you and me. Don't get me wrong, Tracey, I'm a fan – I wouldn't be alive now if it wasn't for him. I don't think any of us would. But he's got a few issues, and one of them is that he's a control freak. The fact that he's having to rely on Joseph to map the route, on Beth, Samantha, you, me, all of us... Well, all of it is out of his control. It's not the RAMs or even other men like those who kidnapped you that he's scared of, it's us, Tracey. It's us." Lucy continued to watch Mike as he spoke to Alice. When he had finished talking, the farmer's wife ushered the children towards the back of the barn to help with some banal task so that the other adults could make their plans.

When they were gathered in a loose circle, Mike began. "Okay, firstly, can everybody here drive?" he asked, looking at each of the faces as they nodded. He took a deep breath, grateful that the first hurdle was out of the way. "Great. Joseph, I think you should take the lead in the 4x4. You know the route, and that grill guard will mow down any RAMs that get in the way. Beth, you take the truck and caravan. It's not ideal, but we'll keep Alice and the kids in there, that's where they'll have most protection. Em, you take the box van, and Samantha, you bring up the rear in the ambulance with Tracey riding shotgun." He paused for a moment to check everybody was following his train of thought. "You and me, Doc, we're going to be getting some fresh air on the back of the truck. It will give us a good vantage point if we need to use the guns and it will allow a quick dismount if we need to fight hand to hand. Does anybody have a problem with that? Or any better ideas? Because if they do, now's the time to speak." Mike stood back, his face inscrutable, but inside he was hoping someone might have a plan that sounded a little less dangerous.

For a long time no-one spoke. Then Joseph cleared his throat to say something; his voice was a little croaky as if he was coming down with a cold. "I wish I could come up with a better plan. Looking around, I can tell everybody wishes they could. The problem is, we've only got so many options open to us." He turned to face Mike. "I can see in your face, lad, that this has been nattering you. If anything happens out there, it's not on you." He turned around to look at the others. "If things go our way, we'll be in Candleton later on today. Hopefully it will be safe, somewhere we can mourn our losses and then begin to build our future. If things don't go to plan, then that's just the way it was meant to be, and it won't be the fault of anyone standing here. It'll just be that the cards were stacked against us this time." He stepped back and nodded as if to say *I'm done*.

"Thanks, Joseph." Mike said, mirroring his nod.

"I've got one suggestion." Beth stepped forward and looked towards her father. "Dad, couldn't we attach a couple of pallets to the front of the bed of the truck in between the cab and the load, to give Lucy and Mike a bit of cover? And maybe some razor wire along the edge as a bit of extra protection."

Joseph looked towards his daughter with a soft smile. If his head wasn't feeling so fuzzy, he would have come up with something like that, but trust his eldest to save the day. "Good idea, sweetheart, give me a hand and we'll have it done in five minutes."

The group disbanded and a flurry of activity ensued. Joseph, Beth and Tracey went off to begin work on reinforcing the truck, Samantha and Emma joined Alice with the children, and Lucy and Mike headed towards the Land Rover in order to gather and distribute the weapons and ammunition.

"Don't get me wrong, I think it's really sweet that you chose me to join you in what is so obviously a kamikaze mission, but can I just ask why?" Lucy said, raising her left eyebrow questioningly.

He stared straight into her misty blue eyes and she could see there was nothing but honesty in his tired face. "Truthfully, Doc, my sister apart, I trust you more than anybody in this place. I trust you to fight, I trust you to do what needs to be done and there is no-one I would rather have standing next to me up there. If I thought for a second I could do this by myself, I would. I don't like the thought of putting you in harm's way, but just knowing that I've got you to back me up makes me feel like we've actually got a chance of getting through this."

"Oh, man. This is because I gave you that whole speech about being on the same page isn't it? Jeez, when will I learn to keep my big yap shut?"

*

Lucy and Mike distributed the weapons evenly among those who could use them, with the warning that they should only be fired in extreme circumstances. They left ten cartridges with each shotgun and kept the rest of the ammunition for themselves. Lucy still had the Glock in the back of her jeans and she wedged the Browning along with two magazines under the tarpaulin with some foodstuffs. Joseph, Beth and Tracey had laid a roll of razor wire around the edges of the flatbed, and two large pallets had been secured into place. The gaps in the pallets were a perfect fit for the shotgun barrels, giving Mike and Lucy an extra level of protection should they need it. Two further thick tarpaulins had been attached to the bed of the truck, so if they needed to dismount from either side without getting ripped to pieces by the wire, all they had to do was flip the heavy cloth cover over and down. Lucy climbed up onto the storage box fixed to the back of the cab. There was a groove in the cab's roof which would give her and Mike something to hold on to when the road got bumpy. Standing on the box gave her a good view, but there were still a lot of blind spots if someone or something got in too close. She stood for a moment and let out a heavy sigh before climbing back down and going in search of her friends.

Lucy got to the ambulance to find Mike kneeling on the floor, hugging Jake and Sammy closely. Emma was standing beside them, enjoying what was left of her family for what could conceivably be the last time. "Now seriously, guys, you behave for Alice. No drinking, no smoking and definitely no swearing, okay?" Mike pulled back with his finger raised and looked at them reproachfully. Both children started giggling and he held them close again, kissing first Jake then Sammy on the cheek.

He stood up and pulled away, but Jake took a tight hold of his hand. "I'm scared," he said, looking at his older brother for reassurance.

Mike was about to speak when Sammy pulled her younger brother's chin to face her. Her warm brown eyes, her mother's warm brown eyes, were confident and reassuring as she answered him. "There's nothing to be scared of, Jake. Mike and Emma are just going to be riding in different cars to us and I'll be with you. I won't let anything happen to us."

Mike picked up his little brother as if he were lifting a small sack of flour. He was wearing a black T-shirt and his muscles rippled as he supported the young boy. "Sammy Bear's right, Jake, there's nothing to be scared of. Now remember what I told you. You be good for Alice." He lowered the child back down to the floor and tousled his brown mop of hair while giving his younger sister an appreciative wink.

At that moment, Samantha came round the corner. Her red hair was tied back in a ponytail, and her normally pale skin was bright pink. "Alice is looking for you two." She pointed to the children in a mock accusatory fashion. "It turns out that they've got a portable TV and DVD in the caravan as well as a good supply of crisps and chocolate, so while we're all busy driving, you lot are going to be watching films and partying. How's that fair?" she asked, smiling at Jake and Sammy. Their eyes widened and they each took one of Samantha's hands as she led them off.

Emma kissed them both on the head as they went by and then she went up to Mike, who had been joined by Lucy. "This is it, then." She reached up to her brother's head, pulled his face into her shoulder and whispered to him, "Don't let this be the last time." She pulled back, her eyes wet.

He kissed her forehead, turned and walked away, too overcome with emotion to speak.

"Don't worry, sweetie. I won't let anything happen to him," Lucy said as she handed Emma a tissue. She gave her a firm hug and then she too walked away in order to ready herself for the journey.

Joseph was just about to climb into the 4x4 when Mike approached him. "Joseph, if things... if things aren't what you expect when we get there... when we get to your brother's place. You're welcome to travel north with us."

"That's right nice of you, Mike, but I spoke to my brother before the phones went down. Candleton was already preparing for the worst. If there's one thing

I'm sure of, it's that we'll be safe there." Joseph nodded in appreciation once more and climbed into the car. He reached across and took a bottle of water from a small bag that Alice had prepared for him. The farmer unscrewed the top and took several thirsty gulps. The back of his throat felt like he'd been gargling with sand. He reached across to the glove compartment and took out some menthol chewing gum. If he was getting a cold, at least that would keep his airwaves clear.

Mike stood in front of the double barn door. He undid the lock and looked first to Joseph, then to Beth, who was behind in the truck. Finally his eyes moved up towards Lucy. She had the shotgun aimed towards the door, ready for whatever was on the other side. Mike's outstretched hand counted down, a digit at a time. Five, four, three, two, one. The engines started simultaneously. Mike ran forward into the courtyard pushing the left-hand corrugated steel door open, eyes darting frantically as he did so, searching for anything that shouldn't be there. The courtyard was clear. He ran back into the barn and did the same with the right-hand door. The vehicles began to move. Mike leapt onto the back of the truck. The tarpaulin protected him from the razor wire and Lucy's hand grasped his firmly as she pulled him to safety. He reeled the tarpaulin in and the razor wire sprang back into place. The pair of them climbed into the relative safety of the pallet cage and then up onto the box. The journey was finally underway.

Mike turned and grabbed his jacket from the floor. It was a mild morning, but travelling at speed out in the open would soon cool him down and he didn't want to seize up at a vital moment. He looked across at Lucy who was wearing a vest covered by a thick cotton shirt.

"What?" she asked, noticing he was staring at her.

"You don't think you're going to be cold later on?"

"Never had you pegged for a sissy, Mike," she said, grinning. He just shook his head in reply as if to say *you'll see*.

The convoy rolled through the courtyard and began to retrace the route the ambulance had taken when they first came to the farm. The dirt track was bumpy, and after each rise, Mike and Lucy looked back nervously to watch the caravan bob wildly like an apple in water. Joseph turned onto a track that Mike hadn't seen before. There were vast fields on either side, once home to hundreds of grazing cattle and sheep, now eerily empty. The track led up a steady incline and while clinging safely to the cab of the truck, Mike and Lucy looked into the distance towards Leeds and the chilling image of countless plumes of smoke.

Mike looked in another direction. It was further in the distance, but more columns of rising smoke were visible.

"What are you looking at?" Lucy asked.

"If I'm not mistaken, Bradford," he replied grimly, "or what's left of it."

Joseph began to slow down and eventually stopped in front of a gate. The rest of the convoy pulled up behind him. Lucy quickly unfurled the tarpaulin and Mike jumped down. He jogged up to the 4x4 and Joseph rolled down the window.

"Alright, Mike, out of this gate we turn left, we take a narrow lane for just on two miles and then there's a gate on the right that will let us on to Woodrow Farm. We can get about another six miles taking the farm tracks there and through to Kent Farm." Joseph spoke with authority. There weren't many farmers in a fifty-mile radius who he didn't know.

"Okay, Joseph, we'll follow your lead. Don't forget, you see RAMs on the road, you don't slow down. You plough straight through them." He looked at Joseph, who nodded confidently.

Mike walked up to the gate with his hand resting on the butt of a machete. He carefully leaned over and looked in both directions. All he saw was a quiet country lane lined with rustling green hedgerows. He slid the bolt across with a rusty shriek and pulled the heavy steel barrier back. Joseph began to move the truck forward and Mike jogged round to the side, where Lucy helped him back on board.

The truck swung out to the right in order to take the left turn without hitting the hedge on the other side of the road. Beth pulled the wheel into a full lock with a grunt and slowly advanced through the gateway. She was almost through when there was a loud scraping crunch and the truck juddered. Mike and Lucy shook too and would have lost their footing if they hadn't been gripping the cab.

Beth jumped down and ran her hands through her thick blonde hair in frustration. The truck was almost clear of the gateway, but the attached caravan had run straight into the stone gatepost. Joseph stopped and got out of the lead car to see what had happened. Mike and Lucy also dismounted and Lucy went to check on the caravan's occupants. Mike headed straight for the road to make sure they were not joined by any unwanted visitors while Joseph and Beth dealt with getting the convoy moving again.

Joseph took charge. Walking to the back of the truck, he unhitched the caravan coupling and unhooked the breakaway cable. He then wound down the jockey wheel and with the help of his daughter pushed the caravan back. Beth climbed into the truck and edged it clear of the gate and onto the road, while Joseph steered the caravan safely through the gateway and reattached it to the truck. Then, without hesitation, he went back to his car.

Mike and Lucy climbed back on board and the convoy began to roll again.

"It's nice to see that things are going to run as smoothly as they usually do for us," Mike said as he looked back towards the caravan.

His body spun around as he heard the Land Rover engine revving noisily. A hundred metres in front were two RAMs, running towards the car like rhinos trying to face off with a jeep. Joseph maintained his direction and speed, and the two creatures launched into the air, limbs flailing as they flew. Each one landed in a broken heap at the side of the road. The truck jerked slightly as the first of the beasts was flattened further by the heavy wheels. Mike and Lucy both raised their eyebrows, surprised that Joseph had kept his nerve.

The convoy slowed shortly afterwards and Mike noticed that Joseph had put his indicator on to signal the turn into the farm. Lucy picked up her shotgun and rested her arms on the roof of the cab, ready to fire if they were attacked. Mike jumped down and swung the gate open, all the while looking around for RAMs or people. Before he climbed back on, he opened the passenger door of the truck. "Beth, are you going to be okay, or do you want me to unhook the caravan?"

"I should be fine this time, there's plenty of room for the turn, but thanks anyway," she replied, her strong arms already working the wheel as Mike closed the door and went to climb back on to the bed of the truck.

The truck and caravan manoeuvred through the gate with ease and the other vehicles followed. The Land Rover stopped and Mike jumped down to close the gate behind them. Joseph had made it clear that his friends and neighbours may still be on these farms, and so their group was to do nothing that would risk the occupants' safety.

Mike leapt back on board and the vehicles began to move once again.

"Y'know, this time last year, if I was riding around this beautiful countryside with the wind flowing through my hair, I would have been in heaven," Lucy said, as she absorbed the view of golden fields and luscious green hedgerow.

"So what's spoiling it for you now?" Mike asked.

The pair continued the ride in silence, their eyes scanning the landscape for any predatory presence and their hands gripping the cab of the truck to maintain balance.

After a few miles, the lead car stopped again, but this time Joseph climbed out and signalled for Mike to join him. "Alright, out of this gate, we're onto public roads. We've got just short of four miles before we can get back on to a farm track. The only thing is, Mike, there's a small village to go through. There's only a few houses, I'd say fifty people at the most, but I don't really know what to expect, so I just wanted to give you the heads up." Joseph's voice was still a bit croaky, but the menthol gum had helped a little. Mike was so preoccupied with the journey that he didn't notice.

The farmer climbed back into the Land Rover and Mike checked left and right before opening the gate. The vehicles began to creep through one by one.

"Joseph says we've got to go through a small village up ahead," Mike said as Lucy pulled him back on to the truck.

"Well, we were going to have to at some stage, I guess," Lucy said, double-checking that the Browning was still in easy reach underneath the tarpaulin. They drove past a road sign: "Billington 1". "At least we're not guessing how far any more," she said, drawing the Glock from the back of her jeans.

Joseph put his hazard warning lights on as the first houses came into view, and Mike and Lucy stood to attention, taking in every detail, every movement.

A row of quaint white cottages stood proudly on one side of the lane, their small neat front gardens bursting with colour, the floral aroma palpable in the warm morning air. Thatched roofs and leaded windows leant intimations of another time and another world. Lucy had her Glock ready. She felt a sense of guilt that such a beautiful setting would now have to be treated like anywhere else. Behind every wall, every hedge, up every small alleyway, the enemy could be waiting to pounce. It didn't matter if it was a picturesque village or an urban slum, everywhere was the same now.

The convoy passed the houses, disregarding the thirty miles per hour speed limit. Curtains twitched, but no-one and nothing came out to greet or confront them. Maybe the village had remained free of infection, maybe they had not succumbed to any raiding parties. Or maybe they'd dealt with their infected only to be robbed and brutalised by their fellow man, so now they just hid in their homes like terrified children, praying that the vehicles wouldn't stop.

Tracey placed the shotgun back on the floor. She had picked it up when she had seen the sign for the village, and she had held it firmly in her sweating hands hoping she would not have to use it. She let out a sigh of relief. Samantha noticeably loosened her tense shoulders and began to sob.

"God, I hope this place is everything Joseph says it is," Tracey said, lifting her hand in front of her to see it visibly shaking. When she didn't get a response she turned to look towards her companion. "What's wrong?"

Samantha wiped the tears from her cheeks with the ball of her hand and sniffed. "I... I just don't know how much more I can take... I'm not cut out for this..."

"Not many people are."

"Some are," Samantha said, looking towards the truck as it headed round a bend out of the village.

"It'll get easier when we get there," Tracey said, extending her hand to Samantha's shoulder.

"You can't really believe that. You can't really believe that, Tracey. This is purgatory, and there's only one way out."

Tracey withdrew her hand. "Don't talk like that. You're stronger than that. You're better than that. People are depending on you."

Samantha sniffed again but said nothing.

They left the village behind and headed into the quiet of the countryside, the peace punctuated only by the sound of the vehicles and the birds in the trees and hedgerows. It wasn't long before the Land Rover slowed down to a stop and flicked on the left indicator. Mike jumped down and opened the gate. They were back on a farm track. He gratefully shut the sturdy steel barrier behind them, climbed back on board the truck and the small flotilla set sail once again.

"This is going a hell of a lot smoother than I expected," Mike said as the truck bounced up and down on the dry uneven dirt track.

"You ever heard of tempting fate, Mikey?"

Suddenly, Mike saw movement. Two 4x4 vehicles were speeding across the opposite side of the field. The engines revved louder as they picked up more speed, reached the corner of the field and started down on an intercept course.

"Oh, shit!" Mike said as he reached for the shotgun, simultaneously banging on the roof of the truck. At first Beth was surprised by the loud noise, and then she saw the vehicles too. She flashed her lights on and off repeatedly to signal her father, who slowed down to a stop.

Mike and Lucy headed straight to the caravan and got Alice and the children out and over the dry stone wall edging the track they were taking. Mike ran along to the other vehicles. He instructed Emma to take the shotgun and go over the wall with Alice and the children, while the rest of the group took cover behind and underneath the truck and caravan, ready for a shoot-out.

Lucy joined Mike on the ground underneath the truck. Her Glock was tucked into the back of her jeans. She was aiming the shotgun, and she had put a small handful of shells between them for easy reach.

"So, Mikey, how smooth do you think it's going now?"

19

The first black Range Rover came to a halt. All the doors opened simultaneously and four gun-wielding figures emerged. The second car stopped and five more figures appeared. All of them spread out, their weapons pointed towards the convoy.

"We don't want any trouble, but you need to get off this land now." It was the voice of an older man with a strong Yorkshire accent.

"Philip, is that you?" Joseph shouted, his voice less croaky now.

"Who's asking?"

Joseph stood up from behind the front of the truck. He put his weapon on top of the bonnet and walked out with his hands raised. "Philip, it's Joseph from Mead Hall Farm."

"Lower your weapons," Philip shouted, as he walked towards the familiar face. The two men extended hands and shook firmly, and the parties on both sides relaxed and disarmed.

"You're one of the last people I expected to see here, Joseph. What gives?" Philip asked, still clutching his friend's hand.

"We're heading to Candleton, to my brother's place. We're doing our best to avoid roads where we can. I'm sorry for the trespass, Philip, but it's rough out there." Joseph relinquished his grip.

"Two groups have tried to attack us. Thankfully, we've got a lot of farmhands and they all know how to use a gun, so we've been able to repel them. We thought you... well, we didn't know what you were doing, but we weren't going to take any risks. One of my workers had a house in Billington. A gang attacked the village, took what they needed and left a number of them dead. He escaped up here with his family." Philip paused and looked behind his old friend to the figures emerging from behind and underneath the stopped vehicles. "Where are your lot?" he asked, scanning the faces as the bodies emerged.

Joseph looked down to the ground. "My two eldest lads didn't make it. Neither did my son-in-law. Beth and Annie were kidnapped, but these people we're travelling with saved them. They saved us." Although his words suggested a huge level of gratefulness, his tired eyes spoke only of the pain as he looked back at his friend.

A frown appeared across Philip's large weather beaten face. "I'm so sorry, Joseph. The loss of a child is something no-one should have to suffer."

Mike and Lucy approached the two men. Introductions were made and not so much pleasantries as acknowledgements were exchanged. Joseph turned to his two travelling companions.

"Philip has just been telling me that before all the trouble started they were due to start work on a National Trust visitor's centre and trail about five miles north of here. There's nothing on the map, but there are plenty of dirt tracks and makeshift roads where all the surveyors and planners have been sketching it out. He reckons we could take those dirt roads and it would bring us out roughly eight miles south of Candleton." Joseph was enthusiastic as he reported his news. He turned back to Philip. "You'd be welcome to come with us."

Mike and Lucy didn't react visibly, but their hearts sank as the words left Joseph's mouth.

"That's very kind, Joseph, but this is my home and I'm not leaving it for anyone. We've got a good supply of food and fuel. We've got workers to harvest crops and defend the place. God willing, we'll ride this out here, and maybe when things return to something a bit more like normal, we'll pop up to Candleton and pay you a visit. We might trade some wheat for a bit of that bread and butter pudding your missus makes." The pair cracked a smile as they recalled happier days, and Philip extended his hand once more. "The very best of luck to you, Joseph, to all of you," he said, looking towards Lucy and Mike as he spoke.

"Thank you, Philip. May God go with you," Joseph replied before letting go of his friend's hand and walking back to the Land Rover.

*

Just as Philip had described, there was a road sign stating "Heavy plant crossing" and a few metres after it, a right turn into a tarmac car park with several Portakabins and a small array of abandoned machines. Between the two temporary buildings at the end of the tarmac was the start of a wide gravel road rising into the distance. Joseph headed towards it and hit the trail with a satisfying scrape and clunk. Small stones flicked up and clattered against the chassis. Every minute he travelled he was getting closer to his brother, getting his family closer to safety. It was good fortune to have run into his old friend, and this shortcut would not only save them time but also reduce the risks of them being attacked.

The road rose higher into the beautiful green hillside. Occasionally one of the vehicles would skid a little where a small section of track crumbled away, but it didn't matter; they were not planning on retracing their steps. This was a one-way journey.

Mike looked across at Lucy who was trying to take in the view with her hands tucked underneath her armpits. She wasn't shivering, but it wouldn't be long before she was. He unzipped his coat, flicked it off his shoulders and hooked it over hers, taking her by surprise.

"I'm not one to say I told you so," he said, smiling.

"No way, Mike, you need this more than me, you've only got a T-shirt." Lucy began to take the coat off in protest, but Mike placed a firm hand over hers and shook his head.

She gratefully accepted and zipped the coat up. Mike's warmth, still present in the coat's lining, quickly heated the blood in her veins. She grabbed the back of the cab tightly, leaned over and kissed him on the cheek. "You're a gentleman, Mike. There weren't too many of them around even before this happened. Your mom and dad would be proud of how you turned out." Lucy smiled as she looked across at her companion and placed her hand over his as they both held onto the cab.

"My real dad was a wife-abusing, child-beating chronic alcoholic who cared for no-one but himself. He would never have given a damn how I turned out. But Alex, my stepdad, he was a good man, one of the greats. If he thought for a second I was standing with a coat on my back while there was a lady next to me shivering, I'd have got a friendly clout round my ear and he'd have taken my jacket off for me, just so I remembered what to do the next time." Mike allowed himself a small chuckle and Lucy joined in.

"He sounds like he was a really lovely guy," Lucy said.

"He was. He really was. If it wasn't for Alex, I don't know how I would have ended up. I got my temper from my real dad, I know that much, and if Alex hadn't come along to keep me in check when he did, I think I could have been a very different person now." Mike looked out towards the trees on the other side of the valley.

Lucy rubbed her thumb gently over his hand. "I don't think so, Mike. I think the good inside you would have come out, whoever raised you." Their eyes met, and for a split second there was something there beyond friendship, beyond the shared experience of the last few days. The truck shuddered over another pothole and Lucy lost her footing. Mike swung his arm around her waist and caught her. Their faces froze in time, inches apart. Their eyes stole each other's image and both held their breath, wondering what would come next, but then abruptly came to their senses. "Thanks," she said, her cheeks beginning to flush.

"You're welcome." He smiled and helped her regain full balance then resumed tight hold of the back of the cab.

Joseph noticed an expansive turning point up ahead. He had drained the bottle of water in order to quell the itchiness in his throat, but now he was parched again and hungry, and thinking about it, he needed to pee too. This was a good place for a pit stop. He flicked on the indicator and the convoy slowly rolled to a halt in the siding.

Everybody dismounted, grateful for the respite. Lucy returned Mike's jacket and went to the ambulance to find hers. Everyone else met up at the caravan and Alice put a large pan on the stove and emptied several cans of chicken soup into it.

Boulders were scattered around the edges of the turning point, and as each of them was served their mug of soup along with a handful of dry crackers, they dispersed to the various rocks to chat and enjoy the food.

"Wasn't there enough soup for you, Mike?" Tracey asked, seeing that all he had to eat was the dry crackers.

"My brother's a vegetarian," Sammy answered for him. "That means he doesn't eat meat."

All the adults smiled at the young girl as she proudly explained to Tracey what a vegetarian was, genuinely believing she didn't know.

"So, Mike, what made you stop eating meat?" asked Tracey.

"I just couldn't justify it any more," he replied matter-of-factly.

"What do you mean, couldn't justify it?" she replied.

"Five years ago, Alex and I were coming back from London and we stopped to get a bite to eat at Watford Gap services. There was one of those huge animal transport trailers, you know, the 'double-deckers'? We walked past it and saw that the sheep could barely move. They were bleating pitifully. The poor little things were terrified. They were in cruel, filthy, horrific conditions and were probably heading to the abattoir. I cursed the driver, the farmer and the owner of the slaughterhouse for allowing it. That night I couldn't sleep, and it dawned on me that by continuing to eat meat I was just as responsible as they were. So I decided from that point on that I didn't want their suffering on my conscience."

He took another bite of his cracker.

"So, you think we're terrible for drinking this chicken soup?" Tracey asked, earnestly.

"My brother and my sisters are drinking it. Alex and my mum ate meat and I didn't and don't think any less of them. Would I prefer it if people didn't eat meat? Yes, of course I would, but it's a decision each individual has to make." He smiled sincerely at Tracey, who instinctively looked down at her mug of soup with a guilty expression on her face.

Joseph was crouching near the caravan, squeezing the tyres like he was in a supermarket checking for a ripe melon.

"Is everything okay, Joseph?" Lucy asked as she approached to return her empty mug.

"I hope so. These aren't really designed for this type of terrain. It'll be playing hell with the suspension."

"Do you think it'll make it?" she asked with concern.

"Let's pray it does," he replied, the back of his throat beginning to scratch again. He stood up and rubbed his lower leg and calf.

"Are you okay, Joseph?" she inquired, falling back into her role as doctor.

"Pins and needles. I was crouched down too long, that's all." Joseph walked across to the group and announced that it was time to get underway once more.

The tyres of all the vehicles made the ground crackle as the gravel fidgeted beneath the moving rubber. The convoy was underway again but this time descending rather than climbing the beautiful hilly countryside.

Mike nudged Lucy and pointed diagonally ahead at a small plume of smoke. "I'm guessing that's Skelton."

"Well, at least we won't have that nightmare to go through, thanks to Joseph's friend."

The lead car came to a skidding halt and the vehicles following it jerked to a standstill, spraying gravel.

"What is it?" Lucy shouted as Joseph climbed out of the car.

"There's no more bloody track," he replied.

Mike and Lucy jumped down from the truck. "What do you mean, Joseph?" Lucy asked.

"Look for yourself. They never got any further than this. The trail just heads down there." Joseph pointed to the right. "That will take us back out onto the road about three miles south of Skelton." He shook his head as he spoke.

"Joseph. I don't understand. Didn't your friend say this would take us eight miles south of Candleton?

Surely there must be another way around?" Mike asked, bewildered.

"They obviously weren't as far on with the development as was rumoured," Joseph replied bitterly.

"So what are our options?" Lucy asked.

"We're out of options. We can't go back the way we've come. I don't think the caravan could take it. We're going to have to go down the track, head north and get through the town centre as fast as we can. Hopefully we won't run into too many of those things if we can make it through quickly enough." As soon as Joseph stopped speaking, Mike's shoulders dropped as if they were being held by puppet strings that had suddenly been cut.

Joseph walked off and knocked on each driver's window to explain the situation.

"Is it just me or is that the worst fucking plan you've ever heard?" Mike said.

As they moved off this time, no-one was marvelling at the green and pleasant surrounds. The track was bumpier than the previous one, and all the vehicles shook wildly from side to side as they descended the last part of the hill and made the transition to flat fields. There were traces of efforts to make the track more passable, but clearly this makeshift road had not been travelled on for some time. It was similar to the farmer's fields they had passed through earlier in the day, but where those had had good drainage and heavily worn tracks from use by multiple farm vehicles, here the trails had worn thin, and heavy rains from previous weeks had left debris on the pathway. They crawled to a stop at a large galvanised steel gate. Beyond lay the grey tarmac of the road to Skelton. Mike jumped down and pulled the bolt across. There was a clang as the gate creaked back. Mike made his way back to the truck; there was little point in closing this one behind them. There were no farmers or crops to protect, merely a broken promise of safe passage.

The vehicles turned right one by one like cattle walking into a slaughterhouse. The lane had potholes, but it was still a marked improvement on what had gone before. The convoy moved relatively smoothly and slowed in trepidation as they reached the brow of the hill which heralded the descent into the town square and uncertainty.

It was like being on a rollercoaster. As soon as each set of wheels reached the sharp decline, the drivers pumped their accelerators and shifted quickly through the gears to reach as high a speed as possible before they ran into any threats. The road down to the town centre was clear, but Joseph could see up ahead that there was an abandoned car. The windows had been smashed and the doors were open. It was in the middle of the street at an odd angle just before the square. He rode the clutch and moved down a gear as the 4x4 mounted the kerb with a whiplash-inducing shudder. The truck did the same with less effort. The attached caravan made a sickening crunch as it mounted the pavement, but the momentum won over and it got round the obstruction and into the square. The other vehicles followed rapidly, and the ascent back out of town was now in sight. Mike and Lucy looked around feverishly. The square of the idyllic market town had a war memorial in the centre where two roads crossed, making it the single most exposed section of the town. Lucy spotted a group of

RAMs in the distance, clearly alerted by the revving engines and the sound of metal on concrete made by the caravan. When they caught sight of the convoy they began to run with purpose. Lucy and Mike grabbed on to the cab tightly as they hit another pothole. Then a horrifying crash sounded, followed by an interminable scraping noise. The pair looked at each other in a breathless panic. Both knew instantly what had happened and, in unison, they hammered on the roof of the cab for Beth to stop. They looked towards the RAMs: they were about three hundred metres away, and more had joined them. They looked in the other direction and noticed another group zeroing in. Lucy leaned over to see the damage. One of the caravan's wheels had come off and the axle had collapsed. The bottom edge of the caravan was battered and broken. Curtains twitched wildly as the petrified occupants looked out.

"Fuck, fuck, fuck! Mike, what do we do?" Lucy cried out.

Mike grabbed the Browning from underneath the tarpaulin. "Doc, show me how this fires."

Lucy released the safety catch and pulled the slide then handed it back. "That's it, now you just aim and pull the trigger," she said, still not understanding his intentions.

He picked up his rucksack and pulled it onto his back. He threw the heavy tarpaulin over the razor wire and brought Lucy round to face him. His firm grip held her upper arms, forcing her to look and listen.

"Listen, Doc, there's no way we can fight it out with these things, we're too exposed. I'm going to unhook the caravan, then I'll lead the RAMs away.

Hopefully they'll all follow me. You get Alice and the kids into the other vehicles and then get out of town as quickly as you can. If there are any stragglers, take them out quietly. You don't want to draw attention." He turned around and started climbing down.

"You can't, Mike, it's suicide," she called after him, tears forming behind her frightened eyes.

"Just do it, Doc. Please." He threw the tarpaulin over the defensive razor wire, which sprung back into position. "It's up to you to get them to safety now. Tell my family that I love them and I'll see them soon." With that he ran to the caravan, released the coupling and unlatched the breakaway cable.

Mike pulled the Browning out of the back of his jeans and then ran to the front of the convoy so he was visible to both sets of advancing RAMs. Joseph and Beth watched from the vehicles in awe as he fired at the first group and then turned and fired at the second. They were too far away for him to get a targeted shot, but the sound grabbed their attention and he became their new quarry. He waited until they were about twenty metres away and then began to run. He was heading in the direction the convoy would take, so at the first opportunity he would need to make a turn and draw the RAMs away from that route. He looked back and fired. One of the creatures floundered briefly as the shot exploded in the flesh of its belly, but then continued in pursuit. He fired again into the mob of snarling grey beasts. His intention was to attract stragglers rather than kill them. Mike began to sprint faster, confident that they were all following him. They were sixty metres away from the convoy and if Lucy and the group acted quickly the vehicles could soon be underway again.

Lucy emerged from her hiding place underneath the tarpaulin and scanned the area. Mere seconds had passed but the imminent threat of attack had lifted; she saw the two groups of RAMs converging in pursuit of their single prey. She looked up and down the convoy, all was clear. There was the sound of gunshots growing ever distant. Lucy quickly jumped down and ran to the Land Rover.

"Joseph. Get everybody out of the caravan and into the other vehicles, and whatever happens, don't tell anyone about Mike," Lucy ordered. She went to the second vehicle. "Beth, grab your shotgun. You and I are going to stand guard in case there are any more of those things around. Only fire if there are no other options. We don't want to sound the dinner gong." The younger woman did as requested.

Lucy and Beth patrolled up and down on either side of the convoy. Their shotguns were cocked and ready. Joseph swiftly evacuated the caravan, distributing the occupants throughout the various vehicles.

"Where's Mike?" Emma asked Joseph as he opened the passenger door of the box van to lift in Sammy and Jake, who were tearful and terrified.

"He's up ahead, dealing with our *problem*," the farmer replied, not lying but by no means giving Emma the full story either. She realised it was no time to play twenty questions and did not press any further. She knew her brother would be doing all he could to gain them safe passage, and he always had a plan.

Mike slowed down to take a turn into a back street, keen to make sure none of the chasing mob lost track of him but mindful that he couldn't afford to reduce speed too much and get caught. Two RAMs were up ahead, the pounding feet of the pursuing mob alerting them to the possibility that dinner might not be too far away. Mike raised the handgun as they converged. He pulled the trigger, click. He pulled it again, click.

"Fuck!" he shouted. He reached round to drop the empty weapon back into his backpack and withdraw his hatchet and one of the machetes, then ran at the two advancing beasts head on. Thick saliva bubbled from their dead grey lips as they approached. Their black pupils were soulless pinpricks in the bright afternoon sun, and their guttural, snarling growl increased in volume with each stride forward. Their hands reached out like hungry orphans in a Dickens novel. They were ready to leap, but Mike leapt first. He rose above them, putting his full weight behind his swinging arms. The hatchet sank deeply into the forehead of one, the sound of breaking bone swiftly followed by a slushy withdrawal. Milliseconds later another powerful crack sounded as the hefty machete sliced through skull, cracking bone on the way in and shattering more on the way out. Both creatures were down before they could even touch Mike, but the pause for their execution and the time it took for him to retrieve the weapons from the bodies meant the pack of ravenous beasts in pursuit had gained valuable ground. He heard a shot, then another, from the direction he had run from. He could only hope there were just a small handful of stragglers for his friends to deal with. He looked back to see that the creatures following him had not been distracted. The leaders of the group were just ten metres behind now. He would have to sprint faster. If they got him, they could still have time to get back to the convoy before it set off.

*

"Get in the car and go, Joseph," Lucy shouted, once Alice and the children were safely dispersed among the four vehicles.

"What about Mike?" he asked, with one foot in the car and one still on the road.

"Coming back here wasn't part of his plan. Don't let it have been in vain," Lucy replied, her voice shaky.

Joseph saddened visibly as he crouched to get back into the driver's seat. Lucy pumped the shotgun and fired at another stray RAM as the vehicles began to pull away. The box van and the ambulance pulled around the wreck of the caravan and headed upwards and out of the town centre. Joseph mowed down two creatures that had been attracted by the sound of the gunshots. Lucy looked around frantically to see if Mike had somehow managed to escape the beasts and got back onto the road, but there was no sign of him. She wept. Mike had willingly sacrificed himself so the rest of the group could live. He did it without a second thought for his own life. She wished she could see him one last time to say thank you, but instead, she could only whisper it as the convoy sped past the boundary of the town. "Thank you, Mike."

20

Mike carried on running, but he was tiring. The pain in his leg was nothing more than a memory as elevated adrenalin levels remained constant in his blood. He could run miles, but not at this speed. The RAMs, on the other hand, showed no signs of fatigue. Their growls and grunts seemed to become more excited with each centimetre gained. He took another left turn and saw a number of large semi-detached houses lining the streets. He looked back once again to see where the pack was in relation to him. The leaders had been joined by a few more but were still about ten metres behind. He was going to have to try and find a way to get to safety, to get off the street. His lungs were burning.

He was heading downhill, which made running easier, and he could see that there was not far to go until he joined one of the main streets through Skelton. Maybe he would be able to give these creatures the slip by sprinting up a side street. Then, at the bottom of the road, a small group emerged. He had underestimated the amount of sound he and his would-be attackers, who now numbered upwards of fifty, were making. The other pack began to run in his direction, the angry growls of these additional eight beasts indistinct from the noises behind him but present nonetheless. At a push he might be able to battle eight RAMs with the various weapons he had at his disposal, but no way could he do it while still being pursued by the others. He would be overpowered in no time. His choices were becoming fewer and fewer as each second ticked by. Sweat was pouring down his forehead and he could feel it dribbling down his back. His breathing was increasingly laboured. Mike knew his body well; he knew he was stronger, fitter and faster than most, but his limits were approaching quickly.

His pursuers had gained more ground. The pack was about eight metres behind him now, and the group coming towards him was just twenty metres in front. Within a few seconds this would all be over. The footsteps and the gurgling growls were deafening as the creatures drew closer and closer.

*

Joseph had managed to cripple a further three beasts as the vehicles progressed swiftly towards Candleton. They were proceeding at sixty miles per hour along the straight stretches of road. They slowed down to thirty to take the shallow bends, but it wouldn't be long before the signs for Candleton began to appear. It wouldn't be long before Joseph was with his brother and his family and friends were safe. It sounded clichéd, but Mike had made the ultimate sacrifice for them to live, so the very least he could do now was to look after Mike's friends and family like they were his own.

Each time the vehicles went round a bend, Emma craned her neck to try and catch sight of Mike on the truck. Each time she failed. She grew increasingly worried that he may have been injured and rather than standing guard he was actually lying down, bleeding out. Her little brother and sister were sharing the seat beside her. Sammy held Jake tightly, more akin to an anxious mother than a loving sister.

"Did you see Mike when we stopped?" Samantha asked Tracey as the ambulance steadily navigated the gentle curves of the road.

"I heard Joseph saying something about him dealing with the problem, so I'm guessing he had his hands full," she replied, before turning around to look into the back of the ambulance. "Are you three okay in there?"

Alice and her two youngest children were sat on the gurney swaying from side to side with each twist and bend in the road. "Yes, thank you, dear," Alice replied, clutching her children tightly.

In the distance, Lucy could see a formidable church steeple. Could that be Candleton? Please let that be it. Please say we're safe, she thought to herself.

*

Mike withdrew the shotgun from his backpack. His decisions were becoming more and more split-second. A shot forward might kill one of the creatures, but the recoil would slow his progress by a fraction. A shot back might also kill an attacker but would propel him towards the other group that little bit quicker. He veered to the right and hurdled a thigh-high red brick garden wall. He pointed the shotgun directly at the large bay window in front of him and fired. Glass imploded, revealing an impeccably decorated living room. He glanced back to see the two groups of RAMs converging and beginning to stumble over the barrier. He fired a couple of well-aimed shots, bringing down two of the beasts and giving the creatures following an extra hurdle to cross. Mike leapt through the window, ducking as he went to avoid any hanging shards of glass. His head twitched from side to side, looking for the best escape. He pulled open the door to his right, revealing a hallway and staircase. He bounded up the stairs as he heard the first creatures displacing the broken glass around the window and gaining entrance to the house. As soon as his foot hit the first step he realised he had made a mistake. The second floor of the house would trap him, but there was no time to double back now, he would just have to figure something out. There was a loft hatch at the top of the landing. It was quite an old house and the ceilings were high, so there was no way he could reach it without the aid of climbing apparatus. More glass crashed, followed by a thud, then another. The first beasts were in. Why hadn't he closed the door behind him? What an idiot. The more he thought, the more he realised the loft was his only salvation. Mike reached the top of the landing and looked around desperately, searching for a chair or anything that could help him. There was nothing. He looked down to see the shadows of the first RAMs heading towards the stairs. There were no other options, he would have to try and balance on the thin banister and post, see if he could get the hatch open and then take it from there. He climbed gingerly onto the thin oak rail as the first creatures barged each other to mount the steps. With one hand pushing up at the ceiling for balance, he took the barrel of the shotgun and levered the loft cover aside. He threw his weapon into the darkness above. The hatch was at a diagonal to the end of the railing. To get into it he would have to leap across and up at the same time, grab the wooden edge of the loft surround and then pull himself through the gap. Sweat covered most of his body now, his energy virtually spent. Everything would come down to this one final action. If he made it, he bought himself time. If he didn't, he would be clawed and torn apart by his assailants.

*

Joseph brought the Land Rover to a standstill at one end of the bridge. There were sturdy metal barriers at both ends which certainly hadn't been there on his last visit. Water gushed beneath, deafening him to every other sound. He looked to the other side of the river to see an army jeep and what looked like turrets on both sides of the road. He climbed out of the car and instinctively raised his hands as he approached the barrier.

"Move on, old man, we're not taking in any strays," a voice shouted from the other side.

He stayed calm but resolute. They had all come too far to be turned away by a hidden voice. "I'm here to see Daniel Masters," Joseph said firmly. The rest of the group watched from the vehicles, worried that their journey was not yet over.

"What's your business with him?" the voice replied.

"I'm Daniel's brother," Joseph responded.

"Wait there," the voice replied sternly.

A few minutes passed as Joseph stood at the head of the bridge. He looked around to the others. Their faces were tired, their hearts heavy. An army Land Rover pulled up next to the jeep on the other side. A uniformed soldier climbed out and headed towards the civilians. His pace quickened as he got closer, and when he reached Joseph, a broad smile broke across his face.

"Uncle Joseph," the corporal said and took the familiar hand gratefully. "We were worried you wouldn't make it. We'd actually begun plans to send a party down to see if you were still at the farm. Dad has been a wreck, worrying about you."

Joseph clutched his nephew's hand with both of his. "Darren, you have no idea how grateful I am to see you. We've got some people with us, friends, people who saved our lives."

"If they're friends of yours, Uncle, they'll be friends of ours. Bring them in and then I'll take you to Dad." Darren released his grip on Joseph and turned around. "Let's get these gates open now," he barked back towards the turrets. Four men in army uniforms appeared and opened the barriers.

Joseph got back in the car and drove across the bridge, pausing to let Darren climb back into his vehicle and lead them in to Candleton. The group advanced carefully, the barriers were closed the instant they were through, and as they drove past the tall turrets, they noticed another four soldiers on guard, weapons raised, covering the ones who were opening and closing the gates.

The convoy proceeded into the centre of Candleton. Villagers gawked at the spectacle. For several days, the only vehicles they had seen had been military ones. Darren stopped in front of the village school and got out. He marched inside and reappeared a moment later with an older man and woman walking behind him. Joseph ignored the pain that was beginning to dance around his leg once again and climbed out of his car. He walked, then began to jog, towards his brother in an uncharacteristic display of emotion. The two embraced, then Joseph pulled away and hugged his sister-in-law before turning around to the other vehicles and signalling for the occupants to follow him.

"I honestly didn't know if I was ever going to see you again, Daniel," he said, sniffing with emotion.

"Well, you're here now, Joseph, and that's all that matters. Who are all these people?"

"They saved our lives, we owe them everything. Everything!"

"Well, bring them in, bring them all in," Daniel replied, putting his arm around his older brother and leading him into the large school house.

"Where's Mike, Lucy?" Emma asked, almost running up to her. Lucy couldn't respond. Her eyes welled up and streams began to run down her face. She pulled Emma towards her and kissed the top of her head as she hid her tears.

"No! No... No!" Her legs buckled underneath her and Lucy gripped her tighter to make sure she didn't hurt herself as she came to rest on the ground.

"He said I had to tell you that he loved you and Jake and Sammy and that he'd see you again soon," Lucy said, desperately trying to speak in between her own sobs. "He saved us, Emma. There was no way any of us would have survived if he hadn't done what he did."

Samantha and Tracey got out of the ambulance and headed towards their friends. Samantha caught Lucy's watery gaze and she knew that Mike was gone. She put the palm of her hand up to her mouth to cover her silent scream and crouched down, struggling to breathe.

Beth sat in the cab of the truck for a moment. They had made it, but it was difficult to find any joy in reaching their final destination. The man who had rescued her and her sister, the man who had saved them countless times since, was lost, and his family and friends were grieving right there in front of her. Is this what life had become? Was it just one nightmarish episode after another, punctuated by death and misery? Beth climbed out of the other side of the cab so as not to intrude on the mourners. She walked back to the ambulance and led her mother and siblings into the old school house.

When their sister didn't return for them, Sammy and Jake got down from the van and went to see where she was. They came around the corner to see Samantha crouched down, taking huge breaths in between turbulent sobs, with Tracey rubbing her back like a mother burping a baby. Then they saw their sister and Lucy holding each other tightly, both women crying uncontrollably. Neither child knew the reason, but instinctively they began to cry too.

*

"Fuck it," Mike said to himself and launched into the air. He grabbed on to the edge of the loft hatch and felt splinters tear through the skin on his fingers. He forced his tired muscles to pull him up. Whereas once they would have responded quickly and powerfully, now the fatigue had slowed them. He rose shakily through the hatch as the first beasts reached the top of the stairs, their grasping fingertips brushing against his boots as he pulled himself through the narrow opening. He sat exhausted on the edge with his legs dangling down, tantalising the hungry beasts below. He caught his breath for a moment before shuffling off his backpack and pulling out his torch. Looking down, he saw the monstrous grey faces and the sickening yellow teeth gnashing between dark grey lips. A chill ran up his spine. The clutching, rapacious hands reached upwards, desperate to seize their prize. Dozens of them lined the staircase and landing, but Mike's feet were safely out of grabbing distance. He had taken enough risks for one day and so he replaced the loft cover and turned on the torch, shining it into the blackness. He found the shotgun and placed it safely back into his pack. The loft was boarded in places and he carefully stepped across to the largest floored area and sat down, pulling the water bottle out of his rucksack. It was half full. He would have to make it last, but he took a few thirsty sips before lying down on the bare wood, completely drained.

*

In the hallway outside the headmaster's office, Emma, her siblings, Lucy and Samantha sat on the floor with their backs against the wall. They held hands, embraced and shared their grief. Alice, Beth, Tracey, Annie and John sat on uncomfortable orange plastic chairs against the other wall. They had gone through the same, they knew the pain, and their grief was far from over too, but the promise of safety now they were in Candleton allowed them to delay their mourning for just a few more hours.

Joseph and his brother were inside the office with Darren and Keith Martin, a councillor, who, alongside Daniel Masters, commanded more respect than anyone in the district. Joseph told a brief version of the story which had led them to Candleton, mentioning the large inventory of food and supplies they had brought with them. On hearing this, the other three men couldn't help but smile. He then went on to explain who the rest of the people were in the group. There would be time to go into more detail later on when they were all settled, but for now, the three statesmen of Candleton had heard enough.

The door to the office opened and they filed out. Keith Martin walked up to the young woman with dark hair who was being held by a motherly looking older blonde. By her side were two children gripping a red-haired girl tightly. All of them had tear-stained faces, all of them were scared, all of them were lost.

"You must be Emma?" Keith said as he bent down in front of the young woman, while making friendly eye contact with the older one. "What your brother did was nothing short of heroic, Emma. He didn't just save all of you – with those supplies that you brought, he saved all of us as well. You, your family and friends, you're all welcome to stay with us. As I speak, we've got accommodation being prepared for you in the local hotel. I think you'll be more than comfortable there. Now, I'm certain all of you have just had enough for today and you want to be alone. I fully understand that. When you're ready, we'll give you a tour of the place. We'll show you what we're trying to do here. One thing you don't have to worry about is your safety." He placed a gentle hand on Emma's and stood up.

"Thank you... erm?" Lucy replied, raising her eyebrows in expectation of being told a name.

"My name's Keith Martin, that brutish looking bloke over there is Daniel Masters and you've already met Corporal Darren Masters. My wife will be across in a minute to take you all over to the hotel. It's one of two places in the village that has electricity, thanks to a small turbine, and I've got some water being boiled so you can have a wash and freshen up." He smiled sympathetically at the group. "If there is anything any of you need, you just let me know."

"Thank you, Mr Martin, that's very kind," Lucy responded automatically.

"Please, it's Keith. We're done with formalities here," he replied, and headed back into the office.

*

Mike didn't know how long he had been asleep. He had turned the torch off, so as not to waste the battery for as long as it would take for him to catch his breath, and then simply passed out from exhaustion. The shuffling, thudding and growling from the floor below was still clearly audible, so it was obvious the RAMs were going to hold a macabre vigil until he reappeared. He turned on the torch and reached down to his rucksack, pulling out the bottle of water. Mike took a few sips then replaced the cap. His stomach groaned for food, but there was nothing he could do to abate his hunger. He looked around the dusty loft space and a black-and-white image of Oliver Hardy popped into his head saying, "Well, that's another fine mess you've gotten me into." And how, he thought. He panned the torch around, looking for anything that might give him a spark of an idea, just one tiny crumb of inspiration.

He was sitting on a small island of floorboards, surrounded by a sea of joists and itchy carbon fibre insulation covering a plasterboard ceiling which would result in his certain death if he was to step on it and fall through to the floor below. There were more floorboards directly surrounding the hatch, but that was it. This loft had never been used in earnest for storage. There were no boarded gangways and no light switch, and it was clear that nobody had spent any significant amount of time there. He became deaf to the angry sounds from below as his mind desperately sought a means of escape.

*

"I've put you in adjacent rooms," Jenny Martin announced as she led the bedraggled group through the foyer of the four star hotel. Keith's wife was the owner of the place. It had been passed down to her by her parents and she took great pride in running it well. Before the catastrophic events which had befallen them, the hotel had been a hugely successful business. They had a full calendar of weddings booked, businesses from all over the country had streamed through the doors for meetings, conferences, team building excursions and, if that wasn't enough, holiday makers flooded the place in summer, desperate for a little evening luxury after exploring the wilds of the Dales during the day.

"This place is beautiful, ma'am," Lucy said as the group made their way through the hotel.

Jenny's hard face softened and she broke into a proud smile. "Thank you. Just because the world's coming to an end, there's no excuse for a lapse in standards," she said dryly, as the rather motley assemblage began to ascend the staircase. "We've got thirty-five rooms in total. We've designated the ground floor as a kind of cottage hospital. It made sense with us having electricity. We've got a young woman who's due to give birth to twins in a few days. She's the only patient at the moment, but I'm sure there'll be more before long."

"Oh! Do you have any medical staff?" Lucy asked.

"Alas, no, but we could really use some." Jenny smiled knowingly at the doctor and then at the young nurse as they advanced down the hallway.

The daylight was beginning to fade and the hotel owner flicked a switch on the wall. There was almost a gasp when the lights went on. It had only been a few days, but they had already forgotten what the convenience and assurance of electricity had meant to them.

Jenny walked along the corridor, opening the doors as she went. "You can choose your own rooms. I'll have my staff bring some hot water and towels up for you.

"You still have staff?" Lucy asked, amazed.

"My husband and Daniel were insistent that everybody should work towards the village being self-sufficient. As well as getting the hospital up and running, we've got a few other projects on the go in the hotel grounds, so it made sense for my staff to stay on here rather than be reassigned elsewhere. I'm sure my husband will explain everything to you when he gives you the tour." Jenny made to leave and then turned back towards them. "Keith told me briefly what you've done and what you've lost. We're very grateful to you and we hope you choose to stay here. Your story will bring a lot of hope to the village." She paused for a moment, looking around at the tired, sad faces, and then she turned once again to go back downstairs.

*

Mike shone the torch towards the brickwork of the shared wall between the two semi-detached houses. The cement was old and the odd chunk had fallen away through the passage of time. He aimed the light down and saw joists and insulation. If he worked hard, he would be able to tunnel through to the loft of the adjoining property. Hopefully he could then make a careful exit while all the RAMs stood guard in this house waiting for him to reappear. The problem was that it wasn't going to be a quick job. First, he would have to remove some floorboards from around the loft hatch and take them over to the wall so he could stand without the worry of falling between the joists. Then he would have to slowly chip away the cement and hope his torch didn't run out of battery power before he finished. This was going to be quite strenuous and he didn't have much water left. He was already thirsty; he could feel his lips drying as he sat planning. It was going to be touch and go whether he could do this, but the only other option was trying to fight his way out, and he didn't really fancy that.

He knelt up, moved the ray of light over to the hatch and carefully walked across the narrow wooden beams. He didn't have his claw hammer with him so he took the hatchet from his rucksack and chipped away at the wood surrounding the nails which secured the boards into place. Pulling them free still took a lot of effort, but eventually he had enough to provide a good working surface. He carefully carried the planks over to the shared wall and laid them down crossways over the beams.

He then collected his rucksack, put the torch between his teeth and began to chisel using a screwdriver and the wedge end of his small axe. Gradually, pieces of grey cement began to chip away, forming a hole.

*

"You okay, sweetie?" Lucy asked Samantha, tenderly brushing away a matted curl from the nurse's forehead.

Samantha wiped away a tear from the corner of her eye and sniffed. "I still can't believe it." The pair of them sat on the edge of a single bed in a beautifully decorated room. "How are Emma and the kids?"

"Emma's getting them washed and settled. I've given her a couple of sleeping tablets. The poor kid's a wreck. Little Sammy's convinced herself and Jake that Mike's coming back. She said that if Mike said he was going to see them again then he would. She said he's never broken a promise and she's insisted that the room next door to them is kept free for when he gets back." Lucy smiled at the optimism that children allowed themselves, while Samantha sniffed into her handkerchief.

"How are you holding up, Lucy?" she asked, lifting her bloodshot eyes towards her friend.

"I just feel weird. Being in a luxury hotel with electricity after what we've been through is a little surreal to say the least. One of the hotel staff told me that, provided we manually fill the cistern, we can even flush the toilets, because they've got power to operate the pump that feeds the septic tank. Now if that isn't living the high life, I don't know what is." Lucy forced a smile to try and coax Samantha into one. She realised it was all down to her now; she had become the matriarchal figure of this small band. It wasn't the life she had planned. What had Mike called her? Ah yes, a "rock chick". She liked the sound of that, a thirty-four-year-old rock chick. It was a lot more exciting than being Mother Hen, but then again, she was getting good at playing curve balls, so maybe she would adapt. She hadn't known Mike long, but there was an emptiness inside her now he was gone.

"Well, if you need me, sweetie, I'm just going to be next door. Try and get some sleep and then we'll check this place out tomorrow, see if it's as good as Joseph hoped." Lucy stood and, in another motherly gesture, kissed Samantha on the forehead before leaving the room. She passed her own bedroom door and moved on to the next, where she tapped gently on the white painted wood.

There was a pause and she could hear shuffling before a voice said, "Come in."

Lucy entered to see Tracey, half wrapped in a towel. "Hi, I was just freshening up," she said, almost guiltily.

"Don't let me stop you, I was just making sure you were okay before I turned in for the night," Lucy said, not even entering the room.

"It's funny. My dad used to go mad at me for wasting hot water. I'd leave the shower running for about ten minutes before I even stepped in." She let out a small chuckle in recollection. "He used to go, 'I'm not the Sultan of bleeding Brunei y'know. Wait until you've got your own place, you'll understand then.' It was true, I never valued it. My dad was brought up in the East End. The family was poor. There were times when they didn't have hot running water or heating, and I suppose it's only when you've done without it that you realise what a luxury it actually is. When I was locked up in that garage I thought I'd never feel hot water running through my hair or over my face again. I've got a small sink in the bathroom that I've filled with boiling water using a plastic bucket. Twelve months ago, that would have felt like living in squalor. Now, it feels like the lap of luxury. I don't think I'll ever take anything for granted again. I realise how lucky I am to be here, Lucy, and I want to thank you."

"You're welcome, sweetie, but it's not me you need to thank."

"Yes it is. It was both of you. You both played an equal part in getting us here, so thank you," she said again.

Lucy gently closed the door before returning to her room. She unzipped her holdall, pulled out a change of underwear and a T-shirt, then moved into the en-suite bathroom and tugged on the light switch. An extractor fan whirred into action and the small room lit up. Lucy unbuttoned her shirt and removed her bra, then took off her jeans and pants and looked into the mirror over the small sink. She had dark rings beneath her eyes and her face and neck were grimy with the day's travel. Her blonde hair seemed to have become a shade darker with the accumulation of road dirt and dusty air, and even her blue eyes seemed to have lost their sparkle. She poured the bucket of hot water into the sink and looked back up at the mirror. A river of tears began to run down her cheeks, clearing a salty path through the grime. "If you're up there somewhere looking down on us, Mike... We miss you, sweetie... I miss you." The words stalled as they left her mouth and gave way to sobs. Lucy reached for the plastic pill bottle, turned off the light, sat down on the floor, hugged her knees and cried hopelessly into the night.

*

It was slow going. Mike didn't know how long he had been working, but it seemed like an age and he'd only managed to get one brick loose so far. What was more, he was sure the torch was beginning to dim. He turned it off, hoping he could work by touch and save precious battery life, but working blindly would take him twice as long. Then it dawned on him. He had never been subtle in his approach to doing anything, so why try to over-think now? He needed light, so what better way than to smash a hole in the roof? He picked up his hatchet, balanced carefully on the boards to give himself a comfortable swinging action and then began to hack away. Chips of wood flew in all directions. Within a minute, he could see the red tile of the roof. Another minute passed and two tiles had been dislodged, revealing the dusky sky. He demolished a hole close to a metre in length before deciding it was enough. The torch would be needed to provide valuable light when he got through to the other side, and he'd already established that working in the dark was not a sensible course of action, so he took his rucksack and carefully climbed back to the wide island of chipboard. He took a drink from his bottle. There was very little left. He zipped his coat up, put the rucksack underneath his head and, with the growling, bumping, shuffling sounds below to keep him company, he drifted off to sleep.

21

The following morning Lucy did the rounds, making sure her friends were okay. Emma, Sammy and Jake had already been up for several hours and the two youngsters were still in denial, making the grieving harder for their older sister. The emptiness of loss dissipates a little when it's shared and understood, but having to put on a facade while screaming in anguish inside made the process twice as painful. Emma was trying to be a good sister and not dash her siblings' hopes, but it was hard. She and Mike had been through so much together and now it was down to her to fend for the family. She was grateful for Lucy's visit, but she had no interest in looking around the village. She just wanted to stay in the hotel and catch snatches of depressed sleep when Sammy and Jake would allow.

Lucy, Samantha and Tracey went down to have breakfast and Lucy made arrangements for some to be sent up to her friends.

"I hope you were comfortable," Jenny said, as the three women took seats at a table.

They all nodded. "It's a beautiful place you've got here." Lucy had felt obliged to say something in addition.

"Keith is coming round after breakfast to give you all the tour. I'd like to stop and chat, but our patient didn't have such a good night's sleep so I'm going to drop by and see her," Jenny said, turning to leave.

"Would you mind if I tagged along? I'd like to make sure she's alright," Lucy said, reminding herself that she had been a doctor before becoming a gun-toting action woman.

"If you could pop in later and take a look, that would be terrific, but I know Keith's pretty keen to show you around the place first," Jenny replied, as a member of hotel staff appeared carrying plates filled with scrambled eggs, bacon and beans.

All three pairs of eyes sparkled like decorations on a Christmas tree. Another member of staff appeared behind, bringing two six-slice toast racks with large doorsteps of browned bread in each.

The three women began to pile food into their mouths hurriedly, stunned that they had been presented with such a bounty.

"I could get used to this," blurted Tracey, a few crumbs of toast falling from the side of her mouth as she did. "A nice room, hot water and a full cooked breakfast with all the trimmings are a bit more than I anticipated."

"Make the most of it, kid, it won't be like this forever," Lucy responded, wiping tomato sauce away from her lips with a thick white serviette.

*

Mike awoke in pitch darkness. The unnerving growls and thuds continued downstairs, but they were now joined by another sound, something alien. It was the sound of someone shimmying along the joists. The hairs on the back of Mike's neck bristled with terror as he had the overwhelming feeling that there was a presence in the loft with him. He stiffened as he heard the familiar low guttural growl of an infected beast. It wasn't just close – it sounded like it was directly over him. He reached for the torch and swiftly flicked the switch. The demonic grey face of a RAM hung over his with its mouth open. A thick globule of saliva slowly oozed from one corner. The cavernous pupils were unaffected by the dim beam of light and there was a look of pure malevolence on its face as it slowly began to move towards Mike's neck. He was frozen, completely paralysed by fear, until a violent lurch made him spit blood and the beast's incisors ripped deeply into his jugular vein. Mike's whole body convulsed at the realisation that he was about to die and be reborn as one of the creatures he despised so much.

"AAAARRGGGHHHHH!" The loud scream jerked Mike awake and excited the ranks of bloodthirsty beasts below. His whole body was drenched in sweat and he slowly tried to regulate his breathing. It was just a nightmare, a trick of his mind.

"Fuck me!"

The sun was gradually making its way higher into the sky, and there was enough light for him to begin his work. He took his last few mouthfuls of water, rubbed his stomach in an attempt to pacify the increasingly angry growls of hunger and carefully walked across a few beams to urinate before climbing back into position to begin his work. To his delight he found that now a single brick had been removed, the others came away with greater ease. He could only guess at the time by the position of the sun in the sky, but Mike was confident that he could make a hole big enough to climb through before the afternoon. He took off his T-shirt and tied it around his nose and mouth so that the cement and brick dust would not exacerbate his thirst. Then he launched back into the job at hand. Chisel, strike, chisel, strike, chisel, strike, clear and then repeat.

*

"My wife used to use this minibus for guided tours for the guests, and as you're guests of the hotel, it seems fitting that you should be getting one now." Keith smiled as he looked in the rear-view mirror towards the three women, who were greedily taking in the sights around them.

They left the village and drove towards the bridge they had crossed the previous day. The soldiers on guard gave Keith a short but respectful nod as the minibus came to a standstill. He pulled on the handbrake and turned in his seat to speak to his passengers. "Now, I'll show you everything on a map when we get back, but Candleton is in rather a unique position that makes it easily defendable compared to most locations. The village is effectively a small island surrounded by the fast-running waters of the same river... well, a river and a large tributary if we want to split hairs. There's a bridge on this side and one on the other side. We have two sets of gun turrets at both bridges, manned twenty-four seven in rotating shifts. There are thirty soldiers in total and we're also training our own group of reservists. On top of all that, we have lookouts at the most easterly and westerly points of the village and, finally, the young corporal's pride and joy, a pair of Jackal 2 armoured vehicles." He broke out into a proud smile as he finished reeling off the inventory.

"I don't understand how you managed to secure such a large military presence?" Lucy asked, a little confused by the scale of protection for such a small village.

"Well, as you will probably know being an army doctor, things had been getting worse for a while. Groups of conscripts were forming their own militias and gangs, taking over barracks and, in some cases, whole towns. Of course, we weren't privy to this information, but we got a full briefing when Corporal Masters – Darren – arrived. Apparently this had been going on for weeks, but the state news broadcasts and communications blackouts had prevented word of it spreading. The government saw what was happening and decided the defence of the capital was the priority. When the orders were received to head to London, the conscripts at Darren's barracks revolted and took over. A real bloodbath ensued. With a few like-minded troops, he managed to escape with a ton of equipment and ammunition. He realised that the key was to find a suitable base, turn it into a fortress and wait to see if the chain of command re-established itself. Being a local lad, he knew the unique geography of Candleton would make it the ideal place to defend. They got here a few days ago. We had already made fortifications of our own, but the arrival of a small army of well-trained men has turned this village into what I'm convinced is one of the safest places in the country."

"It's impressive, Keith. What's going to happen when the food runs out, though?" Lucy asked.

"I'm glad you asked that," Keith responded, starting the engine of the minibus once again. "To be honest, until you showed up yesterday with your two truckloads of supplies, we were a bit worried. Although there are a couple of fields this side of the river, the majority of the farmland is on the other side. We may be able to get a small harvest from it under armed guard this year, but it will be dangerous. If it's not the bandits, it's the RAMs that we'd have to worry about." He stopped speaking while he executed a three-point turn in the road.

"You call them RAMs too?" Samantha asked, surprised by the use of the terminology.

"Well, yes, I'm afraid some of the soldier's vernacular has been rubbing off on me." He smiled, making eye contact with her in the mirror. He finished the manoeuvre and moved off again. "Anyway, as I was saying, we were concerned we were going to run short of food, but you've given us that one little leg up that we needed. Feast your eyes on the Candleton 'Dig for Victory' campaign," Keith said, as he turned the minibus onto a long residential street.

All the front gardens were a hive of activity. People were digging, planting, wheeling barrows, erecting small poly-tunnels – and not just adults, but children as well.

"We're doing this with every free bit of land in the village. Behind the hotel we're keeping hens and goats. Unfortunately, all the other livestock was requisitioned by the government when the UK was first locked down. We've got two fishing teams: one working the north part of the river, one the south, and we've even turned a few cellars into mushroom farms. Obviously, the crops will take a while to grow, but now we've got a stopgap..." He parked the car in the middle of the street and waved to a few of the diligent gardeners.

"I'm astounded. It looks like you've got everything you need right here," Lucy said.

"Well, not quite. We could really do with a doctor and nurse. Do you know any?" he said, turning around in his seat and smiling.

*

Mike removed the final brick and shone the torch through to the other loft. It was completely boarded and he could even see a loft ladder. He pushed his rucksack through and lowered it to the other side, then climbed into the neighbouring property. Although still present, the noise from the horde of milling RAMs became more muted. He quietly tiptoed across the loft to the hatch. He couldn't hear any activity directly below, but it didn't mean the house was empty. He put his rucksack down and slowly released the catch, allowing the hatch and ladder to open and lower. He carefully extended the aluminium steps rung by rung until they reached the carpeted landing, then he popped his head through and swiftly surveyed the area. The bathroom door was open and a terrible smell emanated from within. He re-shouldered his rucksack and climbed down, making his first job the closing of the door. Mike looked into each of the bedrooms and saw that the beds were neatly made and the rooms were tidy. He walked downstairs and straight into the kitchen at the back of the house. On the counter there was a flyer saying "Skelton emergency meeting, 7pm Tuesday". Mike wasn't sure, but he thought today was Thursday. Had the occupants of the house gone to the meeting and never returned? He opened the fridge and saw a plate of beef, a half-open tin of luncheon meat and a tube of liver pate.

"Yum," he said sarcastically.

In the salad crisper there were a few leaves of lettuce which were well past their prime. Most importantly, there was nothing to quench the insatiable thirst that he now had. He opened the freezer door, revealing a host of defrosted ready meals. There was an ice cube tray on the top shelf. Mike carefully pulled it out to reveal the melted water within. He gently set his lips around the corner of the white plastic tray and tilted it back. The room-temperature liquid glugged down his throat and he instantly felt more energised. He continued his search for food and found that the only thing in the sparse cupboards he could actually eat as a vegetarian was half a box of muesli. He chose not to. Eating it dry might help fill his stomach, but it would almost certainly make him thirsty again.

If nothing else, at least he was out of the loft and his thirst had been quenched for the time being. Now, he needed to figure out how to get to Candleton. He knew it was north, but it would be foolhardy to simply head north in the hope of happening across it. Mike needed a map. A local newsagent would probably sell maps of the area, but better still would be the local library. They were bound to have detailed Ordnance Survey maps, and with one of those, Mike could go cross country and avoid the roads. He looked out into the back garden. There was high panel fencing on all sides, but he could see what looked like an old abandoned mill at the back of the house. He hoped the RAMs would stay near the built-up residential areas rather than the deserted industrial ones. Going in any direction blind was a risk, but this was probably the best option. He carefully opened the door and walked along the fence, crouching a little as he went, giving himself maximum cover from the sight lines of the predators next door. Mike reached the bottom of the garden and vaulted over the wooden slats of the fence, crouching into a roll as he landed on the concrete below.

The street was empty. He jogged down the hill, withdrawing his weapons ready for any confrontation. He came to the junction where the side street met the main street and he peeked around the corner. He could see a couple of hundred metres up the road towards the war memorial. There were a few of the creatures scattered around, wandering aimlessly, but none of them caught sight of him. He looked the other way and saw two RAMs heading in the opposite direction. Beyond them were a number of small brown public street signs. Mike didn't want to risk going back the way he had come just in case one of the mass of RAMs from the house had spotted him and was in the process of hunting him down. The only other option was to try to head along the street, ducking and weaving to avoid being seen. Hopefully one of those signs would at least give him an idea as to where he might find the library.

*

"Okay, sweetie, everything seems to be fine. These little guys are getting ready to come out, but not right this minute," Lucy said to the young woman, who was overjoyed that there was a qualified doctor dealing with her pregnancy.

Samantha helped the woman back into a sitting position and poured her a glass of water.

"Y'know, I was scared to death about giving birth, but having you two here has really put my mind at ease. Thank you."

Lucy and Samantha smiled. For the first time in a long time, things felt right. This was their chosen vocation; this was what brought them happiness, what brought their lives meaning. "Well, it's a pleasure, hon. Now you get some rest and we'll be back to check on you later."

The two women left the room and walked down the long hall. "That felt good," Samantha admitted.

"I was just thinking the same thing. I thought my medical career was going to be restricted to bandaging battlefield wounds from now on. I didn't think I'd ever get the opportunity to help someone bring new life into the world again." She smiled.

"What do you make of this place, Lucy? I mean, not just the hotel, the whole village?"

"I think they've planned and organised everything well. I don't think people are going to go hungry and last night was the first night I've felt safe in quite some time." She looked across to Samantha. "It feels right."

*

There was a loud crack and Mike looked back in the direction he had come from. A fence had been demolished by a group of RAMs – his escape hadn't gone unnoticed. The creatures looked up the street and then down. There was a split-second pause as Mike locked stares with one of the beasts. He felt the hairs on the back of his neck bristle, and goose bumps fanned up his arms. Then, as the sound of their agitated growls were drowned out by the group's thundering footsteps, he turned right and began to sprint as fast as he could.

The two slow-moving creatures up ahead gained purpose as the commotion alerted them to possible prey. They began to charge towards Mike, who had renewed vigour now he was back in the open. He darted behind a van, confusing the RAMs long enough for him to work his way behind them and unleash a brutal blow to the back of each one's skull. He withdrew the hatchet and machete simultaneously. Both creatures stood for a second, a small stream of lumpy blood trickling down their necks, before collapsing to their knees and then crashing face first onto the tarmac. Mike quickly wiped his weapons and continued running towards the signs. The large group of RAMs were at least fifty metres behind him when he spotted the sign for the public library. He turned left as per the instruction. This took him up a short narrow street towards another library sign, this time for a right turn. Up ahead there was a single-storey brick building. The canopied doorway was blocked by a metal roller shutter and the windows were too high and too narrow to gain access, but Mike could see skylights on the roof. At each side of the entrance there were small brick walls with bicycle parking racks attached. Without slowing down, he reached around and placed the hatchet and machete back in his rucksack, then took several short sharp breaths as he launched from the pavement to the wall to the canopy. He hung on like a gymnast on the high bar, swinging powerfully to gain the momentum to push himself up. From there, it was just a short step to the roof. He ran to the back and then flopped down flat next to a skylight. There was no sight or sound of the pack of hunters, and even if they found the building they would not be able to see him.

Mike gazed down into the large open-plan library and saw that it looked just like most others he had visited. It had dingy and uninspired decoration, but there was a wealth of knowledge and promise in the full shelves of books. He turned his attention to the skylight itself. He had seen some that had a mechanism for opening in warm weather, but this particular model was not one of those. He knelt, remaining as low as possible, and felt around the edge. He withdrew the screwdriver from his backpack and levered away a small piece of sealant, allowing him to remove the rest simply by peeling it away. He examined what was beneath and established that the thick plastic was riveted to a raised mounting in four places. He pushed the edge of the screwdriver underneath and then pulled the plastic sharply, splitting it around the rivet. He did the same for the other three, then lifted the skylight to one side and lowered his head through the gap. It was about ten feet down to the floor, but if he lowered himself carefully, the drop would be easily manageable.

He shuffled to the edge of the hole he had created and turned around as if he were climbing in to a cold swimming pool. His muscles tensed beneath his black jacket as they took his weight and slowly lowered him, inch by inch. When his arms were fully extended, he let go and dropped. Then he heard charging footsteps and a maniacal scream behind him.

*

There were three shallow knocks. Emma and the children looked curiously towards the door. "Come in," she said.

The door opened slowly and Joseph appeared, followed by Beth, John and Annie. Emma eased herself up from the bed.

"I hope you don't mind us popping in?" Joseph enquired politely.

"Of course not," Emma lied. All she wanted was to be left alone to grieve. Well, that's not all she wanted. She wanted her little brother and sister to accept what was happening, so that she could mourn with her family rather than by herself.

"Are they looking after you here?" Joseph asked as he and Beth sat down on the bed next to Emma.

"The people couldn't be nicer," Emma replied, struggling with the banality of the question.

"I've spoken to my brother, Daniel, and to Mr Martin. There are a few houses free in the village. A lot of folk went to join their families all over the country when the problems first started, so now they're just lying empty. Of course, you don't have to make a decision now, but when you're ready, if you choose to stay, you don't have to live out of a suitcase. You can have a home here." He put his hand on Emma's and the irritation she had felt dissipated.

"I don't think it's a matter of *choosing* to stay, Joseph. I wouldn't feel confident with just me, Lucy and Samantha travelling the rest of the journey with the kids in tow. I mean, look what's happened to us so far, and we've barely come fifty miles."

"Stories are already going around the village about us, about what we did to get here, about what Mike did," Beth said, trying to make Emma feel better.

The three of them sat on the bed and the four children began talking as if they were in the playground at break time. That small snapshot of normality brought a little comfort to the adults.

Joseph and Beth stood up. "Well, I didn't want to take up much of your time. I just wanted to check in with you and see if you needed anything," Joseph said, placing a gentle hand on Emma's shoulder.

"That's very kind of you, Joseph, thank you. But they're taking good care of us here," she replied, patting his hand twice in acknowledgement.

"Come on, kids," Beth said to her younger siblings as the family made their way out of the room.

As soon as the door closed, Emma reclined on the bed once more, keen to lose herself in her thoughts, while her younger brother and sister began laying out a Monopoly board.

"Do you think she'll be okay, Dad?" Beth asked as they walked down the hall.

Joseph's leg was now constantly numb below the knee, but at least his cold symptoms had cleared up for the time being, although last night he had woken up with the worst headache he had ever had. Now he came to think of it, it wasn't the headache that had woken him up but the agonising cramp in his thigh. My goodness, he was falling apart at the seams. Is this what it was like to get old?

"Dad?" Beth said, surprised that her father hadn't responded at all.

"Sorry, love, I was miles away. What did you say?"

"Do you think Emma will be okay?" she asked again.

"I think all of us are going to be fine," Joseph said, putting his arm around his daughter's shoulder.

*

Mike turned and ducked in one instinctive movement. Three people were running at him. The first was a middle-aged woman with long black hair, flecked with grey, and fierce dark brown eyes. She was the one howling while swinging a chair in his direction. Mike's ducking movement meant she lost her balance and went flailing off to the right. The second figure was a small rotund man, completely bald, his body lost in a thick brown hand-knitted pullover. He tried to right hook Mike, who easily deflected the punch. The third attacker was a middle-aged man with gelled black hair and a thin moustache. He ran at Mike with a broom handle. Mike grabbed it tightly and jettisoned his assailant across the tile floor. All three hurried to gather themselves. Mike pulled the shotgun out of his rucksack, pumped it and pointed.

They froze, instinctively raising their hands. The fear and uncertainty caused by being attacked vanished as Mike looked at the motley assembly in front of him.

"Fuck me, it's the Addams family. You haven't got Pugsley and Wednesday hiding round here somewhere have you?" Mike asked. The three remained silent, angry with themselves for not taking down the intruder. "Who the hell *are* you?" Mike demanded, still pointing the shotgun in their direction.

"I think the more pertinent question is who the hell are you?" the woman asked, trying to control her frustration and fear. The two men remained cowering, looking down at the floor.

"I'll ask you again." This time Mike raised the shotgun to his shoulder and pointed directly at her.

The woman gulped and held her breath, then released it, stuck out her chest and announced, "We're the librarians."

It was totally inappropriate, but Mike burst out laughing. The woman had spoken as if announcing she was a member of the Justice League or The Avengers.

It took a moment before he regained his composure and resumed eye contact with the woman, who looked more indignant than ever. "Look, if I put this away, the three of you aren't going to try anything stupid, are you?" He looked from face to face. Each shook their head vehemently and Mike lowered the shotgun into the rucksack. His attention was drawn to two vending machines, both were open and still half full. He walked across and pulled out a bottle of mineral water and a chocolate bar.

The librarians just watched, afraid to move but curious as to who the intruder was. Mike took a long drink and then wolfed down the chocolate bar before grabbing another.

"So, what are you guys doing in here?" Mike leant against the drab beige wall of the foyer and gently slouched down to the floor. The woman walked across to the vending machine, gesturing as if to ask whether it was okay for her to take a drink. Mike nodded enthusiastically and she sat down opposite, prudishly adjusting her skirt as she did.

"The library has been closed for near on six months, but we've all still got keys, so we pop in regularly to borrow books. Well, on Tuesday, there was an emergency meeting at the town hall and we all agreed to meet here beforehand. We were just about to set off when we heard screaming and shouting followed by gunfire, lots of gunfire. We didn't need to see what was going on to know what was going on." The woman stopped and took a long drink from her bottle. "We yanked the shutter down, put the padlock on and have been here ever since. We keep hearing the odd gun, the odd charging group of what we can only assume are those things, but we're safe as long as we're in here."

Mike took another sip of water. "Trust me, it's not nice out there. How are you fixed for food and water?"

"We're actually quite fortunate from that point of view. As well as the vending machines and the additional stock for the vending machines, we've got a staff room with a water cooler and a dozen replacement bottles, and the library cafe has quite a lot of tinned items. They shut the place down so quickly that they never thought to remove the supplies, so we'll be fine for quite a while." She looked towards her co-workers, who were staring angrily at her for giving the intruder so much information.

Mike picked up on the body language. "Don't worry. I'm not here to rip off all your supplies. I'm after a map."

"What kind of map?" the Uncle Fester lookalike asked with interest.

"I came into town with my family. An army of those things attacked us and I led them off while my brother and sisters escaped. They were going to a place called Candleton. I know it's north of here, but that's about it."

All three librarians sprang to their feet as if their lives had a purpose once again. They hustled through the labyrinth of shelves and headed straight towards the map section. Mike stood up and followed them. As he reached them, the Gomez lookalike had already pulled an Ordnance Survey map from the shelf and handed it to him.

"Wow, I'm impressed, guys, that's quick work." Mike smiled warmly towards the increasingly likeable trio.

"Was there anything else you needed?" the woman asked. Her demeanour suggested she was the head librarian.

Mike was about to say no, then he paused. "Actually, now you mention it, there is something else."

22

Lucy opened the door to Emma's room. The tight-knit group had shared so much over the previous few days that there was no need for formalities like knocking. The children rushed up to her and Sammy flung her arms around her waist.

"Do you want to play Monopoly with us?" the young girl asked, before racing her brother back to the board.

"Maybe later, sweetie, I was just coming in to see how you were all doing." She levered off her trainers and planted herself on the bed next to Emma. Both were in a semi-upright position, able to see the children play contentedly. "They seem to be holding up pretty well," Lucy said, watching Jake throw the dice.

"Yep," Emma admitted, with more than a hint of bitterness in her voice.

"Y'know, we got a guided tour of the village today. It's incredible what they've done with this place, how they've fortified it, how they've planned. I think we're going to be safe here, Emma."

She turned to look at Lucy, her dark eyebrows arched in sadness. When she spoke it was only just loud enough to hear. "I know I should be grateful that we're somewhere safe. I know I should be grateful that we're alive, but right now, all I really know is that my brother's gone. I can't see beyond that, Lucy. I don't want to see beyond that." Tears began to trickle down Emma's face and Lucy pulled her close, like a parent comforting her child.

The pair stayed like that for some time. Eventually Emma pulled away and dabbed her eyes with a handkerchief.

"Have you eaten today?" Lucy asked.

"I don't want anything," Emma replied. The thought of food filling the emptiness inside her was too repugnant.

"Sweetie, if you don't eat, you're going to get ill. You have to look after yourself. Sammy and Jake are counting on you more than ever now. Look, I'm about to go down for some dinner, why don't you and the kids come join me?"

She shook her head. "I'm fine, honestly, but if you'd be willing to take Jake and Sammy, I'd appreciate it."

Lucy looked ruefully towards her. "Of course I'll take them, sweetie."

The children happily followed her out of the room and Lucy closed the door behind her, leaving Emma alone for the first time since arriving in Candleton. Emma edged down the bed and reached across for another pillow, clutching it to her chest as she began to wail.

*

After Mike had checked out the items he needed, courtesy of the three librarians, they all sat down in the comfortable chairs of the reading area. He studied the map while the others talked quietly amongst themselves. When he'd finished, he surveyed the small group of oddballs. The three of them were clearly social misfits: intelligent, geeky and, outside of the confines of this library, very vulnerable. Together though, they were companions, equals, who understood each other's awkwardness.

"Look, you guys." Mike spoke and the other three stopped. "It's late afternoon now, I can't really risk setting off tonight, so I'm going to go first thing tomorrow. Why don't you think about coming with me?"

All three were stunned into silence. They looked at each other, shocked first by the generosity of such an offer from this stranger and then by the mere suggestion that any of them could ever consider leaving the only place they felt whole. They whispered among themselves for a few minutes and then the woman spoke.

"I don't even know your name," she said. The crow's feet around her eyes deepened as her face warmed.

"I'm Mike. Mike Fletcher," he said and impulsively held out his hand.

"I'm Ruth, this is David and this is Richard," the woman said, introducing her two colleagues. "It's a most generous offer, Mike, but we don't really plan on leaving here."

"I don't understand. What are you going to do when the food and drink run out?" he asked naively.

"We've made plans. We've got a few weeks left and we intend to enjoy them together in the place we love. Then, when the time comes, we're all going to leave together," she answered, looking towards her friends.

It slowly dawned on Mike what she was saying. He didn't know if the suicide pact had come before or after the night of the town meeting, but they were clearly resolute. He hung his head solemnly. "I'm sorry. I'm so sorry."

"Don't be sorry. It's what we want," David answered, leaning forward.

"Look, Mike," Ruth said, "it's not exactly a sports car, but I've got a Nissan Micra in the staff car park. I'm not going to be using it again. I don't think it will handle cross-country trails well, but you're only a few miles from Candleton by road and you're welcome to it."

The chance of him finding a vehicle with keys and a good battery had been so remote that he had resigned himself to making the trip on foot, but now this stranger was offering him a passport to his family. It saddened him to think that he wouldn't get to know these people better, that no-one would.

Ruth stood up and went to her workstation. She pulled out her handbag and removed the car keys, then came back round and handed them to Mike. "Honestly, Mike, they're of no use to me now."

Mike got to his feet and took the keys gratefully. "Thank you, Ruth. This is one of those moments in life when the words can't match the sentiment, but thank you. If you could meet them, I guarantee my family would thank you as well. Because of you, I'm going to get to see my brother and sisters again tonight." Mike took her hand in both of his and shook it firmly. "Now, I don't suppose you've got a stepladder so I can get back out?" he asked, smiling.

"You don't need one. The emergency exit opens directly onto the staff car park," Ruth said proudly, as if she'd designed the building herself. The three librarians led the way through the maze of bookshelves to the metal fire door. "It's the silver Micra in the last space."

Mike withdrew the shotgun from his backpack. "As soon as I'm through, get this door shut behind me. I'll take care of whatever's on the other side. And thank you again, all three of you." He looked at each of them before booting the panic bar on the door and rushing out into the late afternoon air like Butch or Sundance making a last run for freedom.

He was immediately confronted by a single RAM sprinting towards him. It would have been foolhardy to give away his position for the sake of a solitary beast, so he shoved the shotgun in his backpack, withdrew a machete and swung. One of the creature's flailing arms deflected the strike and it escaped with just a deep cut. The force of the parry knocked Mike off his balance, and before he knew it, the grey abomination was past him and running towards the open emergency exit. Ruth, David and Richard were standing at the door, frozen in fear, as the creature approached. Other than on news reports, they had not witnessed one of the infected before, but now they saw it in all its terrifying gore. The yellow teeth of the RAM began chomping up and down in anticipation of not one, but three fresh kills. Every fibre in Ruth's body wanted to shut the door, but pure terror had clamped down on her muscles. Her eyes met the beast's, and fear gave way to sadness. The one thing in her life that had been under her control – how she was going to die – was about to be taken away from her. It was just metres away. Mike made a powerful rugby tackle on the fast-moving creature and the pair of them skidded along the concrete. The RAM was desperate to get back onto its feet, but Mike was an old hand at knowing when to release an opponent he'd brought down. When the pair finally came to a halt, Mike let go for a split second. The beast began to get up but Mike pushed it back down violently, giving himself the time he needed to get into position and push the machete firmly up through the base of the creature's neck. He thrust so forcefully that the blade of the weapon cracked through the monstrosity's forehead and scraped the concrete. Mike breathed out heavily, wiped the machete on the RAM's already filthy clothing and stood up.

"Are you three okay?" he asked, walking back to the emergency exit. Their shocked faces looked back at him, unable to answer. "Guys, are you okay?" Mike asked, a little more urgently.

Ruth snapped out of her trance. "Yes... yes. Mike, is this what it's like out here now? Is this what you have to do to survive?" The woman seemed to have aged ten years in those few short moments. Mike noticed more silver flecks in her hair. It was just as well she had decided to stay in the library. This world was far too cruel a place for someone like her.

"If you're out here, these are the least of your worries. They're single-minded animals. You see one and you know what the deal is straight away. Kill or be killed. It's the people you need to watch out for,

Ruth, but then again it's always been the people you needed to watch out for." He released her tight grip from the door and motioned for the three of them to get back inside. "I'm going to close the door now. Take care of yourselves, you three." He gently pushed it shut, leaving the librarians with their mouths wide open, still struggling to come to terms with what they had just witnessed.

He found the small silver car, threw his bag into the passenger seat, put the keys in the ignition and smiled as the small engine burst into life.

*

"So, how's the patient?" Keith asked as he sat down with his wife to join the hotel guests for dinner.

"She's doing great," Lucy answered. She washed down her mouthful of chicken with another glass of red wine. "This place is going to be a whole lot noisier soon." She smiled at the hotel owner and her husband as she answered.

"She's my niece, well, Keith's niece," Jenny said proudly as she cut into her baked potato. "Her boyfriend worked on one of the local farms. A few months ago he said his father had fallen ill and that he needed to go back home to Cardiff for a while. That was the last we heard from him. The poor child has been staying with us ever since. She's a good worker and a lovely girl. I think she'll make a wonderful parent. Good job, really, with that little shit doing a runner."

Jake and Sammy looked up from the plates in surprise at hearing the hotelier swear. The other adults smirked.

"How's Emma?" Keith asked, with genuine concern.

"She doesn't think Mike's coming back," Sammy replied, shaking her head comically. "But that's stupid."

All the adults at the table were trapped between feeling sorry for the little girl and finding her manner and confidence amusing.

"Mike said he'd see us soon and my brother has never broken a promise, never in his life, has he, Jake? And it's his birthday tomorrow, he's twenty-one, and that's a very special birthday and Mike would want to spend it with us more than anything in the world, so I think he'll come back tomorrow and if he doesn't then it will probably be the day after, but it will be soon, because he promised." The young girl's expression became increasingly tense.

"Well, if that's the case, I'm sure he must be on his way here right now," Jenny said, doing her best to placate the young girl. The other adults around the table looked sheepishly at each other. The discomfort of the lie was felt by all.

Lucy drained her glass of wine and quickly refilled it. Getting drunk wouldn't be a bad way to drift into sleep. Sober, she would just lie in bed and relive the past few days, relive the fear, the sheer unadulterated terror and the heartbreaking loss. But drunk, she could pass out into a dreamless coma.

"I have to say, I can't remember the last time I ate and drank this well," Lucy said to Jenny and Keith.

"It's the least we can do. The prospect of delivering twins really wasn't something I was relishing, so to have two medical professionals turn up at our door on the eve of the birth, well... Like I said, it's the least we can do," Jenny said, exuding gratitude.

"Have you thought any more about those houses I was telling you about?" Keith asked as he poured himself some wine.

"What houses?" Sammy demanded.

"Mr Martin has said we can move into a house rather than stopping in the hotel, sweetie," Lucy said, smiling at the young girl.

"Well, it will be just until Mike gets here, because then we're going to go to Grandma Fletcher's house in Scotland." This time Sammy didn't even look up from her plate, she just announced it and carried on eating.

Lucy raised her left eyebrow and gave Keith a look as if to say *this is something we'll discuss later.*

*

Joseph missed his sons desperately, but there was peace within him as he sat at the large dinner table. His leg continued to be problematic and his cold symptoms had returned, but they were just trifling issues. He and what remained of his family were in the safe domain of Candleton. His brother had moved into this house just a few days ago as his farm was outside the village and therefore unsafe. But his wife, Bridget, had worked quickly to make the place her own, and as they all sat, about to say grace and feast on the bounty before them, they realised how lucky they were to be together.

"Lord, thank you for the food we are about to receive. Thank you for guiding us to safety and bringing us to the house of my brother. And please, God, look after those we have lost along the way. Amen." Joseph opened his eyes and looked at Daniel, who nodded appreciatively.

"Well, have you told everybody the good news?" Daniel asked his older brother as he poured water into everyone's glasses from a stoneware jug.

"No, I was waiting for this very moment," Joseph announced proudly. He took a sip of water. "Tomorrow, my loves, we move into our new house. It's got five bedrooms, so there won't be any need to share any more."

The smaller children looked at each other, spellbound. "Goodness, gracious," Alice said, grateful for the prospect of being able to stay busy while she grieved for her fallen sons.

"First thing in the morning, I'll take you all to see it. It's only one street away and, Beth, there's a room there for Tracey if she wants to come and live with us." He looked at his daughter. She had put her horrifying ordeal to the back of her mind, but with the mention of her co-captive, it all came flooding back.

"I'll go and see her tomorrow, Dad. I'll ask her if she wants to." Beth desperately wanted to leave the table. Suddenly the pain of her kidnapping was back. She felt like everyone was looking at her, imagining what she had gone through. There was no need to feel humiliation, but that's exactly what she felt, humiliation and shame. She would ask Tracey, but she hoped she would say no. It was hard enough looking at her little sister. Even her sweet face brought back memories of being imprisoned in that breeze-block hell. Tracey had been the strongest one among them and, as grateful as Beth had been for the camaraderie at the time, now she just wanted to push those memories as far away as possible.

*

Mike made speedy progress out of the town centre and away from the hordes of RAMs who had persecuted him since his arrival in Skelton. As Ruth had promised, the car would not win a grand prix any time soon, but it was a lot faster and safer than being on foot. As soon as he was out of Skelton, the lanes narrowed and were surrounded by trees and hedgerows once again. He looked at the clock. 18:13. There was plenty of daylight left and at this speed he should be in Candleton within ten or fifteen minutes. He noticed the date underneath the time: 22 May. Tomorrow was his twenty-first birthday. Mike sniggered to himself. It wasn't exactly how he had imagined it would be, but if he could spend it with his family and friends then it would be better than any present he could wish for.

The sky was starting to cloud over and he could feel it getting colder. But with luck he would be in the warm embrace of his family long before the first drops of rain began to fall. The tyres screeched as he took a bend and Mike's face lit up as he saw a sign saying "Candleton 4". He didn't understand why, but a tear ran down his cheek. Was it a tear of happiness? Was it just a physical release of all the stress? Or was it because he was scared? Beyond all the hardship and battles he had fought in Skelton, there had always been an underlying terror. Not for himself, but for his loved ones. Had they made it to safety? If not, everything he'd done had been for nothing. He had focussed so much on getting back to them that the nagging doubt had been pushed far to the back of his mind. Now that the answer was in reach, the hammering fist of apprehension was beating inside his chest.

The Micra negotiated another sharp bend in the road before Mike hit the brake, bringing it to a bone-jerking stop. A huge tree lay across the tarmac. Even with rope, the small Nissan would barely be able to shift one of its branches, never mind the trunk. To either side of the tarmac were ploughed fields. If the group had made it this far, no doubt Joseph would have known of some secluded farm track that would have taken them beyond this obstacle. Even if Mike could find such a trail it wouldn't be long before the small Micra got stuck or ran into a ditch. No, the only way forward for him was on foot. The anxiety he had been feeling was replaced by the more familiar feeling of anger as he walked the length of the tree. It looked healthy. To the best of his knowledge there had been no wind or lightning in the past few days. Then something caught his eye: sawdust. This tree had been deliberately felled.

He instinctively withdrew his shotgun. Could it be raiders setting up a roadblock to rob anyone who stopped? Or was it a town or village further up the road making access harder for any enemies? He carefully surveyed the surrounding area and saw no signs of anybody or any vehicle ready to rush towards him. He pumped the slide on the shotgun just in case and walked around the fallen tree. He took the map out of his rucksack and studied it as he walked. If he stayed on the road for the next two miles he could then take a cross-country footpath over a small hill and rejoin the road just before Candleton. Mike took another look around. If anybody was going to pounce, they would have done it by now. He pushed the shotgun into the rucksack, zipped up his coat, pulled up the collar and began to jog.

*

There were three gentle taps on the door. "Hello?" Emma said, lifting her tear-stained cheeks from the pillow and looking up.

The handle slowly turned and Samantha gingerly angled her head around the corner. "Hi, it's just me," she said, entering the room and closing the door behind her.

Emma wasn't in the mood for company but she knew Samantha meant well, so she sat up and tried to look like she was happy to see her. "Where are Sammy and Jake?"

"After dinner, the Martins took them into the bar area. There's a dartboard and a snooker table in there. They looked like Christmas had come early. Don't worry, Lucy and Tracey are with them." Samantha gestured to ask if it was alright to sit on the bed beside her and Emma nodded.

"At dinner, Sammy said it was Mike's birthday tomorrow," Samantha blurted, as if it had been on her mind all night. Emma nodded. It had been one of the things on *her* mind all night.

"My sister would have been twenty-one next month," Samantha continued. "The problem is, you never know when you're going to see someone or speak to them for the last time. There were so many things I wanted to say to Claire, to my mum and dad, and now I'll never get the chance. But they knew I loved them and I know they loved me and sometimes that has to be enough, otherwise you can drive yourself mad." Samantha wasn't looking towards Emma, but staring off into a corner of the room.

Emma sat there, realising that this was one of the reasons she was in so much pain, the sheer wealth of things she wanted him to know. How sorry she was for leaving him to go to London, how grateful she was for how he had led her, Sammy and Jake to safety, and how proud she was that he had done it without a second thought for himself. "You're right. The things you don't say haunt you more than the things you do. And there's so much I should have said to him."

Samantha turned and, using her practised bedside manner, took hold of the grieving sister's hand. "It's going to take time, Emma, but trust me, it will get better, little by little. And thanks to Mike, you don't have to go through any of it alone." Samantha released her hold and stood up. "I know from experience what it's like and I know you'll just want to be by yourself for a while. But if you wake up one day and decide you want to talk, you know where I am." She smiled sympathetically and made to leave.

"Thanks, Samantha, that means a lot," Emma said, lowering her legs off the bed for just the second time that day.

"I really liked Mike, Emma. From the first time Claire brought him home I could tell he was different to a lot of other guys. He possessed an honour and sincerity which you rarely see, and that's what defined him. That's what made him the kind of person who would run towards danger to save others while everybody else was running away. Remember, Emma, day or night, if you want someone to talk to, you just come and find me."

Emma remained on the edge of the bed with her bare feet gently stroking the soft woollen carpet as Samantha closed the door behind her. Hearing that Sammy and Jake were in the bar had given her the urge to drink. Alcohol might numb the pain for a while. Surely anything was better than feeling like this. She reached for her trainers and slipped them on.

She arrived at the entrance to the bar area to see Sammy and Jake taking it in turns to throw darts with Lucy watching them, while Keith and Jenny sat at a table with Tracey. Samantha was standing behind them. All the adults had drinks in their hands. Obviously she wasn't the only one who wanted to blot out reality or at least have a mild sedative. Jenny stood up enthusiastically and guided Emma to the bar.

"I've had my fair share of heartache, girl, and I don't care what anybody says – a stiff drink, a friendly ear and a soft shoulder to cry on make it a lot more manageable. Now, first things first, m'dear, what's your poison?" Jenny smiled.

When Emma had first met Keith's wife she had thought that she was quite cold and aloof, but now she felt the woman's warmth; she was taken aback by her compassion and the surprise rendered her temporarily speechless. She stood there trying to think of what drink would suit her purposes best. The seconds of indecision ran on, and Jenny finally took charge.

"You're absolutely right m'dear. Why just pick one?" Jenny smiled, grabbed an extra glass, put it on a serving tray and then did the same with bottles of vodka, gin, rum and brandy. She walked back round from behind the bar, signalled for Emma to join her and they returned to the table. "Move up, Keith," she said, placing the tray down. "Emma's sitting next to me."

*

Mike hadn't seen a single soul on his journey from Skelton. He had, however, come across four more felled trees. If Candleton was responsible for these, Joseph may have been right about the village's resourcefulness – it was a smart move. With the right equipment and a lot of time, the trees were not immovable, but they would certainly use up effort and resources and would probably demoralise any potential attackers. There was a small sign up ahead. He slowed down to read it and check the map. This was it. This was the public footpath he needed to take. Light droplets of rain began to fall as he left the grey tarmac and began his uphill trek across to Candleton. Even though there was an incline, he was running faster now than he had been. The promise of this journey coming to an end was too much of a lure, and as his tired legs and aching feet thumped against the dirt track, he remembered happier times when he and Alex had gone running together. What he wouldn't give to have Alex there now.

At the brow of the hill he stopped. He could make out a church steeple, and there was the sound of running water. He removed the map once again and checked it, brushing away spots of rain that splashed onto the outstretched paper. He was nearly there. Down the hill, over a bridge, a couple of hundred more metres by road and that would be it. He would know then if his family had made it to safety.

Mike descended the hill in no time, and the pathway levelled off as it followed the dry stone wall of a farmer's field before coming back out onto the road. He could see the bridge up ahead and feel his heart pounding rapidly, partly due to the exertion, partly due to the anxiety.

"Halt!" shouted a gruff voice as the stranger approached the gate at the end of the bridge. "We're not taking anyone in. Clear off."

Mike wasn't able to see anyone, but he'd spotted the two turrets and assumed that rifles were trained on him. "I was with a group. They should have arrived here yesterday," he shouted in the direction that he'd heard the voice. But there was no response. "Please. Can you tell me, did a convoy of vehicles arrive here yesterday? I need to know." Mike put his hands on the gate.

"Stay where you are, son," said a different voice this time, and two soldiers pointing rifles emerged from behind the turrets.

Mike raised his hands. "Please, I need to know if they got here safely."

The soldiers opened the gate and ripped the backpack from Mike. One of them patted him down, finding the knife Mike carried in his boot. He removed it and threw it in the rucksack, which he then shouldered. "Wait here."

"Okay, I'll wait. I'll keep my hands in the air, I'll dance a fucking tango, but will someone please tell me if a group of people arrived here yesterday?"

Rather than being annoyed, the two soldiers looked at each other and laughed at the young man's bolshiness. The one on the right had short brown hair and a squashed nose and was missing one of his teeth. He looked like a real bruiser. Not the type of person Mike wanted to get into a brawl with, but he was prepared to do whatever it took to get the answer to his question.

"Relax, son. They showed up yesterday afternoon," the bruiser replied.

"How many? How many got here?" Mike asked impetuously.

"Fuck me, kid, I don't know. We've not got a fucking signing-in book at the gate. Let's see, there was a Land Rover, a truck, a van and an ambulance. They were all taken away pretty quick. I heard there was a doctor and nurse among them, and a few kids and Mr Masters' brother. The corporal will be able to tell you in a minute. I don't know all the details." The soldier motioned for Mike to follow him and the three of them stood at the other end of the bridge, awaiting the officer's arrival.

An army Land Rover screeched to a halt a moment later and Darren Masters got out. He was almost running towards the three figures.

"This gentleman says he was with the group that arrived yesterday, sir," the bruiser said to his superior.

"Are you Michael Fletcher?" Darren asked.

"Mike, yes." He was a little surprised that the stranger knew his name. The corporal stood there for a moment, smiling. He put his hand up to his mouth to wipe away a stupid grin.

"Sorry, Mike, it's just that I thought that if I ever saw you, you'd be wearing a red cape with an 'S' on the back. I apologise if my men were a little harsh with you, but we got attacked the other day. Just a small skirmish but we killed three of theirs before they fled. My troops are being a little more cautious now." The corporal grabbed hold of Mike's hand and squeezed it firmly in his own. He then looked at the two soldiers and noticed the backpack. He signalled for them to return it to its rightful owner. "This is Mike Fletcher, gentlemen. He took on a group of over fifty RAMs single-handedly so his family and friends could get to safety. It's an honour to meet you," Darren said, still gripping Mike's hand.

"Thank you," Mike replied, clearly taken aback. "Corporal, did they all get here? Did they all make it?" His brow creased slightly in dreaded anticipation of the response.

"Every last one of them, Mike. Now come with me, mate, I'll take you to them." Darren guided the new arrival to his vehicle and the pair sped away.

23

"So how come you're still so well supplied in the alcohol department, Mrs Martin?" Lucy asked the tipsy hotel owner.

"Jenny, please, Mrs Martin's my mother." She giggled drunkenly. "What am I talking about, Mrs Martin's *his* mother. Well, anyway, we used to go to the wholesaler in Leeds twice a year. We'd just stocked up when the bottom fell out of the world. Six months' worth of hotel guests, diners and bar patrons get through an awful lot of booze, dear. Keith and I have tried valiantly but barely scratched the surface." She giggled a little more and then filled everyone's drinks up. "How are you feeling, sweetheart?" she asked turning to Emma.

"I'm still sad, but my lips have gone numb," she responded, drunk but serious.

"That's the ticket. Now you just need to carry on drinking until the rest of you is as numb as your lips."

Jenny put her arm around Emma and laughed, as did the rest of the table.

"Do you have any tonic? I think I'd like a G&T," Emma said to her new drinking buddy.

Jenny gulped down the vodka in front of her. "That's a great idea. Who else wants a G&T?" Jenny asked. She grabbed Emma and pulled her to the bar to help. Everyone raised their hands.

Sammy and Jake were still happily playing darts and the conversations at the table were becoming less coherent, but noisier, as time went on.

"You mix the drinks, sweetheart, I'll cut the lemon," Jenny instructed as the pair went behind the bar.

Emma laid out six tall glasses, added ice and carefully poured in double measures of gin, followed by tonic water. Jenny expertly placed a piece of sliced lemon over the rim of each one.

"The proof is in the tasting," the older woman said and picked up a glass for herself before handing one to Emma, who closed her eyes and took two refreshing gulps.

Emma turned to go back to the table and froze. Suddenly the only sound she could hear was the blood rushing to her head. Whether it was the alcohol or the exhaustion, she was unable to compute what she was seeing. The glass slipped from her hand, which impulsively rose to cover her mouth. Standing in the doorway of the bar, grinning like the village idiot, was her dead brother. Only, he wasn't dead, he was right there, with a goofy look on his face. Tired, windswept, covered in scrapes and bruises, but alive. The glass smashed on the hardwood floor, showering Emma's feet in cold gin and ice, the sound waking her from the trance-like state. Her lips mouthed her brother's name but no sound came out.

"Mike!" Sammy and Jake screamed simultaneously as they ran towards him. The adults at the table had been oblivious to the figure in the doorway, and when the glass dropped they had all looked in the direction of the bar, but now their heads turned to see the children running towards the man crouching down with open arms to embrace his family.

"No fucking way!" Lucy said, knocking her chair over as she stood up. She had cried so much in the past two days, but now it was from joy rather than sorrow.

Samantha was speechless. She grabbed Tracey's arm with a vice-like grip.

Sammy was so keen to hold her brother that the force of her enthusiasm knocked him over and all three of them became one chuckling pile on the ground.

"That's your brother?" Jenny asked, almost as shocked as his friends. Emma's mouth was still agape, taking in deep breaths in the hope that the extra oxygen might coax her body into moving, but she managed a nod. "Oh my God, this is wonderful. This is wonderful. Go to him, sweetheart, you're not dreaming."

Those were the magic words. Emma had been wondering if she was in a dream or maybe just going insane, but now, as she looked around at the others, she knew from their reaction that this was real. She ran towards him, just as he regained his footing, and locked her arms around his neck. Tears flowed as Sammy and Jake embraced the two of them. Everyone else in the room hung back and bathed in the warmth of the scene. There had been very little that could be considered uplifting over the course of the last few days, but now Lucy, Samantha, Tracey and even the Martins were overcome by the family's reunion.

"This is wonderful," Jenny said again, taking a thirsty gulp of gin and tonic.

"Now that's an understatement if ever I heard one," Lucy replied, wiping her cheeks and grabbing Samantha by the wrist. "Come on, sweetie, let's go see our boy."

Samantha finally relinquished her clutch on Tracey's arm and followed Lucy towards the embrace-locked figures.

"Hey, Mike," Lucy said, beaming broadly.

He returned the grin and loosened himself from his family. "You did it, Doc," he said gratefully as he flung his arms around her and kissed her roughly on the cheek. "I'll never forget what you did, never. Thank you."

"Yeah, well ditto, Mikey. I think I had the easier end of the deal." She pulled back, grasped his face between her hands and kissed him equally roughly, square on the lips. "Good to have you back, sweetie." Lucy let go and Mike moved his tongue around his lips, trying to identify the various alcoholic drinks he could taste.

Samantha was in tears as well. "It's so good to see you, Mike." She tiptoed up, kissed him gently on the cheek and held him firmly.

"Hi, Mike. It's great to see you got back safely," Tracey said, feeling like the outsider in the group.

"Trust me, it's great to be back," he said with a wide grin.

Jenny had disappeared, but Keith walked up to Mike, placed his right hand firmly in his and clutched his upper arm. "It's a genuine pleasure to meet you. A genuine pleasure. What you did... I can't find the words, but this village is indebted to you, young man." He spoke with sincerity and the firm handshake reassured Mike.

"Thank you," he replied, a little dumbfounded by the outpouring of emotion.

Jenny re-entered the room and quickly took charge of the situation. "Right, Emma, if you want to show Mike up to his room, I'm arranging to have a bath filled for him right now. Then we'll get the poor lad something to eat, something to drink and he can tell us all about it. Mike, we've got fresh chicken, some frozen steaks, duck, lamb chops, what can we get you?" Jenny asked kindly, desperately wanting to pamper him.

"My brother's a vegetarian. That means he doesn't eat meat," Sammy announced as she came and stood in between Jenny and Mike.

"Is that so, young lady?" Jenny replied, smiling. "Well, I'm sure we can conjure something up for him."

Mike was led away by his family as the remaining adults looked around at each other, still in a state of shock.

*

"Y'know, it's incredible being back with you guys, but you don't have to stay here while I have a bath," Mike said, enjoying the hot, deep, frothy water.

Emma was leaning against the wall, while Jake and Sammy were just outside the open door but out of earshot. "You'll be lucky if I ever let you out of my sight again," Emma replied, staring at her brother, still coming to terms with his return.

"How come this place has electricity?" Mike asked, letting the warm soapy water wash away the grime and horrors of the previous days.

"They have a turbine. From what I've heard, it's a pretty amazing place. Maybe we can take a look around tomorrow. If it's as good as they say, maybe we should think about staying for a while?" Her words hit Mike like a right hook.

"What do you mean? We need to get to Gran's place." He wasn't angry, just shocked by his sister's comment.

A knot appeared in her throat and her eyes began to mist. "Please, just think about it, Mike. I've vowed to myself that I will follow you wherever you go from now on, but if I had to live through the last twenty-four hours again I think it would drive me insane. I can't bear the thought of losing you, and out there, out on the road, that prospect is always just one wrong turn away. We don't even know if she's still alive. But if she is, she wouldn't want us to risk all our lives if we didn't have to. Please, just think about it. That's all I'm asking. Just think about it." She tried to remain composed but a small tear trickled from her eye.

He suppressed his instinct to feel betrayed and angry. His sister had been through enough. "Okay, I'll think about it." The words wounded him as he said them, but seeing Emma in such turmoil pained him more.

Oblivious to the conversation, the children brushed past their elder sister and ran up to the bathtub. "We should have a party. It's your birthday tomorrow. So we should have a party all day," Sammy said enthusiastically. She took Jake's hand and began to dance around the room.

Mike switched his thoughts away from the serious implications of his conversation with Emma and allowed himself to bask in the excitement of his younger siblings. "That sounds good to me," he said, ducking his head under the bubbles for a second. The children ran back out of the bathroom and continued to dance in anticipation of an all-day party.

Emma and Mike smiled. Despite everything they had been through, everything they still had to go through, and the life-changing decisions ahead of them, at that moment they were a family again.

When they returned downstairs, the number of people in the bar had swelled. Joseph and his entire brood had appeared as well as a few villagers who had heard the story of Mike's heroic actions and just wanted to come along to see him in person. Mike was taken aback once again as his little sister dragged him into the bar and he was confronted by all the smiling faces. On seeing Annie and John, she relinquished her grip on her brother's hand and ran over to them.

Joseph had been experiencing palpitations for the last couple of hours and now a thin film of sweat had appeared on his brow, but he was sure it was all just brought on by the stress. It didn't stop him powerfully grabbing Mike's hand.

"It's a miracle to see you back here, nothing short of a miracle. I can't tell you how happy we are," he said as he finally released his grip.

Other people shook Mike's hand, embraced him and patted him on the back. He found it exhausting. He was grateful when Jenny broke through the crowd of unfamiliar faces, grabbed him by the arm and led him to a table where a plate of pasta awaited him. He sat down, the smell of the food making his mouth water. He glanced up to see all the faces looking down at him and immediately felt self-conscious.

Jenny clapped her hands and ushered everyone away. "Okay you lot, let the poor lad have a bite to eat. Come on, we'll go have a drink at the bar." That was the trigger phrase.

As the crowd drifted away, Emma, Lucy and Samantha joined Mike at the table. Lucy had brought two bottles of wine with her. She opened one and poured glasses for each of them.

"So, Mikey. Tell us all about it," she said, as she tipped the smooth red liquid down her throat.

*

By 2am, Lucy, Mike and Emma were the only ones left in the bar. Emma was reluctant to leave her brother's side, but she had been fighting sleep for the last hour and eventually she kissed them both goodnight and made her way to her room.

"That was quite a homecoming. When I was in that loft, I'd have been grateful for a glass of water and a piece of stale bread. I didn't expect anything like this," Mike said as he drained his glass.

"This place is something else. You really need to think about taking Keith up on his offer and staying here," Lucy said. She peered at the bottles in front of her to see if there was anything left to drain.

"I'm guessing you've been speaking to Em?" he said, smiling.

"I don't know your gran, Mike, but if she knew what you'd been through, what we've all been through, if she knew that you could save yourself and your family from having to go through that ordeal again, I can guarantee she would tell you to stay put in a heartbeat." Lucy rose to her feet. "I'll show you around the place tomorrow before you make any decisions."

"I don't understand. Does this mean you're staying here?"

"I want to stay here. Samantha wants to stay here and I'm pretty sure Emma wants to stay here," she replied.

"That didn't answer my question," he replied, as he shakily got to his feet.

Lucy smiled and turned to leave. "I'm going to bed. Like I said, I'll give you a guided tour tomorrow."

He watched her go and then lingered in the bar for a moment, taking it all in. When Joseph had spoken about Candleton, Mike had never envisaged this. Food, safety and even electricity. Once, he had taken these things for granted; now, they were a luxury, but a luxury within constant reach if he chose to stay. He thought back to the conversation he had had with his gran on the morning of Alex's death. *If you can't make it here then at least get out of the city. You've got good instincts, Mikey, trust them. Keep the family safe.*

Mike turned off the light as he left the bar and walked up the stairs to his room. He was about to get ready for bed when he noticed the carrier bag sticking out of his rucksack. He remembered how happy his nerdy librarian friends had been when they helped him make a final selection before leaving. He picked up the bag and walked across the hall to Lucy's room. He knocked gently on the door. Lucy answered wearing just a T-shirt and a pair of pants.

"I forgot. I got you a little something when I was in Skelton." He handed her the carrier. It was folded around the object like Christmas paper.

Lucy had a confused smile on her face as she took the package and unwrapped it. A hand shot up to her mouth to stifle a small cry. The gift was a book. The cover featured a cartoon drawing of a pig looking up at a dangling spider. Below were the words *Charlotte's Web*.

Her eyes watered. She looked up at Mike and gently pulled him into the room, closing the door quietly behind.

"You were trapped, surrounded by those things, away from your family and you..." Her voice was shaky and her words trailed off.

"It only took a minute, Doc. I was in the library anyway. There's no need to get upset. It wasn't a big deal."

"Promise me you'll stay here. Promise me we'll stay in Candleton," Lucy demanded, her voice still shaky, her eyes tearing up again.

"I told you, Doc, I'll think about it."

"No. This is important. This is the most important thing I'll ever ask you, Mike. Promise me we'll stay. Promise me." She was relentless in her demand and becoming more emotional by the second.

Little else had occupied his mind since Emma had first mentioned it, and as the evening had gone on he had gradually found more and more reasons to remain. This wasn't the safe haven he had imagined when they left Leeds, but maybe it was time to heed Alex's and Gran's advice and trust his instincts. Until this moment he hadn't known what to do, but seeing Lucy so fragile, seeing the one person he had relied on time after time so vulnerable, made the decision for him.

"Okay, calm down, Doc. We'll stay. We'll stay. But what's the urgency, why did you need to know this minute?"

She wiped her eyes again and put her gift down. "Because I didn't want what's going to happen next to be the reason."

Mike's confusion continued for an instant and then Lucy stepped towards him. Her cheeks were still tear-stained, but she had stopped crying. She cupped his face in both palms and moved her lips up to his. Her warm wine-flavoured tongue began to explore Mike's mouth. He was mesmerised by the sensuality of the moment and fell back against the wall for support. He placed one hand on her hip and combed the fingers of his other through her hair, to the back of her head. He pulled her closer to him.

Their breathing became rapid as they explored each other with their tongues and hands. All they had experienced and shared in the last few days had brought them closer and closer together. Momentary glances, a gentle word, a soft touch, the danger, the exhilaration, the fear. In the few days they had been together, the pair had experienced more than in their entire lives before they had met. A bond had formed, transcending age, transcending background. There was an electricity between them that neither could explain and neither could deny.

Lucy unbuckled Mike's belt and slowly pulled open the buttons of his jeans one by one, while he moved his hand underneath her T-shirt and caressed her smooth warm back. She delicately manoeuvred her hand down the front of his shorts and slowly and carefully, like a tiger, edged closer before finally taking hold of him.

She pulled her mouth away from him and he stared into her eyes. There was no trace of sadness now, just excitement and longing. She removed her cupped hand from the warmth of his trousers and guided him over to the bed. She pulled off her T-shirt and took down her pants. Her body shuddered with desire as she turned around to Mike and undressed him. As his clothes hit the floor, she moved her hands to his hips and mouthed and nibbled on his lower torso. The pair trembled, intoxicated with the promise of what was about to happen. Then, unable to take any more, Lucy dragged Mike down onto the bed. Despite the exhaustion, despite the stress, or maybe because of it, they made love until the night turned to morning.

*

It was grey and drizzly outside, but in that room, in that bed, it felt like a bright summer day. Mike levered himself up onto one elbow and spread his other arm and leg across Lucy. They grinned at each other and shared their thousandth kiss.

"Why was it so important to you that I told you I was staying before we... y'know...?" he asked, looking down into Lucy's eyes.

"I wanted you to stay for the right reasons. I didn't want you to think I was sleeping with you just to try and make you stay," she responded, gently running her hand through the dark hairs on his chest.

"Just for the record, that would have worked too," Mike replied with a grin.

"That's useful to know. Who knows what else I might want?" She grinned back. "Seriously though,

Mike. You giving me that book. That was the sweetest thing anyone has ever done for me. You're special." She pulled his head down to hers and the pair kissed again.

"Well, I'd better go and tell Em that we're staying," he said, reluctantly climbing out of the warmth of Lucy's bed.

She pulled him back in and kissed him. "I think this is somewhere we can start again, Mike. I think we can be happy here. I mean truly happy. You. Me. All of us."

EPILOGUE

Joseph awoke with a jerk. His forehead was beaded with cold sweat and his mouth was dry. He looked around the room and saw Annie in one corner with a book open on her lap.

"Hi, Daddy, are you feeling better?" she asked, putting the book down and moving towards the bed where her father lay.

"Where's Peter?" Joseph's eyes were glassy and his voice clicked due to the dryness of his throat. "I have to go find Peter. He'll be scared. He's all alone down there."

Annie's face twitched. Her father was making no sense. The young girl did not say anything but ran out of the room to find her mother.

Joseph climbed out of the bed. His feet were bare and he wore nothing except his pyjamas, but he walked past the open door of the kitchen and out into the drizzle of morning before Annie had even spoken her first words of concern. The cold, wet grass